The Monster Vented a High, Agonized Shriek

. . . but continued its rush upon Oghmal. The champion swung his long-handled axe with all the skilled control of his wrists, so that its edge sank through the malformed skull into the brain-pan. Rearing high on its back legs, it combed frantically at the axe with its forefeet while Oghmal clung to the handle. As heavy as the five of them together, it shook Oghmal and Lygi about like small children. Foam dropped in strings from its jaws.

The Cauldron of Plenty

Don't miss Book One of THE DANANS . . .

The Sorcerers' Sacred Isle

D1601116

Ace Books by Keith Taylor

The Bard Series

BARD
BARD II
BARD III: THE WILD SEA
BARD IV: RAVENS' GATHERING

The Danans Series

BOOK ONE: THE SORCERERS' SACRED ISLE
BOOK TWO: THE CAULDRON OF PLENTY

THE
CAULDRON
OF PLENTY

KEITH TAYLOR

ACE BOOKS, NEW YORK

This book is an Ace original edition,
and has never been previously published.

THE CAULDRON OF PLENTY

An Ace Book/published by arrangement with
the author

PRINTING HISTORY
Ace edition/October 1989

ISBN: 0-441-09500-3

Ace Books are published by The Berkley Publishing Group,
200 Madison Avenue, New York, New York 10016.
The name ''ACE'' and the ''A'' logo
are trademarks belonging to Charter Communications, Inc.

PRINTED IN THE UNITED STATES OF AMERICA

10 9 8 7 6 5 4 3 2 1

To my mother, Fay,
who encouraged me to write from the first
and deserved this sooner,
with love, gratitude and thanks from my heart.

THE
CAULDRON
OF PLENTY

Chapter One

Winter still held the earth of Tirtangir in a grip of frost. Its whiteness helped to cover a broad swathe of blighted, devastated ground where a monster had passed some months before. Trees had rotted to the roots in moments when it blundered by. Everything in its path had died. As rime stiffened the soil, that fearful memory made men's minds immobile and hard when they pondered it, and dreaded the Blind Boar's possible reappearance.

Oghmal the Champion was no different. All his courage and prowess had been of no use against that being. He wanted to draw rein at the edge of the monster's track and seek a way around, though he knew there was none—at least, none for horses. Instead, he clicked his tongue and urged his magnificent grey stallion across the strip of devastation. With a creak and jingle of harness, his twenty riders followed. They did not speak until the Blind Boar's track lay behind them.

"The sooner sweet grass grows over that again, the better for us all," said one.

"It will, soon enough," the companion beside him answered.

"Better if it stayed, to make us all remember how much we don't know. Sanhu was a great sorceress, but not great enough to control the earth powers once she summoned them."

"Sanhu was a bitter woman who didn't know much except how to destroy, and that seeped through all the magic she ever worked. You needn't admire her. She only believed she was great."

"I'll admire her for ending the Freth rule, while I live—and if you have a mind to question the rightness of that gratitude, Rieth, with sword or spear, I'll be glad to answer you."

The speakers were true Danans, hot-blooded children of their mother, the Earth-Goddess. No more gifted race in all the arts and crafts existed, and first among their arts was sorcery, which played its part in all their others, from music to flint-working. And war. Yet even they could be overcome. It had happened, and a long decade of subjection to a tribe they scorned had been the result, from which they had only now emerged. Nothing under the sky would be the same for them again, because of that.

Oghmal rode in aloof silence, thinking of the damage which had been done and the years it would take them all to recover. His own cantons had been spared, and Sen Mag, the First Created Plain, which his party was crossing now. His sister's queenly house at Ridai still stood, on the far side of Sen Mag, near the pulsing sea. They had recovered some of the wealth which had been taxed from them, year after year—yet much of that would go to their allies as gifts. If Oghmal had his way, they would spend a generation recovering and building.

The sun crossed a sky of clear, brittle blue, and the frost persisted until almost midday, crunching under the hoofs of the swift horses which only the Danans bred. Usually there would have been races, mock fights, and singing on the way, small merry irresponsible uses of magic, but the Danans of Tirtangir had grown sober for the present. When the bright roof and crystal pillars of Ridai appeared, the riders raised a cheer and increased their pace to a gallop. Oghmal rode before them all, not as well as some but better mounted than any. They swept down the grassy avenue leading to fortified Ridai, and raced between the rings of earthen bank until they reached the stables and exercise yard. Oghmal's companions tended their mounts personally, after their leader's example, before going to the house to enjoy baths and changes of garments.

Oghmal's elder sister Cena, Rhi of all the Danans in the sacred island, greeted him warmly.

"You have been missed, brother," Cena said. "Was it needful to spend the whole winter at your canton? Your retinue could have been fed here, and never have exhausted our larders."

She indicated the heavy crockery pot, so large that her brother's arms could not have stretched around its rim, steaming by Ridai's central hearth. Compared with the other furnishings of her house, it was a graceless thing, dumpy and plain, if strong as a stone. But then it did not belong there. It was Undry, the cauldron of plenty which belonged to the Freth chieftain Sixarms. It could magically feed a limitless number, and Cena was to return it to him at the spring gathering.

"It wasn't the food, though I'm better supplied than many. You must have had half the land coming to your doors through the winter, and I know better than to think you'd turn them away." Oghmal seated himself on a cushion beside a low table. "I didn't want to increase the number, and there was much to set in order."

"And is that done now?"

"You see me here, sister. Yes, the canton can manage the sowing without me, and I doubt that any serious affairs will arise until after that."

Oghmal meant that his clients and household officials could see to the everyday running of his canton better than he could. It was common knowledge that he hadn't the gifts of a husbandman. The soil bore better and the cattle increased more for others. Oghmal did have his people's affinity for the earth but in his case it was for the high, stony moors, not the fertile fields, the deer hunt rather than the cattle drive. It was just as well that the land's fertility depended on Cena and not upon him; he could never have been the Rhi. Nor did he want to be. The loyalty of family, sept, and tribe ruled his life. He was their champion, the fighter who represented them all when fighting had to be done, and died young on their behalf if necessary.

"You didn't have to come, it's true, but Talvi would have been more than pleased if you had."

"You mean she is displeased now?"

"You had better ask her, brother."

"Where is she?"

"You know her. I have no doubt you can find her if you wish to."

Oghmal wished to. He excused himself to his sister and made his way to the long weaving-room of Ridai, where sorcery was woven into cloth with the dye. A low, sweet singing came from the largest loom, where a patterned sail was taking shape in one unbroken piece. Beside it, on a smaller frame, Talvi wove a cloak in subtler colors but even more intricate design. Elsewhere, tapestries and other clothes were partly complete. The weaving-women glanced at Oghmal knowingly. All were highborn, all artists, all skilled in sorcery, but Talvi made the loveliest and most potent creations there.

"Oghmal! Did you have to sit at home all this time?"

"I have a rare talent for doing just that when there is no fighting to bring me out. Was there no company at all here?"

"Enough. The warriors from Alba proved more attentive than you. Most have decided to stay, and the rest have asked me to go across the sea with them—except Nemed, of course. He courted Cena."

"That was too soon after Gui's death. I'll speak to him. He has two wives in his own realm, anyhow, and she has seen them. He's overconfident!"

"So Cena herself told him. She is not about to become one of a collection, as they say women are at the sunrise end of the earth."

"Cena can indeed and truly look after herself. As you can. Have you decided to accept any of those Alban offers?"

"Now there you ask too much, after shirking the ride from Dar all winter, but I do not mind answering. Not yet. It's not easy to decide among so many young brave fellows who talk so well. You could learn something from them, Oghmal. You are blunt as your precious swords and spears are sharp. You always have been."

Talvi smiled contentedly and sent her shuttle flashing through the loom, then took another with thread of a different shade. She was that rarity among the Danans, a black-haired woman. Danan hair ran strongly to brown and red in all its variations. The sable braids of Talvi contrasted with her fair skin and blue eyes to the delight of every man who saw her. Although she found this pleasant, it never overwhelmed her. So far she had been content to laugh with all the men and cry with none.

"Maybe. You would need sharp weapons around you in Alba, if what I'm told of the Firbolgs is right. Some of these young, brave fellows may have come here to escape from them."

"Then they are wise. Besides, I might not wish to be protected from the Firbolgs. An entire black-haired race! Perhaps I'd feel at home among them."

"I'm a dark enough brown."

"True."

"And a ready visitor in the summer months. Were you to stay at Dar over the winter, you'd have small reason to rue that I never left."

"Oh, goddess, listen to this man! Oghmal, Dar has just you and your war-band and the house-servants who care for them. Nothing goes on there but burnishing of weapons, drinking, and long, long stories of raid, battle, and single combats I have seen. Now what is in that to make a woman desire to go there? Unless she was one of Bava's War Crows."

The description of Oghmal's house was somewhat overdone. Still, he acknowledged a basic truth in it. "You would not have to be there alone. There would be enough other guests to save you from boredom, and I would give over burnishing my weapons from time to time."

"From time to time, ha?"

"Maybe even for entire days."

"I will give it thought. Meanwhile I have to practice my own trade. Oghmal, this cloak is meant to make its wearer invisible, and it will, but only if it is woven at one unbroken sitting. You can tell me more of Dar's delights later; I'll come when I have finished."

Oghmal nodded, and with a word of farewell walked out into the liss, the grassy area within the ramparts. It was true that he had not seen Talvi in too long. Last summer scarcely counted. He'd done little then but fight the Freths and recover from wounds—and Talvi had visited his bedside each day while he was at Ridai. It had been neglect to stay at Dar throughout the winter—but there, he had done it. Nor could he truthfully say that he regretted it.

The warriors from Alba Talvi had mentioned were indeed present in numbers. Oghmal knew many of them; he'd fought beside them in the last battles against his overlords. Death had thinned their ranks. The survivors, though, were looking for land and life-mates, and Talvi would be able to pick as suited her.

Oghmal saw Nemed, and shared the seat of honor with him for a while, talking of various things. Nemed said that he would be taking his ships home to Alba soon, and would send to discuss the aid he expected from Tirtangir, in payment for his aid to them. He'd paid himself handsomely in plunder, but Oghmal did not remind him of that. It was true that he was owed a large debt of honor for his help.

"So that you do not ask us to campaign in Alba this summer, or even next," he said. "We have become too thin upon the ground for that."

"Do you think I don't know?" Nemed demanded. "Ten years of Freth rule! All I ask is that when you come, you bring yourself, your following, and some of the Rainbow Men." He spoke of the mounted force the Danans used to keep order within their own borders, seven troops of picked warriors, each clad in its own distinct color. "Not forgetting Undry."

"Undry?" That was the name of the inexhaustible pot. Oghmal frowned into Nemed's languid, foxy face. "You must know we are to give it back."

"Ah, come now." Nemed grew broadly tolerant. "Surrender a treasure such as that, when you won it fairly in war? You are not obliged to do so, and it would be foolish beyond words."

"You forget," Oghmal said, a small flame of anger beginning to burn in him. "The Freths made peace upon that condition only, and they would have gone on fighting if we hadn't agreed. We couldn't afford that, so we pledged our word, and even if we had not, Nemed, we still can't begin fighting anew. We have held our place in this island at a high cost. Now we must have peace to rebuild."

"Strange words from the battle-champion," Nemed said skeptically. "It seems to me that once the Freths have their cauldron of plenty, they will keep their peace no longer than it takes them to raise a new war-host and feed it to full strength. They want you out of this island, my friend, and a war-host is only as strong as its fodder."

"You labor the obvious, my friend," Oghmal said, with stress on the last two words. "They too were badly mauled in our battles; they still have greater numbers than we, but they also lose more when they fight. I don't believe they will fight again while Sixarms lives, and he's scarcely decrepit."

"You talk of what you owe him," Nemed said, growing angry himself. "He's your greatest enemy! I'm your best ally! Who fought for you twice, and destroyed the Revolving Fortress for you? Who carried your other allies across the sea from Alba, and saved your kingdom for you? Surely you owe me something, too?''

"Much! But not Undry. We never promised that, Nemed, and indeed you have known all winter that you would not be getting it. Ask Cena for it if you will. It's certain I am that she will not give it to anyone but Sixarms, and my voice will be against her if she does.''

"And that is all my friendship is worth!'' Nemed's voice caused heads to turn in that hall where quarrels between hot-tempered warriors were far from unusual. "Are you the only ones with enemies? Are yours the only uncertain borders? The cursed Firbolgs have taken all the eastern part of *my* island, and now they press along the shores of Sabra in their leather boats. I've desperate needs of my own, and what's to supply them? The weary remnant of your weary people, facing westward and crying to the Freths, 'Do not harm us'?''

Oghmal prepared to throw Prince Nemed through a wall-partition, but he was forestalled by the harsh voice of Bava, who led Ridai's troop of battle-women. Tall and lean, with a pattern of crow's feathers tattooed on her skin and two short, curved bronze swords in sheaths at her hips, she was as formidable in a fight as Oghmal and quicker to quarrel.

"Who cries that?'' she rasped. "Crimson thunderbolts! We may be hard-pressed in this island, but none has made us leave it yet and snivel for refuge with a foreign tribe!'' Her yellow eyes glittered perilously. "Suppose you and your insults take a little walk outside with me and my talons.'' She touched the grips of her curved Scythian swords significantly. "Then we will see who comes back.''

"Oh?'' Nemed's mouth twisted a little. "Do you now avoid paying your debts by picking a quarrel and—as you think—slaying your guest? It's a pretty scheme which has been attempted before—''

"And did it work for you?'' Bava interrupted. "Outside we go.''

"I forbid it!'' Cena was there, her face angry. "Nemed, I would not insult you by seeming to protect you, but by the goddess, I did not hear you sparing any insults just now. You're still my guest. Bava, if you must fight someone, I'm here, and I have not forgotten how. It's with you that he quarrelled, brother. Do you wish to fight him?''

Oghmal considered the tall prince, older than himself and

losing hair, but very dangerous for all that, a fighter whose capacities the champion knew. He also knew his own.

"It seems that you go back to Alba without the clay cauldron," Oghmal said. "You may go back without your life, too, if that pleases you better. Just take that small walk outside with me. Bava, you may have what is left when I have finished, like a right War Crow."

Bava laughed, cawed, and made pecking gestures.

Behind his smiling mouth and eyes, Nemed calculated. It was important that he go home and turn back the Firbolg advance. The Danans of Tirtangir, if they remained in his debt, could be of use. Or . . . there was a thing vastly more useful than the aid of their weakened strength.

Nemed let his eyelids droop, to hide the sudden glitter of resolution. He said smoothly, "I ask pardon. I said in anger what I did not mean."

"I was angry too," Oghmal owned, "but I said nothing I did not intend. Well, if you will let the challenge pass, I will."

"Happily," Nemed said.

"I do not trust that smiling fox," Bava said when Nemed had gone. "No, not a feather's weight. I wish you had taken off his head."

"I confess, so do I. Let's hope we never rue this missed chance."

"Let's be sure that Undry is guarded beyond a demon's power to steal," Bava suggested, more practically. "If it vanishes . . ." She made a throat-cutting gesture.

With Rainbow Men at each of the hall's doors, the cauldron was well guarded already, as Oghmal pointed out. "Would you replace them with your War Crows?"

"They'd be harder to deceive, and more alert," Bava said, "but not enough of us are here. This we can do, though—"

That night seven crows, more huge than eagles, perched in the rafters of Cena's house, watching the hall below with merciless eyes. Their shining feathers merged with the shadows. Oghmal himself slept close to the hearth, with one eye open and his sword beside him, a slim length of beautifully worked bronze with a reinforcing central rib. In the champion's hand it struck like red lightning, as everyone knew.

Rainbow Men of the red troop stood three at each door, spear-armed, in crimson leather tunics and cerise cloaks, even their jewels blood-colored garnets. Oghmal respected their abilities, but thought their sameness of dress somehow degrading. His own war-band was worth all of them, and his men flaunted a decent individuality, with clothes of many styles and hues, their own emblems on their shields, and helmets of their choice or none at all. The notion of making all the men of a fighting band look alike had come from Gui, his sister's leman, dead in the recent battles. Oghmal hoped it never became a common thing.

Nemed noticed the extra precautions, not being blind. Instantly his pride sprang to arms, shield raised, axe lifted, ready to defend itself.

Insult. Insult added to niggardliness! He'd asked for the loan of the cauldron in a decent way, and been refused, despite the way he had fought for these people. The skinflints would not even lend it, when in fairness they should have given it to him! Now they mounted extra guards over it, in the shape of those evil crow-women, and set their champion to sleep beside it like a watchdog. They might as well have said to his face that they feared he would steal it.

It would serve them right if he did.

Why should I not? There is danger and difficulty in it; what else makes worthy feats? I could feed a war-host that would stop the Firbolgs, with all their bows and numbers. That cauldron must be mine.

Nemed chose not to remember that he had decided upon the paths of theft while he was speaking to Oghmal. The Danans of Tirtangir had given him a hugely generous share of the wealth they had received back from the Freths, and allowed him first choice of his rewards, which lay aboard his ships even then. Their hospitality towards him and his men had been greater than they could afford, in their circumstances, yet they had stinted nothing. One thing only had they refused him, and that not theirs to give or lend, as they had made clear from the beginning.

Nemed put that from his mind also.

His intention was just. Of course it was.

A different part of him came back to ask unsettlingly: Was it? Could it ever be right to rob one's hosts? Robbing an enemy, yes; that was something to boast about. Would he ever care to boast about this after he had done it?

The colder, wiser part of Nemed's mind, the greater part, began to function again. His offended pride was nothing; the whining of a puppy. That cauldron was essential to him, and he meant to take it. Cena's people undoubtedly would follow and try to get it back. Oghmal in particular, and Bava's crow cult, would be relentless. He'd have to be prepared for their attentions. Cena too would be furious, and he knew her resourcefulness, yet she would not be able to follow him herself. As the Rhi, she would have too much to do in Tirtangir. Losing the cauldron would surely mean renewed war with the Freths. They would have no strength to spare for Alba then.

Unless they lost, and were driven out entirely. Then the survivors would descend on his coasts like packs of starving wolves, bitter for their vengeance. Nemed thought long about that, and decided to take the gamble. He had been a gambler, an adventurer, too long to resist it. Cena's people could do nothing to him that the Firbolgs were not all too likely to make his grandchildren suffer.

Nemed stared at the carved ceiling. Had he been sleeping beside Cena tonight, as custom was for an honored guest among the Danans, he would have found it much harder to reach such a decision so coolly. Maybe it was as well that they had quarrelled after the scene in the hall. Then he smiled bleakly to himself. No, he'd have stolen the cauldron named Undry in any case. He knew that. Now it was only a matter of how best to go about it.

The thing was as secure as it could ever be. Getting it out of Cena's house, past the encircling earthen ramparts and down to his ships, would require either great stealth or an onslaught by the full strength of his own forces; and in the latter case he felt sure he would fail. His warriors would refuse to do such a treacherous deed. Nemed preferred stealth anyhow.

He rejected magic. Cena was more expert and powerful in sorcery than he. She had Carbri, Loredan, Bava, Alinet the Sunwitch, and many others to call upon if she needed them. Any or all of those folk would at once detect magic used, now that they were alert.

That left ordinary cunning. If a man could not remove a heavy object through the doors or the roof of a splendid house, how, in the many names of the goddess, could he remove it? Through the floor?

The cold days passed towards the turning of the year. Frost still lay on the ground in the mornings, and children jumped gleefully on frozen puddles to make them crack, while bubbles shifted about beneath the surface. The breath of humans, cattle, and horses smoked whitely in the air.

"The Antlered King does not wish to cede the world to the Mother this time around, at all," Carbri remarked, "and he's stronger than usual."

His nails struck the gold strings of his harp, bringing forth a cold, brittle chiming, and icicles grew heavier on a railing nearby. The music became warmer, more fluid, and so did the air around them. Water dripped softly from the ends of the icicles. Tight, frozen buds on a nearby bush opened a little.

"Someday, brother, you will forget yourself, and we shall have the seasons out of turn," Oghmal said, only half jesting. "That, or the Mother will bear two suns in a single day."

The Danans believed their mother, the Earth-Goddess, gave birth to a new sun each dawn in the form of a fiery golden bird which flew up to the zenith, then descended west, aging as it went. When it touched the horizon, the Mother swallowed her child and renewed it through the night. Her power to produce strong new suns was less in the winter, when her body was bound in cold shackles and her son, the Antlered King, ruled in her place. The two advanced and retreated around the cycle of the seasons each year, one gaining a small advantage, then the other. Any careless action of a mortal's could upset the balance, which was why powers like Carbri's should not be used lightly.

He accepted the caution, and even the implied stricture. If they needed anything now, his people needed a warm summer and a mild winter in succession. Nothing but Undry had averted famine in the past months.

"Two suns," he mused, "and the earth would scorch white until one slew the other. Now that would make a fine story, brother. The idea is yours; why not polish it and tell it?"

"Because you would do it better."

"I have a repertoire of three hundred and eighty, and those are only the well-known ones. A single tale will occasion me no fearful loss, and you seldom tell stories."

"I haven't the gift for it."

"Talvi will want something more than talk of weapons at Dar."

"Brother, what Talvi wants is her own affair, not yours and not even mine—though I confess I'd like to make it mine. Let's talk of something else. What became of that mare of yours that you thought would have trouble foaling?"

Carbri sighed. "As you wish. Have trouble she did. I was with her the night long, I and young Mahon, who has a rare soothing touch in such things. The efforts of all three of us had this reward only, a thin, weakly filly with a flawed hoof. She has never thrown anything like that before. I wonder betimes if the Freths' old women are not practicing their craft against us yet. They know what our horses are to us. May rheumy coughs plague them for all their winters, if they are.''

From Carbri, this was vitriolic bitterness. Oghmal said grimly, ''Agreed. But half our beasts are not faring well, and the cause is more likely hunger than spells. The grazing after Summer Day will cure them better than magic.''

Summer Day dawned blue and bright, with thousands of Danans gathered about the temple of the goddess on Sen Mag. Her image, carved from a living oak by Luchtan, held grain and fruit in one raised hand, bones and decay in the other. He'd meant it to remind the people of her double nature, giving and devouring. For the rest, she was full-bodied and richly serene of face.

The needfires burned in the dawn, giving a scent of ash- and pear-wood, spilling pearly smoke across the plain. Red Danan cattle, driven between them for luck and health, snorted in the smoke, while frost crunched yet underfoot. There would be no washing in dew for hopeful maidens on this day.

Two men, clad as warriors of Winter and Summer, staged a battle. As the figure in black and grey sank down, a cheer arose. Winter had been defeated once again, and the world this year would be renewed, for another round of the cycles. As at a signal, the festivities and trading began. Danan spirits were seldom lowered for long.

''Sixarms has yet to arrive,'' Cena said thoughtfully. ''It's unlike him to be tardy. I wonder—ah, but he's tough as oak. What poems will you make of this day, mother's brother?''

''Hopeful ones!'' Loredan said. ''A mad ardor upon you to race horses, where the serried host is ranged around; very splendid is the bounty of the cattle's pool, the iris is gold because of it. Delightful is the season's splendor, winter's rough wind has gone. Bright is every fertile wood; a joyful peace is summer.''

Cena laughed. ''Yes. We will make it so; we must.''

Some miles away, on the roof of her house, the enormous crows still perched. Watchful, black against the bright shingles of blue, russet, and orange, they scrutinized each man and woman who approached or left. Most carefully did they gaze at any bundle or box which was carried. If they saw a hamper or chest which might conceivably contain Undry, one or two would fly down and croak interrogations in human voices. Faced by those formidable, restless beaks and steely talons, few hesitated to display the contents and allay suspicion.

From within the hall came a sudden resounding crash. Sparks flared high as the roof of the hearth collapsed. The oak tiles of the floor splintered about the falling hearthstones, and fine ash billowed. The warriors at the doors gaped a moment in stupefaction; then they rushed as one man towards the ruined hearth.

They found nothing but a black, empty hole with ash swirling in its depths, making them choke as it rode the billows of air upward. Undry was gone; they saw nothing, groped, and found only the edges of the hole in Cena's floor. From below came a mocking cry of "Mice!"

"Mice!" a young warrior in orange said angrily. "Then I'll be their cat." He tore some dangling cords from a tapestry and gave the tasselled ends to his comrades. "Support me."

They did, leaning back and bracing their heels against his weight. He vanished into the darkness, and found himself blind, an easy victim if one of the thieves should be waiting for him at the bottom. He didn't hesitate. There was need to find out where this hole led, and at once.

Stumbling among hearthstones and ash, he drew his dagger and waited for his eyes to attune themselves to the scant light. He wished someone had been there. He wanted blood. Never had he felt so great an anger before. These cunning weasels had robbed him of his trust, the inexhaustible cauldron, and condemned his people to—harsh subservience again, it might be, or at the best a new wasting war. He wanted to kill them, he wanted their guts. Nothing but the smell of their freshly spilled blood would content him.

He crawled into a patch of deeper darkness which proved to be a winding tunnel. Three comrades followed him, one after another, and they wormed forward, tapping each other's soles every so often to assure the man in front that he still had backing. From the hall behind them, warriors had scattered to spread the alarm.

They were too late.

The cauldron had been taken before they were made aware that something was wrong by the crash and collapse of the hearth. The thieves in their tunnel had worked very delicately with knives, cutting through the bottom of the fireplace from underneath, for only in that one spot in all of Cena's hall was the floor made of bare earth. They had caught the falling sods and coals soundlessly on wet hides, no matter how they smoked, and propped up the stones around the hearth's edge as they undercut them. Then they had taken the cauldron from its place by the hearth, and pushed it through their tunnel, a task for which Nemed had chosen the strongest men he had. One had remained behind to knock out the supports, then, and bring down the entire hearth; and he was well away when his first pursuer came down to clear away the wreckage, groping and swearing.

The tunnel was short. It led to the stables, twisting about to clear the cellar. The warriors emerged behind an enormous manure heap, wrinkling their noses, to find nothing.

"They couldn't be gone so fast!" one protested.

"Somehow, they are," the leader snapped. "And if they dug their thievish rabbit-run under cover of *this* stuff, the odor must have been upon them for days. Had they been in the hall it would surely have been noticed. Here, you!" He seized a groom. "Who has ridden out of here this morning?"

"Why, none, sir, except some of your own order." The groom stared at their filthy condition. "They saddled and bridled when the alarms were given. What's happening?"

"The opening of the earth," came the large answer, "and the falling of the sky."

Death, it hammered in him. Death.

He mastered the dread, and thought a little. The thieves could scarcely be out of Ridai yet. He'd have thought they could scarcely be out of their tunnel yet. Saddling his own horse swiftly, he rode to the gate in the outer wall of Ridai's ramparts, with a warning to let nobody leave until Undry was found.

"Has anyone gone yet?" he demanded.

"Just some Rainbow Men of the orange band, riding for the First Created Plain. They said the Rhi must know, and at once."

"I suppose that's right," the warrior in soiled orange said, "although others can have the task of telling her, and welcome. Meanwhile, have the gates closed and let none out except Rainbow Men."

"Conceited little cock-a-hoop," the gatekeeper muttered after the man had gone. "None except Rainbow Men, he says, as if they were gods."

"What has he been doing?" asked his mate. "Rolling in dung?"

"You'd better ask him," came the dour reply. "Ah, listen to that."

The clamor of Bava's monstrous crows as they flapped into the air was chilling. Their wings shadowed every part of Ridai and the woods outside it before they had finished searching, and they found nothing. They flew to the sea, screeching vengefully, and discovered the purple band before them, taking care that Nemed's ships did not sail until the cauldron was recovered.

Frustrated, the War Crows winged back to Ridai, and found a troop of men in purple tunics and fringed violet cloaks there also, their horse-harness gemmed with amethysts. Not until then did it enter their minds that anyone could wear purple. They had only flown above the beach, not landed to investigate more closely, and the delay gave Nemed his chance to depart with a favoring tide. Fifty horses which he and his chief warriors had been loaned for their pleasure were left behind on the shore, each with a purple cloak trailing over its saddle as a signature of trickery.

Undry was aboard one of those vanishing ships. The War Crows flew after them, shrieking, but even they could not fight seven ships' companies, and Nemed's ships were the only places for them to land, besides being swifter than any vessels of Tirtangir.

"Burn his grandmother!" Bava raged. "He'll see Alba again!"

"Yes, lady," Oghmal agreed, his soft, somber voice charged with anger, "and so will we."

"No," Cena said, blanching white. "Oghmal, no!"

"There's no doubt," the champion said. "Nemed is away, with all his ships, and Undry has gone with him."

"No! Sixarms will be here, tomorrow. I've promised him to give the cauldron back. What can I say? *'Oh, it's been stolen, I let it be stolen; such things do happen.'* Oghmal, you and Bava suspected him! You had the guarding of Undry. How could you let him steal it?"

"Because he was too cunning for us, and still our guest, and we supposed our precautions would be enough to discourage him. They were not. He even took advantage of them." Oghmal's voice was like metal. Only one who knew him as well as his sister could have seen the depth of passion he contained. "I will follow him to Alba and bring Undry back, no matter what I must do to obtain it; and I will kill Nemed in plain justice, as a second purpose. But you are the Rhi. It's you who must face Sixarms and tell him. I'll be there, backing you.''

"What if he doesn't believe me? Goddess! What if he demands Undry back with instant war as the forfeit? He's patient, and once he was a friend, but his patience has its limits and this will bring him to them. Brother, our people cannot endure more war!''

"Yes, they can. They can endure it if they have to." Human feeling rang through the metal of Oghmal's voice again. "They can even hold the Freths at bay now, from their fortresses. Yet there is a chance it will not come to that. Sixarms is wise, not only patient; and we won't know until after we have told him.''

"This is the worst dishonor and shame I've ever known," Cena said, her rich voice shaking. "You take it so lightly."

"Sister, if you believe that, there is nothing you will not believe.''

"And now I'm a fool to you!" Cena screamed, seizing her heaviest jar and hurling it at him. He swayed aside, caught another object, then caught her as she flew at him, striking with a warrior's power and skill. "Who let his trust be stolen from under his fool's nose? Who leaves me the task of explaining? Champion! Great champion of our people! What of the tribute-children the Freths hold? A beetle could have done better!"

Oghmal agreed with her, but it would have been ignoble whining to say so. He defended himself against her blows until her rage dissolved in the anguish flowing up from within. She wept as stormily as she had expended her fury, and then she looked at Oghmal with eyes like drenched stones.

"You allowed this to happen. You dishonored us all before Sixarms.''

Dishonor was a word none had ever been able to use to Oghmal before. He felt it like a bath in fire now. He'd been tricked, and with laughable ease. He should have made certain he knew where all of Nemed's men were, at all times, and ordered his ships drawn up on the shore and dismasted until Nemed was ready to leave. That no guest had ever been insulted like that in Cena's house, and that she would have been the last to do it herself had she been there, meant less than nothing. The responsibility had been Oghmal's. It was still his.

He nodded mutely.

"I will look my best when I face him, though," she said. "Send in my girls, Oghmal, and make sure you are at your most splendid, too. Sixarms is not to think he is declaring war on beggars.''

There was no danger of that. Cena appeared again with her hair and face well washed in pure water, her cheeks clear, her eyebrows tinted a dark brown, and her lips reddened. She wore a long tunic of indigo silk, worked with trees half in summer leaf and half in flames, with a necklace of gold and sapphires at her throat. Over it, because the weather was still cold, she had cast a cloak of shaggy white fleece. Her red-gold hair was coiled and piled on her head, with combs of silver and pearl in it, and ornaments of twining animal designs graced both her shoulders.

Oghmal greeted Sixarms in a tunic of shining black linen, bordered with gold, with a belt of heavy gold links. Over it he wore a four-cornered cloak the color of flame, held on one shoulder by a jewelled brooch in a pattern of flying birds. His long sword with its golden hilt hung by his side in a sheath adorned with bronze leaves and branches, all in blue enamel. His dark brown tresses were braided, and he had never looked more like a champion.

Their guest contrasted mightily. By their standards, the Freth was ugly, with a remnant of grooved forehead, beetling brows, and a nose with no bridge to speak of, but plenty of width. He wore the plain hooded tunic and hide leggings he generally did, with his stone-headed club on his vast shoulders, and stumped in with his bent-kneed gait.

Yet he was nothing laughable, despite his grotesque appearance. Sixarms not only held great power, he used it well. Under his kingship, his tribe prospered, and the chiefs of all other Freth tribes acknowledged his superiority. He was the one chosen to represent them before the Danans. Once he had led them in war against the invaders to victory, and once to a drawn conclusion. His name had been given him because of his prowess as a builder, and the lands he ruled were fertile and productive under his kingship. The Freths would never have a greater lord.

He heard what Cena had to say, and she said it like a ruler, with dignity and courage. Sixarms, for once, nearly lost his massive composure. Doubt, great anger, mistrust, could be seen battling in his bearded face, in the stance of his body. At last he said in a voice like querning stones:

"Is this true? If you are lying to keep the cauldron yourselves—"

"She is not," Oghmal said flatly. "I am the one who lost it

when I had the duty of guarding it, and it will soon be in Alba, so you must accuse me. Nemed has robbed us both.''

"It makes no difference! What do I care whether you are trying to cheat me or whether you lost Undry to a trickster? I will have it back. You must bring it to me by Midsummer, or face war with the Freths again. War, for as long as it takes to drive you out of the sacred island wholly. You know that this is not a threat to laugh at.''

"We are not laughing, as you see. Neither will Nemed, for very long," Oghmal said.

"Sixarms, you know we know what this failure would cause for our people," Cena reminded him. "The agreement was that we restore Undry to you in the spring, at this gathering fair. More than that! Some of our children, a third of them, are still . . . fostered among you. Are we such fools?''

"It seems so. What of my people? I feed them from the lip of Undry when the hard winters strike. Shall I go home to them and say, I, your mother's brother, can do this no longer? The cauldron was loaned to your enemies by me, and they were careless; it is gone.''

"It will be recovered," Cena said. "Give us until Winter Eve instead of Midsummer.''

"Midsummer is long enough. If you cannot find Undry within three full cycles of the moon, you probably cannot do it at all.''

"You do not trust us to go to Alba, or bring back the cauldron if we do go. That is what you mean.''

"Trust between us has worn very thin, Cena. Has is not?''

"I will give hostages, then—and be one, if you wish.''

"That you will not, sister." The champion was determined. "You are the Rhi. You cannot do this to ease the shame you feel when you are needed here to stand for the tribe before the goddess.''

"Besides," Sixarms said in his deep, slow voice, "we Freths have all the hostages we need. The Undry must be returned, and that you may have a chance to do this, I will check all retaliation—until Midsummer.''

"And after that?" Oghmal asked, very quietly, very gently. Taller than Sixarms, long-limbed and relaxed, he was yet almost as heavy in the chest and shoulders as the Freth. Nothing had ever escaped Oghmal's long hands when they gripped in earnest.

Sixarms looked back at him, steadily, calmly, a brown gaze centered in many wrinkles meeting a pale blue one which had become relentless. Sixarms knew the champion's loyalty to tribe and kin; there, if nowhere else, they had something in common. He also knew death when it looked at him. However, he had not been shaken by the certainty of death in many years.

"After that," he said, "we will do as pleases us. Don't look for understanding; I'll hear no excuse. You have some time, and that is all I can give."

"It will be all that we need," Cena said. "We will restore Undry to you."

Chapter
Two

The wide circular hall at Ridai clamored with tongues. Men and women of the highest standing spoke for and against each other's ideas. Cena, her hot passions but partly curbed by time, rulership, and children, sat on cushions like the rest in the Council circle, her apple-wood throne with its copper ornaments abandoned for the present. Light streaming through the sun-windows above made her hair a treasure of red gold. The only head brighter in all of the room belonged to Alinet the Sunwitch.

Loredan, her mother's brother, sat beside Cena, legs crossed beneath what had once been a comfortably round paunch but was now flatter. Much as he liked his comforts, the master-poet did not eat as he pleased while his people went hungry. Cena had ruled with his help from the beginning, finding in his mildness and detached intelligence a counterweight for her own fiery nature.

Across from her, yellow-eyed and savage, sat Bava the War Crow, with Hol next to her, a chieftain of middle rank only, though in terms of cattle and followers one of the strongest in the land. Young Mahon Stagshanks sat awkwardly in the circle, the master of Lost Star Lake since his closest kin had died in the war with the Freths; a difficult situation for him, since he'd been fostered among the Freths and hardly knew Danan ways any longer. He'd become a client-follower of Cena's, and accepted her guidance. Shaui the pirate, just arrived from his island stronghold, was another of her clients, having become such in return for the cancellation of a gambling debt it would have inconvenienced him to pay. Chieftains, leaders, and judges, they filled the center of Cena's hall, sitting or lounging by low tables. Outside that circle, in partitioned booths against the wall, sat the major artists and craftsmen, like Talvi the weaver, Gavidu the flint-worker, and Beren the bronze-worker, each one adept in the particular magic of his or her calling. Short of a full assembly of the free folk, which would have been held outdoors for lack of room, this was the most representative gathering possible.

They all knew what had happened, and agreed that the cauldron must be recovered, the thief punished. The only question was how. Shaui suggested a swift raid from the sea, to capture it and be gone before the thief could respond; retribution in kind. Bava wanted to attack from the air with her flock of shape-changing women, an even swifter raid. Some of the younger chiefs spoke for a full war against Nemed, and were laughed to scorn by most of their elders. Their people could not afford a war with anyone.

"This is not a matter of glory," Cena said. "If the Undry is not with Sixarms again by Midsummer, war will result, and that we cannot have. I favor sending a small band or warriors and sorcerers, chosen by me. They will leave at once for Alba, and only I will know who they are. If they fail, we will need every great fighter we have, here in Tirtangir; the War Crows, the Rainbow Men, the chiefs' retinues, Oghmal's war-band. None can be spared on a venture like this." Cena had almost said, a forlorn venture like this. "I think only a small group could succeed."

"This hospitality-breaker Nemed has warriors of his own," Hol growled. The veins in his heavy neck swelled. "Good ones, as we know from his fighting while he was here, and a fleet of metal ships. What can a few do against them?"

"What could our full strength on the sea?" Cena countered. "I know what Nemed will do with the Undry; use it to feed the

host he means to raise against his own enemies, the Firbolgs. His
ships will not be left out of such a scheme. Where they are, he
will be. He won't be hard to find, but cunning must do the rest.''

Loredan supported her, as did her followers, and she had her
way after some intemperate argument back and forth. Nothing
had ever been settled among Danans without high words and
challenges flying. The only thing to do was enjoy it. Cena
generally did, but not this time. Too much was at stake.

With her uncle and brothers, she settled the details in private.
The names of those who were to go had to remain secret, or as
secret as possible; and Oghmal was determined to be one.

"If it comes to single combat, and it may, I'm the only one
who can surpass Nemed," he said. "I should have challenged
and slain him here when I had the chance. If it comes again I
will not let it slip."

"I go too," his twin said. His harp added a crashing emphasis
to his words. "You for the fighting, I for the enchantment,
brother."

"I haven't seen you backward when there was ever sword-
work to be done," Oghmal answered. "But it's your other
talents we will need. We two. Who else, then?"

"A sorcerer. You, mother's brother?"

"No," Loredan said firmly. "A sorceress, young yet highly
skilled. Alinet."

"Alinet. Yes, she would go. She's powerful—but only by
day. You should have another with you."

"That we can decide later," Carbri said, breaking in eagerly.
"In what guise should we go? We cannot cross water without a
ship, and if we cannot be open war-men we must be traders.
That calls for a knowing captain and some good sailors, for by
the Powers, Oghmal and I are none! What of Shaui?"

"Once that raider got within arm's reach of the cauldron, I
would not trust him," Loredan said, shaking his head. "Choose
a real trader instead. I'm not acquainted with many, but I believe
Tringad is in port, and he knows the seaways around Alba from
Ettins to the Isle of Tin."

"He's a fine drinking partner, and I judge him trusty enough,"
Carbri declared. "Except when lying about the voyages he's
made, and that is to be expected. He and all his men are fighters;
they have to be stronger than any pirate who might rob them."

"Tringad, then, if he'll agree, and I must enspell his memory if he doesn't. We cannot have him talking in his cups until the Undry has been regained, brothers."

"I'll talk to him, and I'll take care."

"One other sorcerer and three more warriors ought to suffice, then," Oghmal said. "For the fighters, three from my own war-band are as useful as any I know, and besides their skills of the warrior, each has a wonderful gift. Arn can carry any burden a pack-horse can carry, and farther, and the burden he carries can never be seen, from before his face or behind his back. Tavasol has such a light tread that he can walk over the thinnest crust of a bog without breaking through, or run over the tops of the trees in a wood without needing a road. As for Lygi, when he comes to a farmstead or village, and is in want of anything, he can withhold sleep from every person there until he gets it."

"If it were Carbri or his friend the sea-captain saying that, brother, I would never believe it!" Cena laughed. "But you I know for a most serious man. Did you think we hadn't heard of those three, or some of the others? Bring them by all means. The business looks more hopeful by the hour. Let you go to Dar and see them, while you, Carbri, ride to the harbor and sound out the trader. Loredan and I will decide upon the second sorcerer while you are gone. Do you trust us for that?"

"Yes," Carbri said at once, teeth flashing white through his moustache the hue of new copper. "Still I would rather that second sorcerer was you, mother's brother. A taste of adventure would do you good. There are more things in the world than advising and adjudicating, or even than poetry."

"Adventure, my child, is better told than lived," Loredan said, "and any stories of adventurers decently fed and clothed are just that—stories. You will be longing for the bath-houses of Ridai, and fit to be passed through a sword-ring without brushing its inner surface before you see me again. Of this I assure you."

"If we don't succeed, you may wish you were farther away from comfortable Ridai," Oghmal said dourly.

"None of that," Cena said warmly. "I know you will fight and strive to succeed after ten other men would have yielded, brother, so why use dismal words? Do not forget to take leave of Talvi before you go."

"Talvi?" The girl might have been in her grave three years the way Oghmal said it. Cena colored with a woman's anger, and Carbri shook his head, despairing of his twin. "Yes, I'll see her now."

"By the grass of the First Created Plain, don't put yourself out!" Cena said hotly. "Nor suppose that she will always see *you*."

The harbor was not much of a place to a man who had seen the ports of Crète and Egypt, as Tringad claimed to have done; merely a bay with various bothies and tents by the shore, and one hall with age-blackened thatch where indifferent beer was brewed. Tringad's ruddy face lit when he saw Carbri saunter in, the harp of bog oak on his back and his ornaments chiming. The short, chunky, balding man bounded to his feet and shouted across the rush-strewn floor.

"Carbri, you royal songsmith! What kept you? There was a bond-girl from Illyria would have suited you well, pretty and far-travelled, sold up the Amber Track and then brought west—so the factor told me, and if I'd learned later you were deceived, I'd have drowned him when next we met. But at least there is still a jar of the southern wine unopened. You are the one man here who appreciates it. When are you going to sail a voyage with me? It would be the making of you."

"I'm a landsman bred," Carbri answered, lowering his rangy limbs to the bench beside Tringad, after unbuckling his sword and dropping it on the table. Tringad couldn't help a quick, expert appraisal of the workmanship in the hilt, or the gold and jewels, equal to anything from the east he had ever seen.

"Many another seaman once said the same. There are no ships like ours anywhere in the world, even the timber ones we are reduced to building now. We would rule the seaways from Spain to the Amber Country if our numbers were greater and we weren't so aloof."

"It's hard-pressed we are here, just now. Even in Illyria you must have heard something."

Carbri had not the slightest notion where Illyria was, and doubted whether Tringad did either. The captain had not actually claimed to have been there, but neither did he quarrel when Carbri assumed it.

"Yes, I have been told. Is it bronze for weapons you need? Man, with a hundred warriors like your brother I could take control of the Isle of Tin and hold it against all rivals. You would have bronze enough to make the foundations of your houses from it. The poorest bondman from the fields would carry a metal axe when he went to war. None could resist you. You'd take Tirtangir in a generation."

Tringad had his extravagances; indeed, he spoke little else, but within them there usually lay central specks of reality. Carbri reached into his saddlebag and placed two shining silver cups on the board. Gold filigree circled the rims, and intricate gold bosses gemmed with jet adorned the bowls. The captain's eyes glistened as he turned them over slowly, delighting in their beauty.

"They have never yet been wet," Carbri said, "and they might be moistened worse than in the cause of helping us talk."

"That's only the truth," Tringad said, and filled the cups with ruby wine. "You are not here only to trade drinks and lies with me, are you, Carbri? Tell me about it after we have well and truly moistened these cups and our own gullets, for I tell you the salt of the sea will need some washing out of mine—and I never knew the time when a bard did not need to be drunken."

"You have it wrong. A bard is always drunken, on a hotter, more ethereal fire than dwells even in wine . . . Words, Tringad, words and fancies. But as you have noticed, we don't scorn wine on that account. Some of my richest invective is kept for those who do, should I meet any."

"I admire that." Tringad swallowed smoothly, with the fine drinking manners of even the roughest Danan. "And how do your kin fare?"

"Cena shines with health, man, and so do her children. Our cousins are well. You know that Garanowy was killed at the Battle of the Waste?"

"I did. Waste, indeed, of a merry youth. He should come back through the Cup of Rebirth as a skylark. Here's to it."

Carbri drank to that gladly. Garanowy had received a month-long wake and some of the best funeral games seen in Tirtangir for a generation; but grief remained, with the hope that they might recognize each other in some future life. Bard and sea-captain drank half their wine and ritually spilled the rest.

"You taught the Freths their lesson in the end, though," Tringad said. "They rule you no more."

"Between us we wasted and maimed half the sacred island first. As you say, we're free and at peace, though it is held in place by a spiderweb and a breath just now. And what of your kin, Tringad?"

"As usual. My wives are pleased when they see me, pleased

when I depart again, and the children change out of recognition while I'm away. My sisters are well, but the black Firbolgs menace everything. The day will come when someone else menaces *them*, and they have to turn back, to deal with it. May it come soon, Carbri.''

Carbri doubted that it would. But he saw that this matter would require careful handling. Tringad knew the seaways they must travel as well as anyone. However, with his kin at risk from invaders, he was not likely to help the folk of Tirtangir flout a man who fought those invaders. Carbri felt free to lie, deceive, and outwit Nemed in any way possible; but he did not award himself the same freedom when it came to dealing with Tringad.

At some time during the talking bout which followed, he gained Tringad's agreement to take himself and a small band of companions across the sea, there to get back the Undry, which had been stolen by their treacherous guest. Unlike his brother, Carbri saw little gain in trying to keep the matter a secret. There never had been one. All knew that Sixarms's inexhaustible cooking-pot had been taken, and by whom. Nemed certainly knew that his former hosts would appear to relieve him of it, and swiftly. It would not strain Tringad's powers of thought in the least to infer the reason for a party, which included Carbri, taking ship for Alba. Nor would a disguise of illusions remain secure for long in the intimacy of a trading ship.

''No, we have to have a skipper we can rely upon,'' Carbri explained, ''and if it's Nemed you side with, say so now, Tringad, for that's a thing I can understand. It would not be healthy, though, for you to strike a bargain with us and then deliver us to that traitor, or to tell him the smallest thing that we might not want him to know. Powers greater than any of your own would be drawn against you then.''

''No threats.'' The captain drank deeply again. ''No more of that. Carbri, I mean no offence, but you are a bard, and that means you believe the fancies you sing. You think Nemed and this cauldron will turn back the Firbolgs, that his return will save Alba—and that nothing else can. Other and better war-leaders have been leading that fight the whole while of his years in exile! Saran-ve the Hundred Fighter, and Redern, and Fanareith the Young—who's Nemed to compare with them? A crafty pirate! He slew two men who were like brothers to me while he was outlawed, and if I can help you do him some harm, I'll be delighted. You need a sea-captain? You have found your man.''

Carbri smiled, painfully. ''Maybe. Our need is for a ship to take us to Alba now, and to go where we bid, anchor where we wish, follow our instructions from now till Midsummer—or tell us why those instructions are unwise. We don't know those waters; you do. Are you prepared for that?''

''If you hire my ship at the right price.''

Carbri rode back to his kindred's royal house well content, and immediately told Cena he had found a captain.

''Good,'' Cena said seriously. ''That's excellent, my brother. For I will be coming with you.''

''We were agreed that you couldn't do that. You are needed too greatly here.''

''No, brother. How I am needed, and for what, is mine to decide. The Rhi who fails her people is not one. Well, nothing counts for more to the people now than the recovery of this one lost treasure. It's known and arranged who shall succeed me if I die; Loredan, Hol, and Bava will see that it happens. You need a second sorceress. I am that, and no mean fighter, either. My magic is potent by night as well as day. I can assume more shapes than one. How could you do better?''

''*We* could not. Sister, are you doing this to escape the harder part of sitting at Ridai and waiting?''

''Of course I am! And never will I lead the Danans back into a ruinous war. Rather would I die or live in exile than that. No lectures from you, Carbri, who have been out drinking merrily when you were on a mission so serious. Cowardly it may be to shirk waiting. Let it be that way. I never could endure to wait, and I shall not stomach it now. You have said yourself you could find nobody better.''

''That I did, sister.'' A coppery lock tumbled over Carbri's eye. His mouth quirked.

Oghmal rode back that night with the warriors of his choice, Arn, Lygi, and Tavasol. All were young, personable, and quick to laugh, skillful with weapons, fine and daring riders; not so very different from some hundreds of their fellows, except for their unique abilities. Slower-spoken and more deliberate than the others, Arn was tall, broad, and strong. Cena thought he might have trouble keeping his girth within allowable limits when he was older.

The light, wiry one with the sandy-reddish hair and sharply

defined features could only be Tavasol, who ran over the tree-tops in a wood, requiring no road. That left the well-knit auburn one with the curling hair to be Lygi, and Cena found that she remembered them all right.

The next morning, as she played with her children, a bird with fiery golden feathers flew to Ridai from the south and perched in a linden tree, dazzling among the green leaves. Macha, the eldest child, ran to stand beneath it and stared in wonder. The burning tail was three times the length of the bird's body, which in turn was the size of a youth or a small woman, and its wings, outstretched, had spanned nine yards. The leaves turned crisp and sere where the bird's plumage brushed them.

"Don't look at her too long, Macha," the Rhi warned. "She will weaken your eyes, for that is Alinet the Sunwitch."

The bird fluttered to the ground. Macha felt uncomfortable warmth reach towards her, and moved unwillingly away, much as she would have liked to touch those glorious feathers. Then their colors changed, forming a pattern of black, white, and orange, while the shape of the bird changed also. In a moment a woman stood there. Of a light, fine-boned build, like Tavasol, she had heavy, gleaming yellow hair and skin of a warm apricot tint. Her eyes flashed blue as a spring dawn. Although tiny, she was vivid enough to make the striking Cena seem almost wan. Over her three-colored gown she wore a black cloak embroidered with fiery red wheels.

"Good day to you, my lady," she said, rather as though she were the Rhi, greeting a visitor. "You sent for me, and such a great stir there is in the land, because of the missing Undry and Sixarms's anger, that I can guess why. When shall I leave for Alba?"

"Not you alone, cousin." They were in truth second cousins, but because the relationship existed through Loredan, a man, it was not taken very seriously. Like all her people, Alinet reckoned her descent through the female line. "Seventeen of us are going, myself included, and not all of us may return. The man we deal with would slay to keep what he has."

"I remember Nemed. Wasn't I at Ridai several times while he was here? He could not keep his eyes off me. He courted you too, for a while, although Gui was your man and he had two wives in Alba. Perhaps they would like to know how he behaved here."

"Perhaps. Did you ever bed with him?"

"No, cousin. He took too much for granted, and I like what I grant to be recognized. He—it was too plain that he was only passing the time in his exile, ready for any mischief. It seems he still is."

"Now that he's home again, he may remember that he has things to lose, and be more steady. But I doubt it. He left again quickly enough when I called him to Tirtangir. He's the roving sort. His wives won't hold him in one place."

"He will remember me too well. He won't have spoken of me to his wives, though." Alinet smiled confidently. "We might visit them while he is away, and wrest the cauldron from their keeping. Do you know them? Are they easily deceived?"

"I don't know them, although I have seen them. Vivha, I think, would do as she pleases in any circumstances, and she's a sorceress to rank with us. We can only see when we get there. He will surely spend some time at home before he takes the war-trail."

"This Vivha must hardly know what her man looks like any longer!"

"True. I have seen far more of him these seven years than has she, and she won't love me the more for that, if she should discover who I am. We are going to her own place, where she practices her own sorceries and knows the local earth. There will be danger, but I cannot wait for a better time. We don't have the time. Will you come, Alinet?"

"I will, and do not fear. There will be a way."

Cena did not like being reassured by a woman young enough to be her niece—almost her daughter. Then her sense of humor came to her rescue. She said dryly, "You have not had time to learn much about fear, cousin. The earth men have always been very agreeable to you, as they should, and jealous of each other over you, which can be pleasing. It is different when one looks at you with the eyes of a foe. I could wish you had been trained for a warrior."

"Everyone else has," the Sunwitch said. "You may need someone to charm a man while you are all clashing your bronze elsewhere. It's true that none has wanted to be my foe yet."

Anhir, maker of stars! Cena thought. *With looks like yours you will have Oghmal's young fighters tripping over their own feet before we clear the harbor. I have misgivings . . . ah, but maybe I am jealous.*

"We need you, cousin," Cena said. "Don't fail us."

"I will not." Alinet grew sober for a moment. "You needn't think that men will distract *me*."

Again reassurances. It struck Cena then that perhaps it was the Sunwitch who needed them, in which case it would be better not to caution or chide her.

"Come and meet them then. See what you think of them."

Alinet had known Cena's brothers since she was an infant, and was at least acquainted with all the warriors of their followings. Tringad and his nine sailors she had never met before. The captain greeted her civilly, the crew with respect tinged with awe and a lust they kept hidden, not even expecting ever to do anything about it. They liked the shapes they wore.

The ship put to sea the next day.

Chapter
Three

Oghmal, in a dark red tunic with zigzags of white woven through it, sat by the ship's railing with Alinet. Water-tight as a nut and almost as round, the vessel had been built to the highest standards of Danan artisanship, every joint, seam, and treenail so close that it rode the water like a living thing. Stylized waves were carved along the gunwales, and the forepost ended in the shape of a leaping cod with a comical expression. Alinet had laughed when she saw it.

She said pensively, "Do we need trickery to do what we came for? You could challenge this man. Maybe if you joined one of the other chieftains who are fighting these invaders, and talked of Nemed's treachery and kept talking of it, loudly, he would be shamed into meeting you. Carbri could satirize him the length of Alba if he did not."

"It's been thought of," the champion told her. "By the oath of our people, it was the first thing I thought of, the cauldron to go to the victor. But supposing I do get it that way, the chieftain I fight for may be tempted by it just as Nemed was. Neither is he the kind to respond to a challenge which is not in his interest. He wears armor in battle, you know. I never fully trusted him after I saw that. It shows a vein of cowardice somewhere.''

"A crafty coward, a breaker of hospitality, a thief and trickster—and something of a lecher, or so he seemed to me." Alinet looked across the white-capped waves to the dark mountains of the nearing coast. "Yet he's famous as a warrior, too."

"I'd never detract from his skill. But to fight him I will have to lure him into a situation where he has something besides honor to gain from it. His home is there, among those mountains, and we'll have to go there—or some of us will, whom he does not know.''

"He must know your warriors, and he will surely remember me."

"Yes. I should have said, whom he does not know *well*. They will just have to stay out of his way. Between them they should be able to get the cauldron, and with that in our hands again, Nemed's pride and purpose will be nothing until he takes it back. It's for me to see that he doesn't survive the attempt.'' Oghmal shrugged. "That's the plan. Something is sure to go wrong with it so that we must make new ones as we go."

"You doubt a lot."

"Here, I think, comes the first of my reasons to." Oghmal gazed at the mountainous cape they were approaching. From its direction, cleaving the wind-ruffled water like a fine blade despite its crew having to row against the breeze, came a metal-hulled ship with its mast lowered.

"One of Nemed's?"

"I don't doubt it.''

By the time the vessel drew alongside, the party was disguised by a glamor. They wore the semblance of men, wives, one old man, two children, and a few animals huddled together, evidently seasick, and just as evidently related. Their appearance said that they were farmers.

"Who are you?" demanded the leader of the spear-bearing men in the metal ship. The narrow-bladed ash oars combed the water to hold it beside the wooden trader.

"Who asks?" Tringad inquired.

"Prince Nemed's men, through my mouth, and I'm Sheirvand Bru."

Tringad gave his own name then, and told his business. "Why

is the prince concerned? If this was a fighting longship, I'd understand, but anyone can see this is a trader.''

"Trader or not, if it comes to his shores from Tirtangir, he wants to know," Sheirvand replied. A burly, heavy-featured man, he wore a doeskin tunic and carried a shield with three running horses painted thereon. "He's at feud with the Rhi for tricking her. Are you pretending not to know?''

"I know what I heard in Tirtangir," Tringad replied. "They're saying that after being her guest for years, he robbed Cena of her best piece of plunder from the war, and now the Freths are ready to march again because of it. That's why my passengers are leaving,'' he added.

"Running away?" Sheirvand asked, looking them over.

Carbri answered, in the creaking voice of the old man he now resembled. "We've had too much of living under Freth lordship, warrior. It isn't right for a Danan. Farmed our farm since me mother's mother's time, we did, but they beasts left little of it, and now they'll burn the rest, if they come again. Urggh.'' He made a horrible noise. "Rather take our chances in Alba, which our forebears shouldn't ha' left.''

"You won't find the Firbolgs any softer, old man.''

"What about your lord, then? Does he have land to offer? We can grow barley in anything but the white sea sand, make a dead cow give milk.''

"My lord needs warriors," Sheirvand said flatly. "He marches when the seed-time is over, and that won't be long. If he gave you land yesterday, you'd still be too late to plant. Try south of Sabra. Is that where you are headed, trader?''

"In the end. I'll do some trading along the safe shores, keep wide of Sabra, and make for the Isle of Tin. Hides and copper are what I have aboard now, and some old bronze for reworking.''

"Put in here. My prince will take your bronze at the best price you are apt to get. All the smiths are making weapons.''

"Say yes," Cena whispered, through lips which never moved.

Tringad agreed, and followed the mirror-blue hull landward. Cena—her tall, mature body hidden within a toil-bent illusion with arthritic hands—felt excitement surge through her, heady as young love. As easily as that, they were landing on Nemed's shores. They would probably not be noticed by the man himself, and she could befool any of his warriors who had been in Tirtangir with him. She remembered them all, and knew their individual natures. The cauldron of plenty seemed almost near enough to touch.

Tringad's ship put in at a creek-mouth where, not far in, a waterfall dropped like a narrow streak of silver through ferns and willow. Cena gazed longingly upward, to the mountains she knew enclosed Nemed's home. For her it was too perilous, though. Once before she had gone to the prince's home in disguise. He knew her resourcefulness. She wished now that she had made rather less of a parade of it on that occasion.

"Sir," she said to Sheirvand, "will you ask your lord to spare us a plot of ground for a farm? However poor and stony it is, we will work it as it never was worked before—"

"I've told you," Sheirvand said, bored. "No. If you haven't the courage to stay with your family's land, do not come begging for it here. There isn't a farm in these mountains but has been worked for a thousand years if it can produce at all."

Cena retreated, muttering under her breath. It would have looked strange had they taken no for an answer too readily. She thought she had been just importunate enough to convince, without drawing too much attention.

Some of Nemed's household officers came down to the shore, with scales and goods, and spirited bargaining followed. Tringad cried that he was being robbed; the prince's officers declared that he was taking advantage of their lord's generosity and his lady's. In the end they made their bargain. It hadn't been a bad one for either side.

"Calling for warriors, is he?" Tringad asked, as though it was news. "Should I mention it in the south, or did the word go forth last autumn?"

"Carry the message if you like, but you'll find the prince's ships ahead of you. They have gone to Arcaness* and the Isle of Tin with the news, like a flight of sea eagles. You will follow as a fat goose paddles."

"What?" Tringad laughed aloud. "You sneering clown, if you tried to manage any ship, you'd capsize it! This one handles cleanly; she's the nut of my heart. Were you at sea under my command for a month I'd work some goose grease off you."

When they were private again, he looked inquiringly at the sorry band his lordly passengers had become.

---

*The Devon-Cornwall peninsula.

"What's your will now? I've said that I go south. It will look mighty suspicious if we don't."

"The prince's ships are there, raising a force," Tavasol said, his light, quick voice issuing strangely from the loose-lipped mouth he now showed the world. "It's an easy way to join him. Nothing would look more natural."

"True. But to go all that way, then come all the way back—"

"—at someone else's speed, or—"

"—when we are here now—"

"Stop!" Cena's voice cut through the babble. "We know the prince will look closely at any strangers who come here, in any guise. We can be lost in a war-host, few of whom he will know at all. Arn can carry the Undry through the midst of it, with nobody the wiser. Any of the men could, if he wore the cloak of invisibility."

"I'll take it now, and steal the thing," Oghmal offered. "How long will it take me, walking?"

Cena told him, she having been there before, alone of them all. " 'Ware horses and dogs. They may not see you, but they can smell."

"I'll have a care."

"What am I to do, then?" Alinet asked. "Sit here in the guise of a farm girl with a face like uncooked bannock while others do the work?"

"You will work as hard as any before this is over," Cena promised. "And it is not that bad. The face I conjured for you is no worse than *cooked* bannock."

Oghmal the Champion drew on the cloak Talvi had woven, with its varied and subtle earth colorings. As he fastened it and drew forward the hood, he vanished from the sight of all living things, yet continued to see. Walking forward past the cargo space, he sprang ashore in the footprints of Nemed's people and entered the woods. The seamen stared as a branch bent back under no evident pressure, then whipped forward again. It had disconcerted them to see six and a quarter feet of tough-muscled manhood vanish while they watched.

Oghmal came to the glacial valley where Nemed's manor stood. Narrow between the mountains, it contained a long narrow lake, with the prince's dwelling set far above the water on a slope. Circular in plan, like most great Danan houses, it had a

slate roof and pillars of red yew. Covered porches looked over
the valley; gables rose like folded dragons' wings above.

Oghmal followed a swineherd driving his charges home along
the lake's margin. Those animals too sensed his presence and,
being cleverer than dogs or horses, began a grunting, squealing
clamor the champion thought would give him away. The swineherd made signs of protection and drove his beasts faster. Whatever troubled them, he did not wish to know about it.

Thus Oghmal approached the house and, after cleaning his
shoes, entered it behind a couple of late arrivals. Treading with
care, he reached one of the great hall's upper balconies and
looked down into it. Entering it would be ill-advised. Wolf—and
deerhounds—cracked bones by the hearth. They would pull down
even the champion of Tirtangir if they shut their jaws upon him.
Oghmal surveyed the hall carefully from where he stood, and did
not see the cauldron.

Prowling the house, he searched it as well as he could from
cellar to roof. In the process, he learned that being invisible was
not the all-permitting freedom boys dreamed that it granted.
Cena had warned him of watchdogs. He soon realized that if
anyone suspected he was there, he could be trapped in many
ways. He could not open a door or chest where anyone might see
it move. Instead, if a passage was not empty, he had to wait for
someone to use the door he wanted, and then follow him closely.
That too had its dangers. If he trod too closely on the person's
heels, he risked jostling him, and even if he avoided that, there
were many ways to betray himself; a stir of air at his guide's
elbow, a loud breath, the warmth of his body, a footprint in dust
or moisture.

Stealing food and eating it had its drawbacks, too. Oghmal
visited the cookhouse only once. An entire roast duck vanished
under his magic cloak while he was there, and he found a hayloft
wherein to eat it so that nobody should be amazed by the sight of
portions hanging in the air, and diminishing bite by bite.

Then he returned to his search. He looked in storehouses, in
Nemed's chamber; he stood within reach of the prince while he
ate, and thought grimly, *I could slay you now, with one blow,
where you sit fancying that the world is yours.*

He couldn't do that. His honor forbade it. Besides, even
invisible, he would never escape afterward; he was here to find
the cauldron, not to take vengeance; and he wanted Nemed to
know who was slaying him, when the time came. Still, it was

satisfying to stand there, while Nemed laughed and drank in the yellow orb-light, and to know that he held the prince's life squarely in his hands. One day Oghmal hoped he would have a chance to tell him.

He followed the prince as closely as he dared, and both his wives, the extraordinary Vivha and the merely comely Siranal. None led him to the Undry. Oghmal would have thought that Nemed must be constantly looking at his treasure, to admire it, to be sure it was still there, and to dream of what he would achieve with it. Seemingly he had a stronger will than that. Perhaps he had stowed it in some hiding place that only he knew, and left it there until he required it. Nor had Oghmal all the time in the world before he must return to the ship. It would arouse suspicion if the trader loitered, doing nothing.

Oghmal left, disgruntled. It made him even more out of temper when a dog attacked him by the lake. Dragging it to the water, he drowned it before it could rend his throat, but he sustained a mauling before it died. He went on his way with his bites stinging.

At the ship, once he had made sure it was safe, he threw off the cloak with joy. "When I see Talvi again, if she asks me, I must say to her that I felt like a walking ghost in that," he growled. "Only thieves and mice could like it. Nor did it do any good. Nemed has the Undry hidden away somewhere inaccessible, and wouldn't lead me to the place. I suppose he'll bring it out when he needs it to feed the war-host he's gathering, and not before."

"Still, it was worth trying," Cena said, folding the enchanted cloak and returning it to their chest, now disguised through illusion as a wicker hamper. "Since it didn't work, we can go south now, as you said, captain."

"There's something you could have done, surely," Alinet said incredulously. "You were *there*, in the house, unseen, and you could think of no way to provoke him into running for what he values most? I'd have fired the place, burned it to ash, then watched to see what he did. The cauldron would have been in your hands within an hour."

"And a hundred warriors would have been racing to surround this ship in the same space of time," Carbri added. "They'd have beaten one man with a heavy load he must be careful not to break. The Undry is pottery, you know, not metal. How would we have explained that one of us was missing?"

"It was worth trying," Alinet repeated. "Your own words. We're treading so cautiously that we achieve nothing! We haven't much time. Do you truly think he will march by Midsummer?"

"No," Cena said, "but I'm sure he must bring the cauldron to feed his increasing host before then. Oghmal did rightly."

"Rightly?" Alinet stared at her relative. "You're old," she said at last. "All of you. Being conquered by the Freths and then holding them to a bare standstill has made you frightened of a risk. You're quivering scared lest they make war again. Nemed is braver than any of you! Oghmal the Champion," Alinet demanded, "what has happened since you slew the serpents of venom at Incar?"

"Enough, brat," Oghmal said coolly. "Enough. It's because of us, old though we may be, that you never saw those serpents crawling across your own grass. If you think Nemed is braver than any of us, it is strange notions of courage you have. The man robbed his hosts. As for you, little one, you are speaking in a manner which will get you thrashed by me if there is any more of it, so bridle that tongue to a courteous pace."

"You thrash me?" Alinet jeered. "I'd scorch your hands off! And if I'm not to speak when I see our mission failing for lack of will, why am I here?"

Cena felt anger and amusement blended. She controlled the first and concealed the second, remembering days when she had been as young and hot as the Sunwitch, as sure that there was nothing in all the many worlds her powers could not deal with. That fierce girl lived within her yet, impatient of restraint; but ruling and raising children alike demanded it.

"You are here, as we are, to save our people from another war," she said. "That mission hasn't failed, and none of us are weak-willed, least of all Oghmal. It is better to deal with Nemed in the south than here in his own place, where he is most secure. His senior wife is as noted a sorceress as I, and I'd rather she was not near him when we lift the cauldron. We have sufficient time to do it this way; not too much, but enough."

"Indeed," Carbri said, "so do not be in too great a hurry to burn houses or scorch off hands. You may be forced to do such things sooner than you like."

Cool, rippling sounds came from his harp.

"I cannot be gulled or soothed that easily, cousin," Alinet told him, from behind the plain illusory face she wore. "The power of your music, I know. Now, I was at fault in my rudeness, but my opinion is unchanged that we are missing a chance here which we may not have again. Arn, Tavasol, Lygi, what think you? It is you who must parade in borrowed guises to do this thing.''

She freighted her tone subtly with scorn, and had she worn her own face and shape in that moment, they might have expressed dissatisfaction with the plan of their lords rather than look mean in her eyes. They were as ready as most young men to be influenced by a lovely face. However, they were also Oghmal's warriors, three of his companions.

"And we'll do it well, lady," Arn said.

"That we will," Tavasol supported him, gleefully. "Never will this prince or any henchman of his be able to keep what is rightfully ours."

"It is not rightfully ours, though by the rights of war-spoil we are better entitled to the Undry than he." Cena's words were a judicious warning. "When we have it, it goes back to the Freths. Let you all remember that."

"It's a waste," Lygi said.

The whimsical cod that was the ship's figurehead goggled across the water, looking south and farther south. The mountainous cape that was Nemed's home receded astern, and a headland covered with dense dark woods grew closer before them.

"Once we round that, we'll have half a dozen islands and any number of mainland bays to shelter us," Tringad told the Rhi. "The cursed Firbolgs are swarming the region; even so, there's so much more coast than there are ships to use it that we shouldn't need sorcery to hide us."

"You never talk of them without a curse," Cena remarked. "Now, we've had them in Tirtangir sometimes, but only as traders. I've never seen any at Ridai, and had no complaints of them. That they are a scourge to Alba, I don't doubt."

"That isn't possible to doubt," Tringad said. "Be careful of them. First traders, then raiders, then settlers. You must have heard of the way they are wrecking the Circles of Heaven."

"Yes, It's the worst deed of theirs of which I have heard."

The temple named was a triple circle of bluish stones, quarried long ago by the Danans in the hills beyond the woods, and set up there at a great focus of earth power, aligned according to the equinoxes and the positions of certain stars. Within the Circles of Heaven, it was said, there was access to a different Otherworld each night of the year. The Firbolgs had heard of the wonder-working properties of the stones and decided to possess them for themselves. Having overrun most of the coasts of Sabra as it was, they had only to fight and win a few battles to dominate the hills where the Circles of Heaven stood so grandly.

"They have built a road, toiling like ants, and they are sledding those stones to the sea, one by one. Then they carry them east by water to the center of their own tribe's power, and, as I've heard, set them up in circles there." Tringad scowled in the direction indicated. "They have to fight Danan raids and risk Danan ships all the way! I don't know how many stones they have carried successfully to their destination yet, but for every one I'll wager there are three at the bottom of Sabra."

"And how many Firbolgs have been slain by the earth power they ignorantly tamper with?"

"That I don't know either, lady. I'm no sorcerer, and I haven't been to the place to see, but there must have been many in the early days. Now, though . . . there has been so much digging and so many of the stones taken that the power of the Circles of Heaven is done. The Firbolgs do not even know what they have destroyed."

"Like rust on the wheat! The Freths say the same of us."

Once she would never have said such a thing. Now, with a decade's endurance of the two peoples' enforced mingling behind her, and the changes it had brought daily before her, she saw that there was no avoiding it. Danans would conquer Freths in the end. It seemed unlikely now, yet she knew it would happen. The older people had won an advantage, and a temporary stay, yet in the end they would be unable to withstand the Danan ships, Danan riders, or Danan bronze. Just as the Danans could not avoid the intermingling that had begun.

Soon after they ventured across the mouth of Sabra, a blustery wind carried them farther into that sea than Tringad had wanted to go. While making south to the coast of Arcaness, he was also driven a day's sailing eastward.

"It'll take us a nine-night to work our way along this coast and cross to the Isle of Tin," he grunted. "Maybe more, if the winds continue against us."

To help the merchant ship move, Carbri summoned a wind out

of the east on his harp. The bark plowed the blue water before it, passing rugged cliffs and many a small sunny cove. Grey tors reared from the high moorland behind the shore. After two days, they reached a river estuary winding far back into the hinterland, its banks wooded with oak, osier, and thorn, its waters a living clamor of birds. Here stood the gathering camp Cena had described.

Brushwood shelters and camp hearths lined the bank. Danan boats lay drawn up on the shore, unmistakable in their sweet lines and ornate carving. Unmistakable, too, were the sails and oars no other people in the western lands used. Tall, fair-skinned warriors in tunics and kilts danced recklessly between whirling spears, tossing them to each other like flashes of light and receiving them back in the next heartbeat. Men came dripping out of the water with broken-necked teal they had caught bare-handed.

The trader seemed incongruous at such a gathering, but as Danans the group was made welcome. The warriors asked innocently what sort of fighting was imminent, as though they did not know. The assembled men were not backward in telling them.

"Prince Nemed wants the greatest host he can gather. His captains swear the Great Oath that there will be no trouble about food, and no halting until the last Firbolg is driven out of Alba. We have heard that before, but we're all willing to try again, and again till it is done. What of you? Are you with us?"

"I would be, save that I'm for the Isle of Tin and a ship to take me south," Carbri said. "I'm outlawed."

"Bah, man! Nemed of all lords won't mind that! Wasn't he outlawed for years?"

"His captains are gathering fighters in the Isle of Tin, too, but why go there when you can join here?"

They talked the matter back and forth. In the end, Arn, Tavasol, and Lygi remained by the river while the others continued west, to see for themselves what was occurring at the Isle of Tin.

Some twenty miles out in the ocean, a place of shingle beaches and granite with the sea booming whitely against its cliffs, the Isle of Tin was strongly held by great seamen. In no other way could it be held at all. A chain of trading stations reached thence all the way to the original home of the Firbolgs, which Danans averred lay on the borders of death, if not within. A Danan Rhi named Deso ruled the island, and no pirate had ever achieved anything he desired there.

Cena had learned to be doubtful of seamen's tales. However, she trusted her eyes. She saw long thatched boathouses holding the biggest, most seaworthy hide-covered wicker canoes she had ever beheld. Their crews were Firbolgs, not unlike the ones she had seen, mingling in peace with Danans. Lyran vessels rode at anchor without benefit of the spells which normally made them invisible. Their crews, men and women with salt-white skin and strangely hued hair, walked unarmed. Deso's warriors kept the peace, and private quarrels were to be left so.

The finest sight to Cena was that of two ships with shining metal hulls. Here she could confirm, from Nemed's own captains, if the prince was indeed taking his scheme forward. While she did that, Tringad could trade. It would help show Nemed's men that this voyage was only what it seemed—a merchant venture.

"You may not carry weapons here," a warrior told them. An old sword-cut showed through his beard as he spoke. "Only knives, and if you use them to cut anything but your meat, it's swift hurling from the sea-cliffs."

"I never heard of anything like that elsewhere," Carbri blustered, in his character as a new-made outlaw. "Never to bear weapons at all? It's unmanly."

"Stay aboard your ship if you'd rather."

Carbri explained that he was an outlaw, and might be slain without penalty if his enemies found him. He might, he said, be followed even here.

"It's forbidden to spill blood here, though it be fifty times an outlaws," the warrior assured him. "The man who slays you will die for it himself, and we'll give you back your weapons when you leave."

"Aye. That'll be a vast comfort to me if I'm lying dead!" Carbri answered shortly. "I cannot get away from this island too quickly."

The warrior shrugged and held out his hand for Carbri's weapons. He surrendered them with a growl. Oghmal did the same, and they walked abroad on the Isle of Tin.

Grass and wildflowers filled the air with scent. Deso's hall had been built of driftwood and imported timber, with a roof of slates, but its furnishings were rich. The Rhi—a hard, hale, grey-haired seaman—sat on a throne of eastern cedar covered with hammered gold, and drank from a glass cup wrought in Crete. Not one of his warriors but wore a breast-plate of enamelled bronze. There was more of the metal here than Cena and her brothers had known could exist in any one place.

The three sat in Deso's hall as guests, not far from Nemed's captains. Without being blatant, they studied the pair and watched their movements. Here, too, they found desperate warriors ready to fight without quarter against the Firbolgs, and here too they recruited them.

Nemed's captains also went away with three sacks of the knucklebone-shaped tin ingots. For most tribes, including Cena's own, that was more than a year's supply. Nemed's smiths must indeed be busy, forging the weapons for the mighty host he was gathering.

Cena seethed. "Never could he bear the cost of this, if it weren't for us! Never could he feed such a host if he hadn't stolen the Undry!"

"Easy, sister," Oghmal said quietly. "There are ears all around us."

Cena mastered herself, though it was hard. All that Nemed was doing, he had done at the cost of her shame, disgracing her before a true friend, before all her people—and he had slept with her before committing his treachery, taking the whole of her hospitality, feigning friendship. Why hadn't she seen what he was? *How could she have let herself be fooled like that?*

She bit into a piece of baked meat, wishing it had been Nemed's throat.

Later, by the cliff edges, she gazed across the roaring sea. Gulls, puffins, skuas, and gannets populated the cliffs. They filled the sky and raided the sea. She wondered how Deso and his people endured such noise, year in, year out. Perhaps when they were born to it, they did not even notice it, or came to enjoy it.

"We have learned all we can, here," she said. "I'll put on my dolphin's skin and follow those ships to whatever haven the war-host is using, and there I need to know only one thing. Where will he send the Undry?"

"In his place I would not send it anywhere, but bring it myself," Oghmal said.

He stroked his long sword as he spoke. Not that he would mind confronting Nemed with an axe or any other weapon, so long as the crafty prince faced open combat for what he had done. Like Cena, Oghmal felt shamed in a way that could only be wiped out in blood.

Chapter
Four

The blue-hulled ships slid like knives through the sea, impelled by their long ash oars. None remembered any longer when those metal keels and ribs had been laid, or covered with their pliant, indestructible skins, or how. Like the days of the glaciers, they were remembered only in legend.

Cena, frolicking through the sea as a white dolphin, was pleased that they were so rare, and that Nemed possessed the last—or almost the last. The dolphin's senses could detect those hulls at a distance of miles, and distinguish them with ease from anything else in the sea.

Changing her shape felt very like being young again, the wild, vibrant woman who had never known defeat. The dolphin's brain, or the eagle's, had no room for the doubts and reservations one gathered in more than thirty years of human living. They could hold to one definite purpose, and revel in the sensations of riding the wind or slanting through emerald coolness after fish. She leapt high out of the water for sheer joy. None could see her from the ships. They were too far ahead.

The green sea swallowed her again. She sang the croaking, burring songs which came back to her as reflected shapes in her mind. The ships still rowed north, towards a certain bay which faced a place she knew as home, when she walked upon two legs; a place whose name she couldn't remember, as the dolphin. It didn't matter. She would be able to guide Tringad there unerringly, later.

Her brother's three young warriors had already reached it. Crossing directly from the camp by the river estuary, in another of Nemed's ships, they had come to this far greater camp on the shore of a deep, wooded bay. Five miles of forest, at the most, separated them from the Firbolg road leading down to the sea from the Circles of Heaven.

Nemed's plans were easy to discern. The Firbolgs themselves would have to gather in great force to stop him, and their own high chieftain was far away, at the heart of the plain to which the holy stones were being removed. This was to be more than a raid. It was a battle, to destroy the Firbolgs' pride, their work force, and their equipment.

"And the great shame is that it's nothing to do with us, really," Lygi mourned, "for I would be glad to show these invaders the consequences of breaking a temple of their betters. Well, there may be a chance to do it, before all's done."

Arn was more single-minded. "Do not even wish for it. We must take the . . . object . . . and one of the ships besides, and that's enough even for three such as we."

"I take it for granted," Tavasol said loftily, "that if we find ourselves in a fight we are not going to shirk it. But the prince must feed us *before* the fight. So far we've eaten well enough on the hunting and gathering in these woods. The way new fighters are coming in, it won't suffice much longer, though."

"Are you perturbed? All that is good. It means we can have little longer to wait."

"Too short a time, maybe. The others could come late to the feast. They needn't have gallivanted off to the Isle of Tin."

"The Rhi must have thought it needful, and I doubt that she will come late. More likely Nemed will than she. But if he does this precious army of his will melt away, and he'll have to begin his war all over again."

"Oghmal would never let that happen."

"He'd never rob a friend, either." Lygi shifted on his seat of bracken, which crackled under him. "But these aren't safe things to talk about. Anyone might hear. It's not a bad force his henchmen have brought together.''

For a group of placeless men and outlaws, it was not. The three had faced closer inquiry than they had expected before being allowed to join the gathering host. Nearly all its members were well-born warriors fallen upon ill times. Nor were they unwilling to talk about it. Most of the time, though, they were too occupied to talk. The prince's representative here was Brasc, a hard little man who had organized a rabble into troops which he kept marching and drilling. There was not a day that any man had shield or spear out of his hands, unless, like Arn, he could assist at a furnace. These smoked and rang all night, producing spearheads.

No people but Danans on the ridge of the earth could have moved so swiftly, or achieved so much, in so brief a span of time. Nemed's messengers had gone forth in the shape of birds, or riding the wind-swift horses the earth goddess's children bred, and fighting bands from all parts of the country had come together in similar ways. Craftsmen and weapon-smiths produced in days what would have taken other races a full cycle of the changing moon—and still it was not soon enough for their leader's purpose.

"I cannot sleep," Tavasol said abruptly. "I'll go for a walk across the treetops and look at this Firbolg road."

"I can." Lygi yawned. "Tonight I could do little else, and tomorrow won't be any softer. Have a care, man. I'd go with you, tired or not, but . . ."

"None can go with me on such walks as these. Rest."

He clapped his friend on the shoulder. Lygi had wrapped himself in his cloak and was burrowing into the pile of bracken already.

Above the treetops, clouds raced before the wind. The waxing moon vanished and reappeared, a pale reminder that time was passing. Tavasol walked through the camp, hearing virile voices singing around a fire, the shouts of a sudden quarrel, and the pacing of sentries. He stopped at the mossy bole of an oak tree and put his hands on it, sensing its slow, stately life. Earth power flowed through it, upward to the smallest leaves.

This was the power which made Danan wagons float above the ground. Being alive, and having a particular gift, Tavasol could tap the same power through green growing things. He climbed the oak as though weightless. Looking across the tossing forest roof, he shed his cares and began to run. His feet barely brushed the insubstantial leafage, yet it upheld him. On the ground he would have had to struggle through underbrush piled and tangled in a solid mass, and could not have done it in less than days. Here, he was unobstructed, and gaps in the forest roof were few. When he came to one, he skirted around it, or leapt recklessly across.

It was dangerous. There were clefts of blackness which he could not always judge rightly, sharp-eyed though he was. They might be filled with supporting leaves or with void air through which he could drop, surprised. Several times it happened, and he must catch a branch—or fall across one, winded but laughing. The danger made it fun. Since childhood he had regretted never having been able to teach another the trick of his leaf-walking. It had always come so naturally to him.

A league and a half from the sea, he reached the Firbolg road. It cut through the forest, indifferent to the natural flow of earth power, made by men not even aware of it. They filled in morasses with stone and brush, then surfaced the fill with split logs in days and days of unremitting brute labor. It never occurred to them that the Mother's body contained energies which could make some parts of her skin buoyant as the sea—and a far cry more trustworthy. When they were told, they didn't understand.

Yet, somehow, they were able to be a threat to Danans. Tavasol gazed at the cleared track leading down to the sea, and let his glance travel the other way, towards the hills. He found that he no longer felt restless. He needed sleep. Descending through the branches, he found a wide fork where he could make himself comfortable by bracing his shoulders and a foot. There, his unfolded cloak warm about him, he rested if not precisely slept.

Before dawn, he was back in his own camp. There had been no traffic on the Firbolg road through the night. He hadn't expected it. They would all have been asleep in the hills by the Circles of Heaven, gaining strength to resume their digging, prying, and toppling in the daylight.

Well, Nemed would surprise them, as he and his friends would surprise Nemed.

The prince arrived that day. Yawning, dishevelled, Tavasol turned out with the rest to welcome him, standing in the cluster of his troop and lifting his burnished spear. Nemed came ashore in his tunic of scale armor and a magnificent cloak, his balding head covered by a helmet like a star. The segmented guard hanging from the back of the helmet covered his neck and even his shoulders. His companions stood behind him.

"My men," Nemed addressed them. "Though I never saw you before, you are as my brothers because you are here to battle the black invaders, the destroyers, the plague that walks. All this they have been to you. Loss and grief they have caused you. Now we are gathered to strike back.

"The land that was yours, the tribe that was yours, the murder of kindred—all this you have to avenge. There is nothing these verminous thieves will not take! Even now, they rend apart the most sacred temple and the strongest focus of power in Alba, for nothing but their own glory. Will you let them have it without paying a price for it? Or will you say to them, with point and edge, "You have come as far as you may. From this day you retreat only, driven by the Earth-Mother's true children who bear her name—*the Danans*!

"Are you with me?"

They clashed spears on shields and roared as one man. The three young spies roared and shouted with them, nor were they false in doing it. They were more than prepared to battle the Firbolgs on their way to lifting Undry from the man who had no right to possess it.

"It's the answer I looked for," Nemed purred, well pleased. "Yes, and because I know you have hungered of late, many of you, I do not ask you to fight on empty bellies, or to chance your rations. You will eat well, constantly, from the never-exhausted cauldron, the Undry. Myself I obtained it, in Tirtangir, from a cave guarded by a monster."

"Cena's hall is a cave," Tavasol said, dryly and low.

"And Oghmal is a monster," Lygi returned, in the same manner. "Quiet you now, for I want to hear what other lies this hero tells."

He made his exploit sound glorious, a match for any of the lost Danan heroes who had battled the Ice Giants or the Poison Warriors in times ancient beyond memory. Whether or not they believed, his hearers enjoyed, and none with more delight than the trio of spies. Tavasol, more demonstrative than his companions, hugged his sides and sputtered through his teeth.

Then the Undry was carried ashore. The three went up with their troop to eat from it.

"Do not judge by appearances," Oghmal had cautioned them

once, "either Sixarms or his cauldron. It's nothing you would look at twice if you did not know its properties. A rounded crockery pot, ugly, lumpy, tough as stone, which a man cannot surround with his two arms, and a thick rim folded outward; that is the Undry. The colors it has are a dingy yellow-brown at the top, shading into a charcoal hue near the bottom."

The cauldron they saw fitted that description to the least detail. No novices at campaigning, the three had brought wooden bowls and spoons in their satchels, equipment as necessary as helmets. Lygi even saw some members of his troop using their helmets as bowls, and wrinkled a fastidious nose.

"It's hard to know which will suffer most," he commented; "their food, or their hair."

The Undry had been placed upon a bronze grid over a charcoal fire, which nine well-born young women gently fed and fanned. Arn's eyes brightened to see them, especially one, a short girl with a merry face and the black hair unusual in their race. But Prince Nemed and his entire war-band surrounded them, shining with weapons, while a leather awning sewn with copper bosses covered the cauldron above. Strings of bells dangled from the awning's edges, ready to chime if any careless or larcenous hand so much as brushed against them.

A dozen huge hounds lunged against their chains, watchdogs to aid the human guards of Undry through the night hours, no doubt. Tavasol repressed a grin, thinking of what he would do to these careful precautions. It was going to be a feat worth telling about.

A cook ladled portions of food to the men in their turn, according to rank and prowess. You could not tell what it would be before you received it: savoury venison, a rich broth, thick sausage, beef, pork, curds, or a steaming stew. The cauldron seemed to produce every sort of food at random, but it was always of the best, and always as much as the eater needed.

"No wonder—" Arn said, and stopped, the words unsaid.

"No wonder, what?"

"Why, I was about to say something unwise, which in this crowd could have been overheard." *No wonder Sixarms was angry when the cauldron disappeared.* "We'll do well here, I think. Better than living on frogs and tree-bark in the forest. A few more meals like this one and the host will march to the heart of Firbolg power itself, to fight them there."

"Maybe that is what Nemed has in mind."

*   *   *

They spent that afternoon mending their equipment, greasing the leather with mutton fat, honing their weapons, and taking any which needed an armorer's repair to one of the forges. Although they ate twice more from the Undry, they came no closer to finding a way to steal it. The cauldron was always taken aboard Nemed's own ship after the host had been fed, covered by the awning, surrounded by hanging bell-sewn straps, and guarded by warriors and dogs.

"I could carry it off, once I got my hands on it, and none would see," Arn muttered. "It's the getting hold of it that looks difficult."

Soon they marched.

Five miles of forest and marsh separated them from the Firbolg road. They widened the game trails with their axes, crossed streams, hacked their way through thickets, and at last came to the wide avenue Tavasol had looked on from the treetops. A heavy sled lay abandoned in the road, its oak runners sinking into the earth under the weight of a large bluish stone.

"Huh!" Brasc grunted. "They tried to get it through before we arrived, and were not quick enough."

"Then this is one more they won't take to adorn their lousy sty," Nemed said. "We can't carry it with us, and if we leave it, a band will come from the other end and drag it to the sea. But we can give it a decent burial in the marsh."

This thing they did, quickly but with respect, as if the stone had been a fallen fellow warrior. Bubbles came up through the murky water as the weighty monolith tilted and sank tracelessly from view.

"Pardon us that we did not keep you better," Nemed intoned, "and trust us at least to avenge you. Lie here in Danan earth. May all Firbolg feet that tread past your resting place be troubled, and fail to come to the sod where their true home will be."

He sounded honest. Lygi marvelled that he could, with the cauldron of plenty behind him on six men's shoulders, knowing how he had obtained it. Well, it wasn't impossible that he would sink to rob his host if that host was a foreign Rhi, yet burn to expel foreign interlopers from his own soil. It might even be admirable, save for one thing. Lygi felt sure Nemed intended to advance his own reputation and power by doing it.

They continued up the Firbolg road, tramping and jingling. All walked, even Nemed. They had not been able to transport or feed any horses for this fight. The rough hills where the stones had been quarried and set up did not suit their horses anyhow. This battle would be foot to foot, hand to hand.

The notorious Firbolg arrows began to fly from ambush. Men fell with broad flint heads driven through their bodies, or—sometimes—with a narrower bronze point nailing their shields to their sides, although these were very rare. Bronze could not be wasted like that. Flint or metal, the hissing, unseen death they carried was the same, and had its effect on the nerves of the marching Danans. They became apprehensive—but they also became angry. The prince's bard walked brazenly ahead, shieldless, clad only in cloth, his harp shouting defiance while he sang an old, old war song that Danan warriors, it was said, had once caused to be heard among the stars. Three Firbolg arrows hummed nastily by him, and he never broke stride. One transfixed the arm which carried his harp, and though his step faltered and his music came to a tangled, crashing halt, he kept walking. Placing the quill plectrum between his teeth, he used this free hand to break off the arrow and remove it from his flesh, throwing the gory shaft away. He did it without dropping his instrument or even letting it slip. Then he walked on, playing again, his music mocking the unseen archers for cowards, daring them to come out and face their enemies in the open.

Three arrows thudded into his body together. Their impact drove him the first backward pace he had taken, and it was necessary to kill him to achieve that. Down he fell in the path. His harp jangled once and was still at last.

"Place him on a bier and carry him ahead," Nemed ordered. "He led us living, and I won't take the honor from him when he died to earn it. Shame eternal to any one of us who turns back now!"

On a litter of spearshafts, the bard led them, carried by six men who slung their long wicker shields on their outer, exposed sides. Deeply though he was affected, Tavasol saw that Nemed uttered his ringing words from within the ranks of his personal companions, surrounded by their shields.

They came to the hills. The road rose and wound, through grass, furze, and boulders. Now they began to see their foes, big, broad-faced men in trousers who raced into the open, shot their arrows, and ran away. Some men of Nemed's host grew so angry they threw aside their shields and pursued them, unencumbered. Leap and dodge though they did, they died for the most part when they came too close to their quarry. Only one man caught his chosen prey, and after a fierce combat, sword to spear, he came back bearing the Firbolg's head, which red trophy he tossed into the bard's litter.

"This first death I give to you," he said.

To the wail of pipes and bold rattle of kidskin drums, they went on, with the silenced harp the most powerful music of all. On a small open fell where the Circles of Heaven had once stood intact, the Firbolgs awaited them.

They were not like the Danans, who adorned themselves most splendidly when they went to fight, perhaps die. They did not have the brilliant, subtle dyes their enemies did, for one thing, and they were a rougher folk. Yet they cried a rowdy welcome to their foes, shaking their wide-headed spears aloft, twirling their short-hafted axes, and stamping their feet. On a low rise behind these warriors, groups of archers with stone bowguards on their hands stood ready and watchful, making no noise at all.

Farther back still stood the workmen, the laborers and foremen and haulers, the loaders and drivers, many of whom were Danan subjects performing forced work. Some of these had run away when word came to them that Nemed was tempering a force to attack their masters; run away through the forest and joined the host fed by Undry. Hardened by dragging stones, armed with hammers and whatever else they had managed to get, they had come back for their vengeance at Nemed's heels.

The prince walked forward, his armor and helmet coruscating with light, his shield of wicker and bull's hide covered with a thin layer of beaten bronze. Worked in the bronze and silvered for contrast was a charming relief of a fawn dancing on its hind legs. Drawing his sword, Nemed announced his name and rank, in a voice which carried to the violated stone circles.

"Who wishes to fight me? Who thinks he can? I have heard that Tarkovets leads you. Is Tarkovets frightened? Or what of Jerduhn? Is Vazhimag there? Surely they have not all remained behind?"

A huge Firbolg warrior pushed through the mass of his fellows and strode down the slope towards Nemed. Topping the tall prince by a head, and considerably broader, his craggy face wholly surrounded by the black curls of his hair and beard, he carried a long, heavy-headed axe which he wielded with both hands. He studied the prince as if he were a tree the Firbolg meant to cut down.

"You called for some great men," he said. "I am Shurn, and you will not need those others to give you your death."

"We will have to prove that." Nemed smiled. "I won't ask your rank. Firbolg standing is worthless anyhow. You came here in bad company, for an ill purpose, and you must take the consequences. Begin when you think you are ready to die, you striding great oaf!"

Shurn handled the axe as though it grew naturally from his hands. He struck at Nemed's knee, shoulder, hip, and head, while the prince moved about, no longer speaking, shifting quickly to dodge the thundering axe-strokes. He tempted his foe by letting his shield tilt forward, exposing his side, and Shurn drove a blow which would have caved in the smaller man's ribs even through his armor.

Nemed interposed the shield again. It buckled and split as the axe-edge crashed through it, but Nemed's sword flashed for the first time. He sent his point precisely through the giant's eye, into his brain, and twisted it free as he fell.

"You ruined my shield," he said to the agonized, fallen man, "and it was worth four of you."

Shurn vented a groan as he died. Nemed, his blood now racing, called out to the noted fighter Vazhimag. He, too, came down the hill, carrying a wider sword than the Danan's, and a lozenge-shaped shield of plain, thick timber, bound with leather at the edges. Nemed held out his hand for a new shield himself, and received his choice of several. He took an oval one as long as his leg.

Shurn, although mighty, had been simple and lacked the prince's skill. Thus he had never made a great name. Vazhimag, a trader, had fought for his goods against a hundred seasoned warriors who would have taken them from him. He had fought men who impugned the fairness of his dealings or the honesty of his pottery weights. He went about the business gravely, careful of his strength, never committing himself rashly as Shurn had done, but he fought with verve despite that, quick to see his real chances as to reject the false ones Nemed offered. It was a better match and a far longer one. The bronze swords were notched and dripping before the end. Both men breathed harshly from lungs that burned, and nothing in all their world was real but the striving, inexorable need to kill the other.

Vazhimag's thicker shield had withstood punishment better. Since Nemed's borrowed one had been hacked through the rim and weakened, its upper third wobbled. Only the bullhide covering still held it together. The next time they strove body to body, Nemed slid his shield behind Vazhimag's, locking the two like the antlers of fighting harts. With all his strength he shook them. The top of his own rattled in Vazhimag's face. For an instant the Firbolg was distracted. In that instant, Nemed drove his lean sword up at an angle, into Vazhimag's throat.

The trader stiffened for an instant. Then he hurled Nemed off and rushed at him in a fearful onslaught, while blood spilled from his neck. There was nothing to lose now. So long as he gave the same mortal blow he'd received, before blood-loss brought him down, Vazhimag did not care.

Slipping the shield from his arm, he threw it skimming at Nemed's knees, but the prince sprang high over it and thus avoided crippling. Vazhimag struck many hard blows, which all landed on the surface of Nemed's shield or on his unbreachable cuirass. He felt them; they hurt, even through scale, leather, and padding, but they did not kill or maim. He could afford them.

He took advantage of the other's frenzy to drive home a thrust to the belly, and last of all to deliver a backhanded slash which nearly removed his head. Vazhimag crashed backward, to lie dead on the trampled grass. Nemed gave him a weary salute, then retreated through his shouting front ranks to allow someone else the honor of single combat.

The Firbolgs, though, were not minded to engage in any more of it. Their warriors raised a shout and charged, the downward slope adding to their impetus. The bowmen remained where they were.

With a crash like part of a forest toppling, the two forces met. A racket of booming shields and cleaving metal sent flocks of birds whirring, startled, from the marshes and the trees. Danans in kilts, tunics, and many-colored shirts, with spirals of paint on their limbs, speared trousered southern invaders, or were axed down and trampled by friends and enemies indifferently while the battle spilled over them.

For an unknown length of time they grappled. Then auroch horns bugled with deep voices from the hill-crest. Intermingled with their foes though they were, the Firbolgs at once fought to win clear, struggling to regroup and run, while the Danans rushed after them, eager to complete their rout.

"Fools!" Nemed bellowed. "It is a trick. They would not break so soon."

Bull's horns bound in bronze and silver cried his caution to the running host. The retreating Firbolgs had withdrawn together into a great knotty mass, while the Danans were more scattered still. As the Firbolgs drew near the crest of the long slope, their bowmen drew and loosed with a deep, vehement shout. Arrows sleeted among the pursuit. A second flight of flint-headed slaughter sang upward and dropped.

"Kneel under your shields!" Nemed fumed. "Oh, idiots, have you forgotten all that you were told? Didn't we practice this?"

Some remembered. Yet they raised their shields as individuals, or in small clustered groups, the overlapping often imperfect. Arrows rattled off when they struck glancingly. A straight hit was enough to drive the heads even through bull's hide and wicker, and into flesh.

The sharp reminders brought back their lessons. The Danans, though hotheaded, were stubborn beneath their flash. Drawing together, they moved forward, watching the bowmen now as well as the spearmen and axe-men. When the arrows flew again, they knelt as one, and their shields rose with a linking, uniting clatter. This time there were few casualties.

Rising, the Danans raced on, rather too soon. They ran into a second flight of dropping shafts, and more of them staggered, screaming, or fell to the grass while racing companions hurdled them in their eagerness to come to grips. Then they were too close for further shooting to be useful, and the opposed tribes met again.

There was no science now, no planning. It was hand to hand, fighter to fighter, until one side fled. Tavasol, the helmet long since knocked from his sandy-red hair, did brisk work with his narrow spear. For a while he fought beside a man and young woman who were either lovers or dispossessed kindred with wrongs to avenge. He didn't know and never had the opportunity to ask, but they fought their share before the chances of conflict separated them, and went on afterward to do more than their share. The Firbolgs had no women warriors among them.

The fight spread and sprawled. Hundreds of combatants covered the slope, striving to hold or to gain the crest, beyond which lay the Circles of Heaven. Tavasol reached the top for the second time, and met Arn there, barely recognizable through blood and grime. The bier on which the harper's body lay had been set down there, because three of its bearers were dead.

"Tavasol!" the wide-shouldered man croaked. "Pick this up with me. We'll carry it forward. They'll follow. The Firbolgs are ready to break . . ."

"What? Man, we've done our share. This fight is not even ours. Remember why we *are* here! Do you remember?"

"Demons devour that! We cannot let . . . the Firbolgs win." Arn gulped. More steadily, he said, "The Undry may fall into their hands if we do. Hai! Comrades! Help us lift this bier!"

The men he addressed turned away, as if they hadn't heard. Arn snarled a curse. Tavasol bent, shouldered the poles, and suggested sardonically that Arn take his portion of the weight, instead of swearing at the lack of heroism in the world.

"If we set an example," he added, "maybe someone will follow it." In the loudest shout he could raise, he cried, "Here leads the harper! Who comes with him?"

They trotted forward without waiting to see who answered, the dead man weighing heavy as a young tree on their shoulders, and growing heavier with every step they took. The Firbolgs waited like a solid wall across the fell, across the world, and Tavasol knew he was trotting to his death, yet his heart lifted, and he found his feet moving faster, strength flooding into him from somewhere beyond himself, the strength of the fighter who has made his final commitment and can lose nothing now, only win.

Someone was racing beside him, someone he didn't know and yet recognized as a brother. Someone else ran ahead, beside Arn, and the companion at his own shoulder said impatiently:

"Man, do not be greedy. You have half the burden. Give me one of the poles . . . as we go. So. I have it. Now . . . move over to . . . the other. Match your pace to mine."

They ran on, the bier supported by four men now, and a roar like the sea rising at their backs. Tavasol never knew clearly how he came through subsequent events alive, only that wherever he went, Danans seemed to rise from the earth around him to guard the harper's bier and strike down all who would approach it from the ranks of the enemy. Once, he set it down himself, to strike with a sword not his own, and fought in a knot of five warriors like a rock in an angry sea. His muscles were stiff and his sinews loose when that sea finally ebbed. He could no longer stand, but by then he did not have to. The Firbolgs were melting away, through the rocks and furze bushes, yet they paused to shout a threat and a promise. Most of them cried in their own language,

knowing no other, but those who could shouted it in the Danan
tongue so that their enemies would know it.

"We will return! We will come back!"

"The stones are no longer yours!"

Bold talk, Tavasol thought. *But we've given you the lie today
at least.*

In the ecstasy of weariness, he walked forward with Arn
leaning on him, forward to the violated circles which gleamed in
the sunset's fire. Three complete rings of stones had once graced
this place in the hills, each stone taller than a man and shaped
with Danan skill. Now they were spoiled, from the outer to the
inner. Nearly half of them were gone.

Yet the ones which remained were worth fighting for. Even a
rascal like Nemed found them worth it. Tavasol was glad he had
not esteemed them less. He sat in a daze, an exalted daze, hardly
aware of his wounds, while Arn's were tended as befitted a hero.

The black-haired girl Arn had noticed was there with water
and herbs. She did not treat Tavasol with much patience.

"Get away from here," she said sharply. "Your friend is
worse hurt than you, if you have not noticed. Since you can
walk, go back to the physician's shelter and get your own hurts
tended. You warriors are stumbling children with weapons out of
your hands."

Tavasol blinked, but he obeyed. Trudging towards the makeshift shelter, through the welter and rubbish battle left behind,
the cries for water and those other incoherent screams which
would continue until death ended them, he reflected that the girl
perhaps was right. Battles, like feasts, began better than they
ended. Yet at least they had won this one.

"Who is she?" he asked, to distract his mind from his many
aches. "The little black-haired one with the sharp tongue, among
the nine that warm the cauldron."

"Her? You don't know?" The man who answered him was
from Nemed's own mountains. "She's Rosgran, sister's daughter to Siranal, the prince's own second wife. He chose none but
well-born women for that function, you safely may swear."

"Then my friend is in good hands? I'll believe she can tend a
cauldron, but do you know if she can tend wounds? He's worse
hurt than I." Light-headedness assailed Tavasol. He dropped
through red gulfs of vertigo before he came back to the world.
"Maybe he should be here, not with her, much as I know he'll
prefer her attentions! She's no physician."

"It's a matter for debate whether we will be tended by one either." The other's tone was dry. "There are more wounded than there are physicians, if you have noticed, and the prince's leech is eager to put as many as possible below the ground himself. If you truly care for your friend, you should hope he does not receive old Morgoth's attention! Rosgran will be better for him in every way."

"Oh, that is good to know."

Tavasol hoped the man's sour assessment was correct. He was too much a stranger in this place himself.

Biting a wooden gag, he had his wounds searched and sewn and dressed, and fell into troubled, night-long sleep. Too weak to move in the morning, he had himself carried on a litter to where Arn lay in Rosgran's care. Lygi, almost unhurt, helped to bear him, and twitted him about his laziness on the way.

"Some men will do anything to escape the effort of walking," he remarked. "A few little scratches, and you lie on your back moaning. Since there is no Rosgran for you, I suppose it's I will have to fetch for you and wash you, sword-brother—a doleful fate."

"For you or for me?" Tavasol whispered. "Arn . . . if he's maimed, or dies . . ."

Arn lay pallid and sleeping. Rosgran sat by him, equally pale, and looking as though she should be asleep. Lygi said something of the kind.

"I soon shall be," she answered. "There's no more I can do for him at present. A good friend of yours?"

"A good friend," Lygi agreed. "What mean you? There is no more you can do?"

"Just that. He's asleep, which is the best thing for him. The Mother witness, he's sore hurt, but not in the lungs or belly."

"Where, then?" Anxiety sharpened Tavasol's voice. "I did not even learn . . ."

"What good would it have done? In the thigh. Someone hacked him there foully, with a heavy knife. He will not walk for some while." She looked at Arn. Her crisp tone softened a trifle. "Brave he is, indeed."

"Will he live, then?"

"Not forever. I see no cause why he shouldn't live as long as you or I, though." She smiled at them. "You will protect us if the Firbolgs keep their promise to return."

Lygi and Tavasol made the appropriate confident brags, even

though the latter lay flat on his back. Lygi was thinking, *Arn, who could bear the cauldron away with none observing it, now cannot even carry himself! Tavasol might have taken it over the treetops to the shore, but even he is helpless. I'm the only one left spry, and I do not see how forcing this entire camp to stay awake will help our purpose. Better far if I could force them to sleep.*

Surely I can steal the cauldron without sorcery!

He devoted his time to thinking of ways. None seemed promising. Certainly he could not dig a tunnel as Nemed's thieves had done. He ground his teeth in rage when he thought of that. Eating the delicious, ample food which poured from the Undry nearly choked him, yet it was his due as much as anybody's, surely more than Nemed's. That was the unbearable thing; to eat from it as Nemed's bounty.

The broth which brimmed from it sustained Tavaşol and the other wounded, though. The curds and thinner, milder soup seemed to help Arn, what little he could swallow the first couple of days. But nothing could help his pain.

Meanwhile, those of the host who were able did all they could to render the Firbolg road to the sea impassable. They set the laborers they had freed to tearing up the fill of brush and stones, wherever their former masters had lain it, so that seeping mud returned to its rightful place. They propitiated the tree spirits with offerings and explained why their needs demanded the action; then they dropped large oaks across dry sections of the road. All this could be repaired, as the stubborn Firbolgs would do; but it would all demand time, far more than the sabotage consumed. Until it was done they would sled no more stones to the sea.

"I'm going to find Oghmal and the others," Lygi said, picking a time when Rosgran was well out of earshot. "They ought to have reached this coast by now."

"Not if the winds are still against them." Tavasol was healing swiftly. "You are not expecting them to paddle in, towing the ship?"

"They'll find a way. Besides, we don't know that the winds have been contrary. I'm going hunting."

"Have a care that nothing hunts you."

The advice was sound. Firbolgs had attacked many of the work parties as they labored to destroy the road. Sudden little red skirmishes and deaths by arrow occurred daily. In the forest, though, the advantage lay with one man when it came to hiding. Lygi sought no trouble.

Buckskin-clad, he slipped away, armed with two spears and a dagger which had belonged to a Firbolg. Moving quietly down out of the hills, he gained the forest and its game trails. While he didn't know the region well, the coast lay a bare six miles to the westward. He could hardly miss that.

A marsh he did not remember forced him to turn aside. By the time he found the right direction again, it grew dark. Lygi spent the night in a tree, and saw dawn and the sea from its highest branches in the morning. Descending, he caught some food and set off again with confidence.

That confidence had eroded somewhat by the afternoon. He still did not admit to himself that he was lost. By nightfall, he had to. And not only lost, but desperately hungry. He'd have to spend the next day hunting, lest he weaken and become even more careless. Goddess, how stupid! But it did no good to say that.

His second night in a tree left him stiff-limbed and light-headed. When the dawn came—and not where he had expected it—he remained in its leafy top for a while, scanning the west with care. He *knew* the sea lay in that direction. All he had to do was find a game trail leading there.

Suddenly his eyes were smitten by the glow of a second sunrise, a smaller one, in the west. A shape of golden fire flew across the sky towards him and descended into his tree, sending rays of warmth through his body. Perched on a branch some yards away, it preened lacy, firelike plumes and regarded him with an exasperated, commiserating eye. Relief expanded within Lygi. He hadn't found the others, but at least they had found him.

The glorious sunbird flew and hopped to the lowest branch, then fluttered to the ground. The filtered, shady dimness there became full daylight in the radiance of its feathers. By the time Lygi had clambered down, the radiance had gone and it was Alinet who stood there, tiny and yet expansive in humor.

"You've given yourself a bad time, haven't you?" she asked. "Lygi, why didn't you just remain with Nemed's host? You might have known we'd seek you there. You didn't even know which bay or cove we'd land in. This must rank as the most foolish thing you've ever done."

"Maybe. I'd much appreciate it, though, lady, if you would

not go on about it, but lead me to some food if you have it. That, or the road."

"Say that you've been a fool," she commanded, smiling at him, "and I'll consider it."

With a growl and a leap, Lygi was on her—but she had vanished and stood behind him. As he spun, disconcerted, she laughed in glee. He had enough presence of mind not to try to seize her again. This was a situation he couldn't escape from looking anything but foolish.

"Come," she teased. "Try again, or confess."

"I've been foolish," Lygi said ruefully, "but it's unkind of you to make me look more so. We all have things to do."

"Yes. Never fear. With me you will survive to do them, not adorn some Firbolg's spear with your head."

She became the sunbird again, and Lygi followed her through the deep glades until he reached the road. There he sat exhausted until a returning work party met him, and halted to hear his tale. First, though, they gave him bread, cheese, and cooked rabbit, which he ate ravenously.

He did not mention any such thing as a sunbird.

Chapter
Five

"How is one chosen to be a cauldron attendant?" Arn asked. "Did you offer, or was there no choice?"

"A strange question, that, and even a bit of an insult," Rosgran commented. "Surely I had choice, and so had all the other girls you see fanning charcoal by the Undry! We're none of us bond-women. I reckoned it an honor to go with Nemed's force and help feed you when you battle the Firbolgs."

"Honor," Arn repeated, his voice yet feeble. "I'm pleased you think so. They say in the camp that the Undry has to be tended by nine maidens of good family, or it will produce no food ever again. Is that true?"

He knew it was not. The cauldron had come from the Freths originally, and they were scarcely an aristocratic folk. Nor had the Danans of Tirtangir ever troubled to surround the Undry with nine young women. He simply wanted to ask questions about it, and seem innocent while he did so.

"It may be." Rosgran's round brown eyes made her look rather innocent herself. "All I know is what Nemed has told me, and his wife confirmed—his first wife, I mean, not my sister his second. That the Undry can feed an endless number, and will, but that if ever a stranger is turned away from it hungry, it will crack in three pieces.'' She chuckled then. ''I'll admit I cannot see what difference it makes whether it's three or a hundred. The disaster would be as great. Still, that's the story, and if there's a lie in it, be it so; it was not I who invented it.''

''But suppose it were stolen?'' wondered Arn, the convalescent, restless and fretful. ''The Firbolgs could make a sudden raid in strength. They said they would be back. If they cannot retake the standing stones, they might settle for the Undry, which they can at least carry away.''

''The Firbolgs won't get their grimy hands on it,'' Rosgran assured him. She leaned forward confidentially. ''Would you know why?''

''Indeed I would.'' Arn had no difficulty in sounding eager. It required restraint of him not to sound too enthusiastic. ''If there's a reason other than two hundred spears.''

''Oh, there is. Vivha, the prince's senior wife, you know, has enchanted the cauldron. If any but a man of his own war-band tries to lift it, the very earth our mother will hold it down with a weight like that of a mountain, or an ancient tree. It won't budge from the spot where it has been left. Yet a man of the prince's companions can lift it with one hand.''

Arn had known stranger things. Still, he doubted the truth of this one. He'd have given his favorite horse and a toe to be able to test it, yet he couldn't even do that. Here he lay, helpless, while his comrades did the work and he was an anchor at their sterns. And Lygi was missing. With every throb of pain from his injured leg, Arn had another vision of what might be happening to his comrade—a vision more horrifying than the last.

His mingled relief and exasperation when Lygi walked back into the camp, and confessed that he had only been lost in the forest, was enough to endanger his recovery.

''Lost?'' he whispered. ''That was all? You pup of a three-legged hound with your head twisted backward, I am never going to let you forget this! Never!''

''That is what I feared. It even looks as though you are not going to die and let me off.'' Speaking much lower, he said, ''You were frightened that Nemed had learned some truth and was torturing me for the rest, were you not? And that you'd be the next?''

"That is a fine thing to say to a sick man," Arn said. Lowering his own voice, he added—and his natural voice was so weak that Lygi had to bend forward to hear—"Take care not to banter like this when Rosgran is about. I'm chary of her ears and her wits."

"That winsome little darling?" Lygi laughed. "I'd endure a wound like yours to be tended by her! The prince even allows her to neglect her duties with the cauldron to nurse you, sword-brother! Such fine rewards we do give to our heroes."

"That winsome little darling is his second wife's sister. Lygi, what if I say something in my sleep and betray us all?"

Lygi paused and gave sober thought to that chance. It hadn't entered his head before. Although he had been about to tell his friend of his meeting with Alinet, he now decided not to. Small use would it be to burden a wounded man with knowledge he feared he might betray.

"So," he said lightly, after a space of silence. "Doubtless I could cut out your tongue, but that seems too extreme. I'll take my chances of your discretion."

"What is this talk of cutting out Arn's tongue?" Rosgran asked. Lygi, startled, had not seen her approach, much less known that she had overheard anything. In that instant, he altered his estimate of the danger of her ears to a closer accord with Arn's. "Why, he hardly speaks a word as it is. Are you afraid he will tell me something about you?"

"Yes," Lygi said instantly. "He threatened to. The greedy fellow wishes to keep your company for himself alone, and revel in your care."

"So? What could he tell me, then? That you, like Nemed, have left a brace of wives somewhere?"

"He *could* tell you that. It would be a lie, of course. No, my fear was that he'd tell you the truth; that I am a Firbolg spy come to steal the Undry, and now that I have seen you, thinking of dragging you back to my tribe's lands besides."

"Your daring I admire"—Rosgran laughed—"but not your good sense—and you are as likely to succeed in one project as the other."

Arn waited until Rosgran had departed again. Then he said quietly, "She told me there is a spell on the Undry, so that only one of Nemed's companions can lift it."

"Ha. You believe her?"

"We'll have to—*you* will have to determine it. Supposing it is true, and you try to take it, not knowing? They will have you in pieces and hanging from hooks.''

"Something in that. What excuse can I make for testing the matter? No, better to make none and do the thing openly."

The next time a meal was served from the cauldron, Lygi attended his troop's serving cheerfully drunk, and sang until his turn came. Then, with a whoop, he threw his arms around it and cried, "I wager I can lift this, food and all!"

With a grunt and heave, he did as he promised, slopping food over the rim. He also put it down again quickly, having burnt his hands. Even as he blew on them, feeling the blisters rise, he deemed it a small price for the knowledge he had won.

"Drunkard!" Nemed barked, striding forward. "Who bade you touch that cauldron? By the Earth-Mother, if you do so again I'll cut off your hands. Have you heard me?"

"Ah, lord, it was only in fun," Lygi protested. "My friend told me no man could lift this cauldron. I said that I can."

"Suppose, instead, you had shattered it? Thank your tribe's god it does not shatter easily, and get out of my sight."

Then he said slowly, consideringly, "Wait." Lygi liked that one cool word less than he liked all Nemed's anger. He faced the prince, anger of his own smoking within him, feeling his face redden. This thief, this breaker of hospitality, dared call him to account? Well, if he questioned too closely, the last thing he felt in his present life would be Lygi's knife shearing through his throat.

Nemed looked at the young warrior, his gaze intent as though it would cut through the false appearance he wore, pierce the bones of his face and lay bare his very thoughts.

"Who are you?" he demanded.

Lygi gave the false name and history he used for his deception. Nemed looked at him searchingly again. Eventually he said, "I'm told you fought well, and I may owe the battle to your friends. Therefore—be out of this camp by morning. If another does what you did, I will kill him, though he be my own cousin."

"You speak of my friends!" Lygi said. "They are wounded in this camp. I will not leave them."

"You may go with your back marked or unmarked, as you like."

"Then I go with him," one of Lygi's troop said flatly. "We are not dogs, to bite and heel when you bid. We're free men.

You may not drub us at your will because you feed us. We have all repaid that.''

There was a grumble of assent from the rest of the troop, though none spoke as boldly as the first man. Nemed heard their indecisiveness, and attacked it at once.

"Any of you may go. Find another place where you can eat as well! But once you have gone, never think to come back to me. You are here to fight Firbolgs, the year round if needful. *This*''— Nemed indicated the Undry—"is what makes it possible. Shall I endure its being handled lightly? No!''

Plainly, he would not. Lygi felt warmed by the other warrior's support, yet he could not have a stranger with him when he left to meet with his Rhi and his lord, Oghmal. He shook his head.

"No, Cehydo. It's too much. You had better stay here and do what you can.''

"Do what I can? When I too can be turned out for any drunken prank? I'd as soon—''

He paused. He would not really as soon leave before it happened. Lygi was neither kin nor oath-brother of his. He wanted to fight, and to continue eating. Thinking it over, he paused further.

"Well?'' Nemed asked. "Are you leaving or not?''

"He is not,'' Lygi said firmly. "Farewell, Cehydo. Take a Firbolg head for me.''

His fellows in the troop gave him encouragement in words, and put together a parting gift for him: food in his satchel, a spare cloak, some brooches and wristlets to exchange for sea-passage elsewhere if he needed to go. Lygi thanked them and hoped they would meet again. Then he took leave of Arn and Tavasol. The latter, quicker-witted than either of his friends, gathered without being told that Lygi had met with one of their lords while supposedly lost in the forest.

"If you are to leave by morning, you can at least spend a last evening with us, and drink a little more,'' Tavasol said. "Ah, would that we could make it a lot! It's a shame that the Undry gives limitless food only, and scants us on the drink.''

"Talk not of the Undry to me,'' Lygi said sourly. "I'd not be taking to the road again so soon but for that cauldron.'' This was acting, for the benefit of those others who had come by with farewells. "I'll not be going alone, though. A few lads now recovered from their wounds are travelling north. They will welcome a hale man's sword with them, and it would seem strange if I didn't accept their company. This place stinks, anyhow."

It did. Men in too great numbers had occupied it too long. Not for that, however, would Lygi have left it while the Undry was there. During his farewell meal, he found a chance to whisper to Tavasol, "I've met—"

"I guessed it," the sandy fighter murmured. "Then they'll find us again, or they'll find you. Then you can come back. You'd be needing only a new name, and a new appearance on you; a blue moustache, maybe."

"Dye your own blue. I'll be forgetting how I do look, and my own name, at this rate."

"Others will remind you. But see, it is best you go quietly, without making a fuss. You could fast against Nemed for this injustice, and maybe force him to take you back—but then you'd be a marked man in this company. So would we be."

"You needn't assure me, man. It is settled. I'll find a way to turn back, and I'll wait in these hills. Nemed will have to disperse the host before long, anyhow, food or no food."

"Then we had better succeed before that day comes."

Lygi left with the departing wounded at dawn, so complying— barely—with Nemed's orders. As they travelled through the hills, they left the Firbolg-dominated and debatable country, coming once again into Danan land, as yet untouched by the raiding. It seemed to smile. Once all the stones in the Circles of Heaven were gone, it would stop smiling very soon, for there would be nothing to stop the Firbolg advance short of the northern mountains themselves.

Their only trouble was with Danans. A party of obvious robbers barred their way, and the leader, a huge one-eyed fellow, looked them over with disdain.

"There's nothing here worth our while, save your weapons," he judged, "and I wouldn't take those. But maybe one of you is fit to join us. What of you, crow-legs?" He addressed Lygi. "You are walking sprightly enough. Leave these cripples and come with us. We can use you, maybe, and you'll do better with us than with these beggars."

"I like their company better," Lygi replied. "Best you not meddle. You may think us feeble, but the Firbolgs didn't find us so."

"No. They left you so. Well, if you won't join us willingly, you had better fight. I'll see what you're made of." the huge man stepped closer, bringing with him a spear and a stench. "Beat me, and you can all go. Lose, and you join me while the rest go. How's that?"

"A fair offer," Lygi said. He had recognized the voice, and found it hard to conceal his pleasure. It was Oghmal's.

Within moments he was down, beaten, the spear-point moving in suggestive arcs between his throat and belly. The one-eyed face leered at him.

"It seems you are my property, youngster," he said. "The rest of you—go! Cross my path again with nothing to offer me, and I may not be so sweet to you."

Because they could do nothing, they departed. So did the robbers, in a different direction. An hour later, Lygi was settled in a dell among birch trees and violets, telling his lords all that had befallen. Most of the robber band had vanished, having been nothing but illusions. The group wore their own faces now, as a relief. It would save them, too, if the people of the district should come forth to hunt the robbers down. Lygi found it hard to speak directly to Oghmal when his eyes, living their own life, kept trying to shift towards the lovely Alinet.

"Arn cannot carry the cauldron out for us then?"

"Impossible, lord," Lygi said positively. "He will be on his back for days more. Tavasol is wounded, too; not so badly, but still, he can barely walk yet."

"Then we must do without their help," Oghmal said. "They had better stay where they are, fed and tended, and bring no suspicion on themselves. Horvo's lightning, Lygi! You should not have involved yourselves in that battle at all! I did not send you to get yourselves slain on Nemed's behalf."

"There wasn't much else we could do," Lygi said. "Once we'd joined him, we were bound to take part in the fighting or run away from it. Then we'd have been back where we began."

"Warrior's pride," Cena said. "I must respect that. I have it too. Well, Nemed can scarcely doubt that they are genuine now, since they were nearly slain. But their services are lost to us, Lygi, and we are the ones who needed it! Sometimes warrior pride should give way to sense."

"And run from a battle?" Lygi was aghast. "Lady, you cannot mean that."

"I can and do. Next time I expect it, though you be ten times a man of Oghmal's. Now let us plan what to do next." Cena's briskness increased. "The Undry is there, in the camp, and guarded by men and hounds the whole time?"

"Night and day." Lygi described the other precautions. "It stands now at what used to be the center of the circles. They are so broken, though, that the power they used to have is quite gone."

"You cannot know that." Cena's blue eyes grew distant. "It has the power to transport a man into one of the Otherworlds, and some of it may still remain. We will not be using it, though. It's a diversion we need, and I have one in mind. You say the Firbolgs departed, vowing to return?"

"Losers always do. Yet these have a record of coming back as they promise, again and again. They have been driven from the stones in many a battle, yet somehow they take more of them each year."

"Well, then," Cena said, "I think they should keep their word again. They are Nemed's enemies; on that account alone I would not make liars of them."

Cena would not say more. Lygi sat puzzled, while she brushed and combed her hair with Alinet's help. Suddenly she exclaimed loudly, and Oghmal sprang up, holding his weapons, Carbri a bare instant behind him. Lygi was woefully slow, having fought a battle, spent two nights lost in a forest, and walked far that day.

"It's nothing," she said. "No enemy you can fight. A grey hair only, my first—and that dog Nemed has given it to me, with all his other crimes! When I think of what he has done! Murdered my people, discredited me with Sixarms so that he will never trust me again, faced us with war and abandoned us to fight it while he goes about his own amusements, betrayed my hospitality—O my brothers, I know that getting the cauldron back must come first! I've said so, and have tried my utmost to think of nothing else! Still I yearn to drink his blood! Once we have the Undry, I'll make it my business to seek him out and kill him! As Rhi of my people, I say it!"

Lygi whistled his approval, delighted at this sudden appearance of the hot warrior through the aspect of the cold-blooded planner which was all he had lately seen of his Rhi. His way would have been to seek out Nemed first, and do justice upon him. But for Cena to finally vent her fury over a grey hair was funny.

Carbri found it so, too. His sister had always been vain of her appearance. Alinet smiled, secure in her own smooth-skinned, golden youth, and brought the comb back to Cena's unbound hair.

"No," the Rhi said. "I'm afraid of what else you may find. Just help me to bind it up, cousin, and then we'll see. We still have the mantle of invisibility, and if I cannot defend myself from dogs, I'm not the woman I think myself. There will be a way."

Ablaze with energy, she strode back and forth, talking. Ideas burst from her, to strike sparks of new ideas in her four listeners, and be discussed, argued, torn down, and rebuilt. In the end, though, they accepted the simplest plan as the best, because it was the one with least about it which could go wrong. Nor did they have to involve Tavasol and Arn in it.

Two days passed. The war-host at the Circles of Heaven, what remained of it, made ready to depart for the sea, where Nemed's ships waited. They would not use the Firbolg road again; they had rendered that all but impassable. No, they would travel through the hills of stone and swing westward; so Nemed had decided. His messengers had gone to the ships with those instructions.

A sudden shout arose, a call of alarm. In the next minute a dozen throats were yelling. Nemed came to the door opening of his tent, stomach tight, eyes squinting in the brighter light, his foxy face alert. If this was a Firbolg raid—

The sunlight struck flame from edged bronze all the way along a ridge to the north. Firbolgs by the many hundreds advanced behind their shields, a deep-voiced chanting booming down the wind. Yes, and there was movement to the east as well!

Nemed did not stay to don his armor. There was no time. He clapped helmet on head, reached for his shield, and ordered a servant to buckle on his sword while he stood with arms raised, letting the shield fall again. The sudden appearance of a full battle-host had shaken him.

"They breed like mice, those enchantment-killers!" he said. "There is never an end to them! The Antlered Rhi himself be my witness, I'll make an end of some today!"

He stepped out, and saw his camp violently astir. All warriors hale to fight, and many who were not, had sprung to arms, gathering in their troops and stepping out with their shields high, though battered from the previous fight. There was a dangerous amount of confusion. It was as though a god had kicked over an ant's nest.

Nemed collected his own companions and set about preparing a solid defence. The Firbolgs came on until individual faces could be seen and remembered. Then their arrows began to hum. At first only a few were shot, to try the range and windage. Then an entire flight hissed over their heads, to fall quivering in the earth or tear through many a brushwood shelter.

Yet—something here was wrong. Nemed did not know precisely what. He only felt it. Before he could realize fully what it was, the Firbolgs broke into a charge, their spears coming down before them in a bright array.

Too bright. That was it. They had not enough human tarnish and dirt upon them, especially for who they were. The Firbolg warriors seemed too perfect, with the perfection of the false.

"It's illusion!" he cried, and wondered at once what might be happening elsewhere while he was distracted here.

He was too late. Cena, her brothers, Alinet, and Lygi were within the camp, the first invisible in Talvi's gift, the others each disguised in a new illusion, more detailed by far than that of the Firbolg warriors. Racing through the camp, shouting contradictory warnings and commands, they caused more confusion, as they intended to. Cena, a flitting ghost, ran unseen for the desecrated circles and the cauldron of plenty on the improvised hearth at their center.

"Oh, I have you now!" she exulted.

Seizing the knobbed, rimmed object, finding it empty and barely warm, she raised it in her arms, casting a fold of her cloak about it as she lifted. Heavy it was, but not too heavy. She could stagger out of the camp with it.

A hurtling giddiness assailed her. She toppled into distances which seemed to lie as much within her skull as outside her. In another way they lay outside the world. She was twisted five ways at once, tumbled, overturned, made dizzy. Then she was gone, and the cauldron with her.

Alinet saw it vanish. Her sorceress's awareness told her how it had happened; she could recognize an Otherworldly gate when one stood open before her. Cena had vanished into a realm unknown.

She ran into the circles, calling the men to follow her. The guards Nemed had set to watch the cauldron came racing to protect it, late for events and helpless to alter what had happened. They turned upon Oghmal, Carbri, and Lygi because they must do something, and weapons rang together in that place where no men had brawled before. Oghmal buried the head of his axe under one guard's ribs, wrenched it out with a demon's strength, and broke a second man's neck with the backstroke. Lygi, his face bitter, drove his spear into the body of a man he had fought beside only days before.

"No, idiots!" Alinet shrilled. "Here! She has gone through this Gateway, the cauldron with her. Unless we follow now, we may not see her again! Come. After me."

Tiny and fearless, she ran for the hearth and sprang upon the exact place where the cauldron had stood. She seemed to fall into an immense distance, dwindling from sight. Oghmal wondered if that had befallen Cena, too, or was she still present though unseen?

No time to settle the question with certainty before acting. Once the champion shouted his sister's name, and received no answer. Alinet seemed sure of what had happened, and had been willing to set the example. There was nothing to do but trust the little Sunwitch. She and Cena might well be in the same place, and needing his help.

He raced for the hearth, planted a foot upon it, stepped up, experienced wild spasms of vertigo, and was gone. His twin followed, the distance of a breath behind him. Lygi was left alone, though not for long. Perhaps Tavasol would have been swifter through the Gate, or swifter to decide otherwise, but he was not faced with the decision. Lygi was aided to make it by two spears which rattled at his heels. He disappeared after his lords.

The warriors who had seen the marvel hesitated to go near the spot. Whatever had happened to the five, they did not wish to learn, certainly not by having the same thing befall them.

"I am not even for talking of it," said one, in the staccato accents of the southeast. "We'd be thought insane."

"Maybe not," another answered, waving a three-fingered hand northward. "There are enough other sorcerous things happening in this camp to make vanishing thieves a trifle. Can't you see that the Firbolgs have gone? They were only a glamor."

"By the White Mare, that's so!"

The dissenting warrior felt sheepish, nonetheless, when he told his unlikely tale to Nemed. Yet the prince did not laugh. He regarded the man from his heavy-lidded eyes, which made him look sleepy when he was most alert, and asked:

"Is this all? You are not forgetting a thing, however small? Nothing they said or did, or some matter of their appearance?"

The man pondered. Nemed allowed him time, aware of the risk he ran in making the suggestion. In striving to remember, this fellow might "remember" something which hadn't been there. Knowing how easily sight and memory could be hoodwinked was the first toddling step to casting a glamor oneself.

Finally the warrior said, "The big manslayer with the axe called out a name, just before he vanished, lord. It sounded like Cena."

"Cena," the prince breathed. Another of the witnesses had mentioned that detail, and here was corroboration. "And she's a sorceress who could raise an army of shadows with ease. Gone with her henchmen, and with the cauldron."

As he spoke the last words, Nemed, astonishingly, smiled. The smile broadened into a laugh until he was quietly, joyfully convulsing with it. He might have been told the most priceless jest it had ever been his privilege to savor.

"Go out, Seithev," the prince said contentedly. "Go out, and tell the host that it will eat as usual tonight."

Softly, he began laughing again.

The warrior Seithev departed, with a question in mind as to whether his prince still had his understanding with him.

He could profitably have asked Cena and her brothers about that.

Chapter
Six

The place was cold. Bitter, numbing cold made the teeth ache and began gnawing at the ears. Drawing a breath was like taking knives into one's lungs. Whiteness crackled and hissed for leagues of barren landscape. Spectral blue-white flames danced in a pallid sky.

Cena stood there foolishly, feet braced against aftereffects of dizziness and the impact of strangeness. She clutched the cauldron as though it contained her life, until she became aware of it, and then she set it down carefully in the snow.

"Cena!" Oghmal shouted. "Sister!"

"Here I am." She unclasped her cloak, shook back its deep hood and became visible to common eyes again. Alinet and Oghmal stood fifty paces from each other, and from her. When Carbri appeared, he stumbled and gazed around, no more than ten paces from his twin, whom he must have followed closely. Long heartbeats went by. Cena thought, *Where is Lygi?*

He might have been killed. She though that with a pang, for she liked brave young men. It would be one more crime to add

to Nemed's debt if it were so. Then she saw him, fully a quarter
mile off, his curling auburn hair conspicuous against the whiteness, his cloak more so. She felt a rush of gladness that he lived.
Oghmal waved to him; the brother she knew, tall and dark-
haired, moving with easy power and saying little, even in this
extremity. Carbri and Alinet were not too controlled to exclaim!

"*Cinalu!* What is this place?"

"Nemed! May all his dearest hopes forever fail! He tricked
us!"

Alinet added furiously, "*Again.*"

She began to describe the fates she wished for Nemed, the
merely humiliating and shameful ones first, the worse ones later.
By the time Lygi reached them, she was describing some rather
appalling torments and finding sweet release in it.

"May his bag-breeches be filled with centipedes and his belt
stick fast—"

"Sister, I see—and feel!—that this is one of the Otherworlds,
but at the risk of being feeble, what happened? Did Nemed send
us here deliberately, or was it our own mistake?" Carbri shivered, and added plaintively, "Also, which of the Otherworlds is
it, and how can we return? If those questions are more than you
can answer, I'll refrain from the thousand others I have."

"Then do, brother mine—do! For I've no better idea than
you, except that I think the worst of Nemed, that crafty, blood-
licking fox. Yet we would not have escaped with the Undry by
his design, and see! Here it is."

Cena began to shiver rackingly in the cold.

"Escape," Carbri said dryly. "Yes, we had better make that
word good, and the first part of it is to find shelter. This place is
not fit for man, woman, beast, god, or demon."

"Lords, my Rhi," Lygi said, stumbling through the snow, his
knees already blue, "*where are we?*"

"You are late, lad," Oghmal told him. "Cena and Carbri
were just gnawing that very question and agreeing that they don't
know. Nor do I. We agree on something else. We are not going
to die here. We will live, and find a way back. Are you with
us?"

"Th—there's a foolish question," Lygi snapped. "Do I look
as though I'd be content to leave my bones here?"

"Mark this spot," Cena said. "We came through a Gate here.
It may be that all we need do is turn around and go through it
again, from *this world*—if we can find it. By the Goddess, I

want that, and two other things! To see my children again, and
to get my fingers on Nemed's false throat!''

"Suppose we share," Oghmal suggested. "You see your
children, and I—'' He spread his fingers significantly.

"Chatter, chatter, chatter!" Alinet said scornfully. "Look.
You came through the Gate first, cousin. There are your tracks,
beginning from nowhere in this snow. I followed you; there are
mine. Oghmal and Carbri passed through next, there and there.
Lygi, you made the transit last, somewhere yonder.''

She moved her arm in a curving track as she pointed to each
location she named.

"You see?"

"I think I do. The Gate is moving, that way."

"Yes. And it's too far distant now for any of us to catch it,
save maybe me. I'm the sole one of us who can fly.''

This was too true. Cena could not transform without her
sorcerer's wands and skins, which she had not brought through
the Gate with her. Alinet had none either, but she needed none.
Though limited to the form of the sunbird, and able to assume
that only by day, she had been born with the power and carried it
with her wherever she went.

In her own world, she did. Perhaps it was otherwise here.

"Transform now, cousin," Carbri said, "and spy out a way
for us to take. The track of this wandering Gate seems as good a
path as any, provided it does not lead us to anything impassable
or deadly.''

He didn't speak his sudden doubt, the suspicion that in this
chilly strange land, Alinet might be unable to change. Her
powers derived from the sun, and he had already noticed that
here the sun was a wan silvery orb which gleamed through
veiling clouds, and could be looked at without hurt to the eyes.

Alinet raised her arms. All the light filtered through the clouds
or reflected from the snow seemed to gather into her skin,
surrounding her with eerie flame. Her clothing became fiery
feathers. A bird with golden claws and a long, slender bill
winged upward from where the woman had been. Flashing across
the sky, she blazed a rich burning gold which shamed the pale
hues of this world.

Carbri cheered; Cena and Lygi echoed him. Oghmal, feeling
the cold bite deeper into his cheeks, drove the handle of his axe
through the snow's hard crust so that it stood upright. He felt

relief as deeply as his companions, but—they had to live to escape.

"We will freeze if we stand here," he said. "Help me build a cairn, here where we entered this place—where each of us entered. We may have to come back this way. The Gate may open at just this spot again. Better if we can recognize it."

Cena slashed her skirt off just above the knees and turned it into makeshift mittens. It would have become soaked from dragging in the snow anyhow. With strips of it wrapped about their hands, the men piled frosty rocks into waist-high conical mounds. They worked swiftly enough to keep warm, while trying not to raise a sweat which would chill their flesh afterward. While they labored, they gave their cloaks to Cena. Later, they took them back, wrapping themselves as closely as they could.

Alinet came back to them like a golden meteor. Taking her woman's shape again, she said, "There's a forest yonder, as strange as everything else in this place. Wait till you see it! Beyond it lies a plain, and beyond that a range of mountains. I cannot tell what's within any of them, because mist covers the plain, but I did see signs that something lives here. The sun is nowhere near setting yet. You ought to reach the forest and find shelter before night."

"And build a fire," Carbri said longingly. "A great, roaring fire of entire branches."

"And obtain some food." Oghmal shouldered his long axe. "The sooner we begin, the sooner we will arrive somewhere. Are your fingers too chilled to play us a song, brother?"

"They won't be so cold until I am dead," Carbri answered cheerfully, "and I'm far from that state."

Rubbing his hands vigorously under his arms to warm them, he took the harp from his back and played a song of summer, to remind them of what they had left behind and had yet to win back.

> "The world is covered with flowers now,
>   The swift herd makes for the stream;
> Fair is the forest from crest to ground,
>   The speckled fishes gleam.
>
> Color has settled on every hill,
>   The shade of the trees grows deep,
> Green, entangled, the comrade of love,
>   Where trysts are joyful to keep."

* * *

Here there were only the pale hissing flames which edged the clouds, and the bright sunbird above them. Not even a wind was alive on the snowfield. Its frozen surface creaked under their feet. On light-teading Danan horses, they might have made short work of crossing it, and with that wish in his mind, Carbri turned to a ballad, about a lover visiting his darling.

> "The first horse that I rode upon
> was chestnut to a hair,
> And far and far he carried me,
> But failed to bring me there.
>
> The next horse that I rode upon
> Was grey as blowing cloud,
> And far and far he carried me
> Until his high neck bowed.
>
> The last horse that I rode upon
> Was sorrel with a mark;
> He took me to my darling's sight
> Before the rise of dark.''

The forest Alinet had told them of grew closer. Carbri had been thinking in terms of the winter forests he knew at home, for this land appeared to be suffering the bleakest winter of his or any man's experience. He had assumed bare trees, frosty undergrowth, and a few defiant evergreens. What he found was unlike anything he had known.

"Child of summer," Cena breathed. "How hideous that is!"

White it was indeed, that forest, with snow and frost, but the trunks of the trees and their forking, angular branches were no less white. They varied with kind, from bleached bone to ivory, chalk, and cream, whites so various that they had the effect of an entire spectrum of color, each tree in full leaf. The silvery foliage rustled and chimed, yet not a bird sang. It seemed empty of animals, too, and unnaturally free of hindering brush.

"We will have a fire, at least," Oghmal growled. He strode to the nearest tree.

"Wait," Cena said. "Brother, I have a feeling that to hack

these down would bring a curse, and that we had better not invite, with our other troubles. Look for one that has fallen.''

"I'd rather bear a curse than freeze,'' Oghmal said. "We can propitiate any such small powers that we offend.''

"Are you so sure, here? Even in our world, such rites don't always satisfy. I'm not being soft, brother. Unless we find dead wood quickly, we must take our chances of bad luck. But let's look first.''

"Bad luck!'' Alinet mimicked, having landed and resumed her girl's shape as the pale shadows grew longer. "How much worse can it be? We're trapped in this pale cold Otherworld, and starving. There seems to be nothing alive here but us and the trees, if they *are* alive, and somewhere Nemed enjoys the warm sunshine, laughing at us.''

"Yes, the back-stabbing thief!'' Cena said furiously. "Let him make the best of his triumph while he has it. I fully intend to see him again. If the Gate we came through does not open for us, we will have to find others.''

Alinet leaned against a trunk which seemed like a number of stems twisted together. She said pettishly, "What became of your cool resolve to have nothing to do with vengeance, cousin, but only to think of the cauldron?''

"We *have* the cauldron now. Besides—the goddess hear me!— if you believe I ever felt so cool about it, you misunderstood me! The Undry goes back to its master before anything else, but once that is done—*ahh!*'' Cena clenched her hands, anticipating. "If Nemed stands in our path before then, even, I'll give him his punishment early.''

"He's escaped it and made fools of us all, so far,'' the Sunwitch said drearily. Twilight and their situation had reduced her spirits. "Maybe he's just too cunning.''

"He believes that, doubtless.''

"And he's the one in the sun! Where are we? He sent us here!''

"I'm not sure even of that . . . I mean that he sent us here knowingly. Our people used the Circles of Heaven as a series of Gates, before they crossed to Tirtangir. Now that the circles are broken and incomplete, they do not work that way, though it may be that Gates still open at random in that place more often than elsewhere. If that's so, we could have gone there at just the wrong time, by chance. Our disappearance may have amazed Nemed as much as it did us!''

"And it was no more than Nemed's whim to place the cauldron where he did?" Alinet was wholly incredulous. "Believe you that, cousin?"

Cena shook her head. "I don't believe, or disbelieve. But it's most strange that he would place the cauldron where he knew a Gate to be. He'd risk losing it—as he has."

Alinet pouted. This pale land with no right sun in its sky oppressed her. Although she could still become a bird of fire, there was not the burning joy she had known in her own world. Flying was difficult. The cold seeped into her bones.

"Wake up, child!" Cena said sharply.

"I'm awake."

"No, you were sliding sideways, about to fall. Let yourself go like that and you will sleep indeed, for a long time. You're younger than any of us, even Lygi. Will you be the first to give up? You said we were old!"

Crossing to the girl, Cena shook her so that her yellow hair flew. "Stay awake!"

Alinet glared, but remained on her feet, blinking. In a while, Oghmal and Lygi returned with arms full of pale wood, which they split and made into a campaigner's fire within a hearth of stones. It burned, although not well, and gave forth volumes of pearly smoke.

"Now for food," Oghmal said, his belly rumbling as he uttered the word. "There must be something in these woods to hunt. I'll find it if I have to trek across them."

"Food?" Cena laughed suddenly. "Oh, we are fools! All this while we have carried the Undry with us, and gone hungry for lack of thought."

Carbri and Oghmal glanced at her, startled. Lygi looked as though the solid earth had quivered beneath him. Only Alinet sat passive by the fire, seemingly without interest, and that was not like her.

"Sister, fools is not the word," Oghmal said eventually. "When we return to Tirtangir, let us say nothing of this. Our people would laugh down the walls of Ridai."

"Hurry!" Carbri urged. "Fill it with anything—wood, snow, leather—then set it on the hearth where it can warm slowly. Will you tend it, sister? One Rhi must be better than nine lesser girls."

Oghmal heaved the cooking-pot to the hearth containing their fire. Then he looked into it. His strong-boned face changed.

"Undry is ancient, is it not? And has cooked the food of many for a long time?"

"Very ancient," Cena said. "Why?"

"This pot," Oghmal said, "is too new."

Cena grew very still. Lygi jumped, reaching towards the pot, and then stopped. Cena went to the hearth like a woman in a dream, to run her hands over the cauldron's lumpy surface. Turning it on its side, she peered within by the smoldering fire's light. Carbri knew she was examining it with magical perceptions as well as the common senses.

She screamed. It was a raging, frustrated scream which Nemed would doubtless have given gold to hear. She raised the cauldron over her head with the white arms trained from girlhood to sword and spear, and smashed it violently down on the hearth. It shattered. The pottery exposed along the broken edges was new indeed, in sharp contrast to the smoked and greased surface.

Cena screamed again, a wordless cry of pure, refined rage which rose to the shaking fires in the sky.

"I'll kill him," she said. "I'll tear out his heart with my hands. On my oath he will *die!* But first, first—I will get back the true Undry, tricking him as he's tricked me! Then I will tell him of it before he dies! He shall feel what I feel now! By the goddess, I vow it!"

Oghmal said nothing. He'd been holding a heavy stick of firewood between his hands. Now it broke with a crack. He did not notice it. For a while he stood rigid; then he relaxed, muscle by muscle, sighed, and fed the pieces of wood into the fire.

"He's still the winner, for now," he admitted, "and we are still hungry."

"Even so, brother, we'd better sleep tonight and hunt on the morrow." Carbri's harp belled his anger for him, beneath and through his words. "We'll be rested, and Alinet can act as the spotter for us. Are you willing, cousin?"

"Yes," she said listlessly, "if there is anything to spot."

Cena looked at her with concern. They huddled together in their cloaks all that night, for warmth, and in the morning they arose, more hungry than ever. Cena looked at the pieces of the smashed cauldron, there by the ashes of the fire, and spoke from the ashes of her fury.

"I should not have broken it. We might have' needed it to cook whatever we can find."

"We'll manage without, lady," Lygi assured her. "I'd take nothing from Nemed, save his life."

"Curb such ambitions," Oghmal said. "His life belongs to Cena and to me, no others. Now let us find something we can eat."

The white forest contained neither fruit, nuts, animals, nor birds that the five saw, though they ranged through it for a morning. Oghmal walked with his darts held ready, Cena and Lygi with spears, Carbri with a sling, and they were as vigilant as growing hunger could make them. Alinet flew from tree to tree, scanning the forest with brilliant topaz eyes. The only living colors to be seen anywhere were her shining feathers, the garb and the hair of her fellow Danans.

The days here appeared longer than those of the world they had left. Although they had no way of judging closely, the time from dawn until midday would have brought the sun close to setting in their own milieu. Certainly the night just passed had seemed very long, but there might have been other reasons for that.

They came to a bubbling, hissing river which ran over snowy rocks. Although its pools seethed, they were numbingly cold. Oghmal dipped the back of his hand swiftly in one, and felt as though fish with razors for teeth had bitten it.

"We cannot wade," he said. "Our legs would be sheathed in ice in moments. I think the man who fell in this would die."

"Talking of that," Carbri said, "your ears look frost-touched, brother, and there's a patch of it upon your cheek."

"What of it? Is there anything we can do?"

"No."

"Then why speak of it? Let's get on."

They travelled upstream, since it was likely to grow smaller closer to its source. Brushing through a growth of oyster-hued fern, they came to a place where the stream surged through a ravine. Of necessity, they climbed its steep banks and followed the ravine into a range of craggy hills. They had yet to see a sign of beast or bird, or even fish.

Higher yet, they entered a valley where the water crashed white among boulders, and they could easily cross with dry feet. They had ceased to be as vigilant, because they no longer expected to find any animal even so large as a mouse. Thus they were surprised when a crackling disturbance of the fern betrayed the movement of something large.

Oghmal recovered first. With a heavy dart in his throwing hand and three more in his left, he trod towards the heaving fern. A head from a nightmare thrust pugnaciously out of the white bracken to greet him; three partial faces on one head, or else three freakish heads imperfectly separated, borne on the same thick neck. The face on the left was smallest, that on the right most distorted, but all were wholly bestial, and all three sets of jaws plainly functioned. Squat and furry, it moved on thick short legs with fearful speed, and bawled as it rushed.

Oghmal flicked a barbed dart into its snout, missing the eye he had aimed for. He sent another into its shoulder, a third into its chest, and the last into its throat as it raised its head to bellow. Then he sprang aside, reaching for the axe slung on his back, snapping the thongs which held it there with a jerk of his arms. The monster swung its triple-faced head towards him.

Alinet shrieked. Cena cast her spear into the shaggy side, and the blood which spilled around the shaft came out smoking. Drawing his sword, Carbri approached the creature's haunches, looking for a chance to hamstring its legs, while Lygi rushed in on the other side to drive his spear deeply into its flank. Hanging on tenaciously, he twisted the shaft and dragged it back.

The monster vented a high, agonized shriek, but continued its rush upon Oghmal. The champion swung his long-handled axe with all the skilled control of his wrists, so that its edge sank through the malformed skull into the brain-pan. Rearing high on its back legs, it combed frantically at the axe with its forefeet while Oghmal clung to the handle. As heavy as the five of them together, it shook Oghmal and Lygi about like small children. Foam dropped in strings from its jaws.

Goddess, what a horror, flashed through Cena's brain. She drew her knife.

Carbri, moving lightly and well, aimed a drawing slash at the creature's leg. Its heavy tail lashed into the path of his blade, and he cut off a third of it. Strong-smelling gore spurted. A backward kick from a clawed hind foot sent him rolling into the stream, where such biting cold gripped his flesh that he could barely crawl out. When he did, he found that he had lost his sword.

He heard it tinkling against the rocks as the stream washed it away. Cena had noticed, too. She bounded from rock to rock, as adroitly as cold and hunger would let her, dropped to one knee and fished for her brother's weapon before it could whirl out of reach. Grasping the blade, she pulled her numbed arm out of the water—if water it was—and stumbled ashore. Through freezing locks of her hair, she saw that the creature fought on, despite the ghastly wound in its head.

Oghmal had dragged his axe free. Whirling it right and left, he opened a fearful gash in one heavy shoulder, and split the paw on the opposite side as the beast struck at him. Cena felt pride and love. Few men could have stood their ground before such a monster, much less struck with such power and coolness while it ravened for their flesh. Then she cried out in dismay, for Oghmal had stood fast a fraction too long, and the gruesome head butted him sprawling, covering him with blood.

The clumsy triple jaws swept along the ground, champing, intent on rending the man beneath.

Cena ran forward stiffly. Oghmal forced his arm into the nearest set of jaws, clamped his other hand on the dripping snout, and strained to force them apart. Powerful though he was, he found the task a terrible one, while he swung and dragged beneath the monster's throat. Growling like a beast himself, he clamped his trailing knees around the wounded foreleg and held on, despite the slippery blood and the overwhelming foulness of the thing's breath.

With all the force and care at her command, Cena drove her brother's sword deep into the bulky neck. Its muscles quivered around the blade. As it continued to savage Oghmal, she threw herself astride it, hanging on by its fur and the hilt of Carbri's sword, which she slowly drew out. The terrible wound in its skull, which Oghmal had inflicted, gaped before Cena's face.

She rammed the sword through the bloody cleft in the monster's skull. Again it reared high with a shattering blare. This time, though, it reared in its death throes, while Cena attacked its blocky, misshapen head and Oghmal struck it in the throat from below, again and again. Lygi had broken his spear by driving it in a second time, beside the spine. Carbri, his limbs all but paralyzed, crawled over the grass towards Oghmal's fallen axe. Alinet, a bird, had sunk her talons into the creature's back, beating her wings in fury. Now she released her grip and flew away, sensing the end.

The beast rolled, convulsed, and bellowed while Oghmal's knife and the sword continued to strike home. With a final sound which sent echoes rebounding among the crags, the beast shuddered and died.

Oghmal, matted and hideous with gore, half-unconscious, struggled to emerge from beneath the carcass. Cena continued to strike, panting, unable to believe that the creature was finally slain. Only as her strength ran out of her, and her overwrought mind accepted the fact of the thing's utter stillness, did she stop the needless, unfelt stabbing. Quaking, she slid down from the shaggy neck. Oghmal crawled from beneath its chest, supporting the massive weight of its forequarters, and rose wincing to his feet.

Cena embraced him, heedless of his revolting state. She was covered with blood and slaver herself.

"Brother! Brother, are you sore hurt?"

"No. Bruised, wrenched, and dragged, that's all. Thanks to you, sister. It never sank its teeth into me."

He spoke hoarsely, but in a steady voice. Looking about him, he assessed damage, wounds, and losses. Lygi nodded and grinned to him over the humped back of their foe. Alinet gave her mellow bird's call from the sky. Then Oghmal saw his brother, struggling on the frosty ground, his flesh turning blue under a coat of crackling ice.

"Carbri!" he gasped, his fortress of a soul shaken for once, and openly shaken. "What happened? You are not bleeding—ahh."

"He fell in the stream," Cena said, "and took a thorough soaking. With me it was only one arm, yet I felt bitten to the bone. I wonder . . . I am not cold now."

"Nor I." Oghmal looked at her, then at himself. "That shellycoat's blood was hot to scald. It must have been that. Lygi! Build a fire at once, and this time I do not care if you have to cut down every tree in this haunted land."

He stripped Carbri of his stiff, crackling garments. He and Cena held their brother full length between them and wrapped cloaks around all three, sharing their warmth. The bard felt like a fish in thin scales of ice. Long shuddering tremors passed from his flesh to Oghmal and Cena.

Eventually the fire began to crackle. Oghmal, about to lift his twin and carry him to the warmth, suddenly had a better idea. He pointed to the furry, reddened heap nearby.

"That is still hot. Take out its guts and lungs."

An hour later, Carbri slept as he had not slept since the womb, snug within the monster's body, its heat soothing the chill of enchanted water from his flesh. By their fire, his companions roasted its heart and drank its blood from containers of bark. They had to conquer a certain revulsion first, and a realistic fear of poison, but neither was as strong as it might otherwise have been. Hunger made a good sauce for anything.

With the monster's blood on her skin and its flesh in her belly, Cena felt strength coming back to her, greater strength than before. The cold of this white land had ceased to trouble her. She didn't question it. They had gained time. They knew now that food could be had here, no matter how dubious. They were surviving—and somewhere there must be other Gates.

"Yet where are we?" she wondered. "Oghmal, I have listened and seen visions, but this is none of the Otherworlds I ever heard of, unless my teachers lied."

"Maybe they did," Oghmal replied. No sorcerer himself, lacking any gift for it, he often doubted their claims to knowledge. That they had powers, he frequently admitted. That they exaggerated them as warriors did tales of their own prowess, or women their beauty, he was convinced.

"Then what do you think this place is? By my hair, it is cold enough to be the home of the Ice Giants in the old tale."

"If we meet any, that will prove it," Oghmal said. "There must be Otherworlds of which we've never heard. Maybe this is one such because it has no people in it."

"Or maybe it has, but this is a waste where no one ever comes," Lygi suggested. "I could understand that."

"So long as we find a Gate to our own world, I'll not care," Cena said. "Time is passing, and—it may pass more swiftly here than at home. I do not want to return to find ten lifetimes gone by, or turn to bones as I touch the earth of Tirtangir."

"Is that likely?"

"I've heard of its happening, and more than heard. Once I knew a sorcerer who aged himself to a dotard through seeking a lost Gate. That is why we must find men and women, if any live here. They can perhaps tell us the way back, and the risks we run in going." She chewed and swallowed a slice of the monster's paw. "This is one more thing Nemed must pay for. I hope we do not return to find him dead. He belongs to us, for all he has done."

"Nemed can await us," Alinet said, shrugging. "I think there has been too much talk of him. Cena, you change your shape

with the aid of beast skins. Can you use that one yonder? Had
we such a thing as that in our company, I do not think we'd meet
many to gainsay or harm us.''

Cena grimaced. "I wouldn't care to don the hide of such a
goblin as that. I might take on its nature as well, and then you
would have to kill *me*. One such battle was enough. You have a
natural gift, cousin. Thus you never studied skin-turning as
others must do it. I'd have to cure the hide in a particular way
for a year, and carve wands to use with it. It was a clever idea,''
Cena said kindly, ''but it will not work. And it's more likely the
folk we meet would run away than assist us.''

She walked to the monster's body and laid a hand on Carbri's
brow. He slept warmly; a little too warmly, perhaps, but at any
rate the heavy carcass was taking long to cool. She did not want
it to freeze solid by morning with her brother inside it.

When the pale sun rose, Carbri awoke, normal and talkative.
As he dressed in the garments his kin had dried over their fire,
he declared that he was ready to tramp across the world. He ate
with a hearty appetite, and for a wonder the cold no longer
troubled him.

"You bathed in the monster's blood as we did," Oghmal
agreed, "only you did it the easy way. Cena and I, we earned it,
while you went bathing in a stream. Have some meat, brother.''

"Ah, the same Oghmal. Jealous because I was wiser than
you.'' Carbri sniffed the roasting forelimb of the dead creature.
"Yes. I'll enjoy that if I do not think of how it appeared alive.
We know now that there is food to be had, and that demon must
have lived on something other than odd finds like us! Which way
do we travel from here? Is it settled yet?''

"Alinet says that beyond these hills there's a plain, shrouded
in mist, with mountains on the far side. It's as good a way as any
to fare, since we've seen no habitations. Maybe in the mist, or in
the mountains . . .''

"Hmm. And if not?''

"Then we tried.''

They crossed a ridge and came to another ravine, which they
sought to cross. Following it, they came to a thing which spoke
for itself; a stone bridge spanning the gap. Carbri stared for a
long, disbelieving moment, then let out a yell of delight.

"Ahé! Men did that, men like us! We'll find what we seek
yet!'' He turned, gripping his brother by the shoulders. "Are

you stone, so? There is nothing more wonderful that we could find!''

''Look again,'' Oghmal said. ''There, at the bridge-head.''

Carbri looked, and his glee did curdle somewhat as he noticed two stone pillars with niches in them. Each niche contained a bare skull, leering at them.

''Men like us, indeed,'' Oghmal observed. ''Maybe a little too much like us.''

''They cannot be too much like us for my pleasure! Ah, we'll set our eyes on some living ones yet, and find some answers! If they prove unfriendly, they won't remain so when I have harped to them a little, and if they do—showing them proof of what we killed yonder may improve their manners. Very well, brother, what *you* killed.''

Carbri carried the monster's claws and teeth in his satchel.

''Let's press on.''

''Wait,'' Alinet advised. ''You are six and a quarter feet tall, Carbri my cousin, and this has the look of an old bridge. A very old bridge. We should cross it one by one.''

Alinet, as the lightest, went first. The bridge held. It held for the rest of them, also. Carbri wondered if she had done it only to have their attention centered upon her, for she was like that, and had played no great part in their battle with the beast. Ah, but what if she did like to strut? If that was to be reckoned a crime, then every warrior, every poet, every bard, was habitually given to it.

On the bridge's far side lay the remains of a little way-house, and a trail leading downward. They were about to continue on their way when Carbri suddenly said, ''Wait, now.''

Returning to the bridge-head, he took one of the skulls from its niche and sat cross-legged with the thing in his hands. Afterward he returned it respectfully to its place and did the same with the other. Then he rejoined the band, looking thoughtful.

''What rite was that, which you found worth sitting in the cold wind for?'' Alinet inquired.

''One known to all bards, and to most sorceresses. See you, sunbird, the head holds all thought, and even after the brain is gone, the skull holds the echoes of those lost thoughts. They can be heard and even seen by a living man with the right training. I wondered if I might discover something.''

''Did you?''·

''A little. They were set to watch that path so long ago that even their bone caverns no longer hold a memory of why. Still, there is someone, somewhere, who sees through those sockets and knows we are travelling this way. Whoever it is, is powerful.''

"That may even be good," Cena said. "He must be a sorcerer, and if so he can advise us. To be sure, he's probably as much a dry skull as his two sentries by now. This path has not been used for long.''

They descended to the plain, an endlessness of feathery grass with occasional bushes, where they found the air less crisply cold. In the mist it was normally chill and damp.

"I'll fly above, to guide you in a straight line," Alinet said. "We will wander in circles otherwise.''

Oghmal shook his head. "I don't care for that. We saw no beasts, and then we met a fearful one. We've seen no birds, yet some larger, fiercer one than you may strike you down.''

"Then you will have to go on without me, that's all," Alinet said. "What if the beast had slain *you*, cousin? The same thing. We'd have had to go on without you. Now, none but me can guide you through this mist, so use me by day and halt for the nights. Nothing else makes sense. Depend on it, if I am attacked there will be enough noise for you to know that something is wrong! I won't suffer it quietly.''

Oghmal had no counter-arguments. Alinet was one of them, and must bear her share of the risks. It was even presumptuous of him to wish to shield her.

Footsore, they followed the sunbird through the mists. Cena, a woman, felt less protective towards Alinet, and took pride in the way she was acting. With her youth, beauty, and powers, the Sunwitch had always been the darling of her clan. They had spoiled her to the point of ruin while they secluded her; yet there had been no complaints from her about this terrible place, and by night if not by day she was the most vulnerable of them all. The smallest, the youngest, the weakest.

Cena admitted to herself that she wished she were the youngest. She'd recover more quickly from events like their fight by the stream. She had found her first grey hair before leaving on this adventure, and been gloomy for hours because of it . . . such a small thing.

I'm three and thirty. That is not old. I'm a sorceress, a Danan, and a Rhi. I may well live a hundred and thirty years more, with my wits and eyes clear. I'm tired, that is all.

They came to another river. This one flowed wide and shallow, at an easy pace. The bottom could not be seen, because the stream contained blood, red and fresh as if it had just flowed from a wound. For a time, none spoke. The crimson river flowed by.

"I know where we are now," Cena said.

"I too." Carbri touched his harp, and sang softly.

> "Then they rode on, and farther on;
>   They rode through red blood to the knee,
> For all the blood that's shed on earth,
>   Runs through the springs of that country."

It was an old piece of knowledge, even then. Down through the centuries it would be pieced into the earth poetry of other tribes and peoples, as would the Danans themselves. But it was no fancy and there was no denying it.

They waded across. Although they could not bring themselves to drink, the thought was in all their minds that they might have to retrace their steps later for that very purpose.

They travelled on. That night they camped in a shallow dip in the ground, among some white bushes, for lack of more substantial shelter. They took turns to stand guard and huddled together to sleep, as before. Once, something wailed in the darkness, close at hand. Pale lights drifted in the mist.

In the morning, they ate the meat they had carried this far, drank the last of their water, and wove carrying bags out of the white grass. With those, and their bark containers and bottles, they could bear away with them anything they found fit to eat or drink. By now they had become far from choosy.

That afternoon, Lygi stumbled over a broken shield. It shattered into fragile pieces when he pulled it from the earth where it had lain partly buried. They discovered other such rubbish of war as they tramped onward; broken leather straps, spearheads and snapped shafts, abandoned tents and wagons, fallen swords, shattered helmets, but nowhere a bone, nowhere the remains of man or animal.

"Once this was a battlefield," Lygi said in a low voice, "but a battlefield where none died, or where all the slain were carried away. How can that be?"

"You know better," Cena answered. "Listen!"

Lygi heard it, muffled by the mist and seeming to come from all directions; the noise of war.

"It is still a battlefield."

They found the source of the noise on a wide heath where the mist eddied ragged. Two gaunt armies grappled there, in the rags of their war-gear. No battle-cries sounded, only dry croaks, while the clash of weapons was a tired scraping. Empty of spirit or hope, the dead men fought their eternal battle.

Something rose in Cena's throat like an aching bubble. It grew, and burst, and suddenly she was weeping hotly, the tears spilling out of her. Carbri held her, letting her cough and sob without restraint. Lygi and Alinet moved closer together for comfort, their hearts chilled by the sight, Lygi the more so because he was a warrior. Oghmal stood where he was, watchful lest the battle should eddy around them and engulf them. What he thought, none ever knew.

Cena's anguish ran dry at last, and she pushed herself away from her brother's sodden chest.

"That will be our folk," she husked, face blotched and dripping. "Ours, Carbri, unless we get back the Undry. Forever at war with the Freths, or driven out by them and having to find new land . . . and fight the inhabitants for that . . ."

"We will get it, sister," the bard said, not with foolish optimism but simply with determination, a will as unyielding as Oghmal's. "But we need you to lead us."

"I know." She straightened, like a warrior who has fought too hard and long but knows there can be no respite yet. "It was a poor time to yield. Bava would despise me."

Carbri supposed that Bava would indeed have contempt for such tears. Maybe she would have been right, but he was not Bava.

"Best we go from here," the Rhi said, "and at once. Alinet, can you lead us on the safest track that skirts this place?"

The sunbird's wings shed beams of brilliant light as it mounted into the sky, like rays breaking through cloud. Some of the dead fighters paused, and raised their eyes for the first time in unknown ages, longing in their gaze. The sunbird passed. They returned to smiting with their broken, tarnished weapons in the struggle whose reason they had forgotten. The noise followed Cena's band for some way through the muffling fog.

They went on because they must.

More leagues of the misty plain fell behind them. With dusk coming swiftly, they heard a new sound, one as unlikely in this place, almost, as the cry of a new-born child. It was the squealing and grunting of pigs.

The Danans looked to their weapons at once, for the only pigs they knew were the grim ones they hunted in the forest, wild, savage, and pugnacious, little better to meet than the monster they had eaten. To their astonishment, sleek white creatures scarcely recognizable as the same sort of beast trotted out of the mist, driven by an ordinary-looking man in a brindled cowhide. Halting, he examined them, noting their weary state and other things about them.

"Live men and women!" he exclaimed. "Here!"

"Indeed we are alive," Cena affirmed, "and mean to remain so! What of you, man? For you appear as alive as we, and that's a live man's task you are performing."

"I breathe air and I eat—here," he said elusively. "You are mortals of earth, children of the Earth-Goddess. I see you, I smell you, I know."

Cena didn't care for that remark about their odor. She felt certain that only the cold made it possible for her to live with herself. She said shortly, "You are right, however you know it. Now if this is the land of Anuven,* we do not belong here, being alive, and your lord should allow us to depart. We haven't intruded here because we wished to."

"Few come here because they wish to," the swineherd answered placidly. "Few confront my lord of their own will, either. Never fear, room can be found for you."

"That we will take up with your lord," Cena said. "Where may we find him?"

"Not I, nor any servant of his knows. One of his dwellings is in those mountains yonder, and you may go there if you wish. Were I you, I would hope not to find him at home."

"Nonetheless, we must so hope, and if he's not there, we must seek him."

"Tell us more of this dwelling," Carbri said.

The swineherd sighed. He seemed less like a normal man now, for while they had spoken with him, he had grown slowly taller and thinner. He said, "If you must go there, you must. But you cannot walk so far into these mountains tonight. Follow me home and help me drive these pigs, if you can. Then you may guest with me, and go to the Rhi's house tomorrow."

---

*Hades; the realm of the dead.

"Gladly," Cena said, after one dubious look at the squealing beasts, "and very gladly we will be your guests. Yours is the first hospitality we have been offered in this land."

"You agree, though? You all agree?" The swineherd looked impatiently from one to another of the little band. He looked no longer, nor differently, at Alinet than any of the others, which proved, Lygi thought, that he was not a normal man or anything like one. "The beasts are scattering already. We cannot stand idle."

Cena's companions all agreed in clear words to the bargain. They would have agreed to more than that for the sake of a roof and walls for the night. They followed the swineherd.

Chapter
Seven

His appearance had changed again by the time they arrived at his house, a long drystone structure as white as everything else. From tall and thin he had become tall and broad, while his hair had darkened almost to black, curling about his ears. He drove the pigs into a series of sties, seeming quite unconcerned about the constant alterations in his form. When he finished his task he had grown shorter, his girth increasing until he was almost as wide as he was tall. Carbri observed that he now had seven fingers on each hand instead of five.

"Who are you?" Oghmal demanded.

"I'm swineherd to the Antlered Rhi," the other answered. "Had I a name, I'd tell it to you, but I have none. Not anymore. When I have served him for a hundred years, if I serve well and patiently, he will allow me to be reborn and I will have a name again. Meanwhile I endure this trying state." He sighed deeply. "There is not much else I can do."

"Why does the Antlered One torment you like this?" Alinet asked. Her young voice flamed like the sunbird's plumage. She misliked cruelty.

"As punishment for things I did in my last life," the swine-herd answered, "and so that I will learn something. More I will not tell—but he's a just lord to this land. You had better not go to him if there is evil on your heads. What are your names?"

"I am Cena, Rhi of all the Danans in Tirtangir," she said proudly. "Not many have linked that name with evil."

"In me behold Oghmal, brother to Cena, son of Siala," the dark-haired warrior said with equal pride. "Battle-champion. If your lord is just, he should have no quarrel with us. If he's not, I'm ready to quarrel with him."

"Though you be the greatest warrior of all the ages," the swineherd said with deep seriousness, "you speak rashly there. Look again at me."

His voice changed as he uttered the words. Soon after he completed them, he became something Oghmal preferred not to see, and it tested even the champion's nerve to follow him as he slithered over the threshold. Cena, pale as the frost, walked stiffly after her brother. Alinet, wide-eyed, announced in a small voice, "I may be ill."

To her relief, the swineherd's shape was human again when she steeled herself to enter his house. Lygi and the bard followed her, lest something foul should creep towards her back. This was a disconcerting country.

They found no cause for complaint in the swineherd's hospi-tality. All the food he served them was white, the bread, cheese, fruit, and meat, as well as certain vegetables they did not know. Cena ate first, considering it her responsibility. She found noth-ing harmful in any of it. The others ate well, after her example. Oghmal was the last to partake, thinking of tales he had heard, that any who ate the food of the White Land could never return to earth—but if that was true they were all doomed, having devoured the flesh of the monster. He cleaned his bowl and passed it for more.

"Good," the swineherd said. "You are willing to trust. It stands in your favor. Now I have advice for you, if you are prepared to hear it."

"Advice is a thing we have hoped for since we entered this realm," Cena told him. "I'd be grateful for it."

"You intend to go to the mountain castle. First settle any rancor there may be among you, any unspoken grudges or hatreds. If such there are, speak of them now and forgive each other. Leave in the morning with concord and honesty between you, or do not seek the Antlered Rhi at all. Take it from me. I *know*! You have boasted that you are honorable folk. Make that good.''

The five looked at each other, from face to face. At last it was Oghmal, the reticent, the taciturn, who spoke. ''Brother—''

Carbri waited. Alone of all the Danans, he had generally known what his dark twin thought and felt, as Oghmal had always been aware of him. Now Carbri did not know. Oghmal's silence lengthened.

''I've long wished I had your gifts,'' he said at last. ''Fluent speech, music, poetry, I covet them all. Once I sought a magician of darkness I hoped could grant me them. He told me they could all be mine—if I slew you and ate your heart.''

Carbri shook his copper-hued head. ''And you never thought you could tell me? Oghmal.'' The word rebuked the champion for lashing himself in silence. ''Did the magician die hard?''

''I slew him,'' Oghmal said bleakly, ''but not then. For three days I lived with his words. More than once I decided to act upon them. For that reason more than any I went back and took off his head. I've lived since with knowing what I might do if I chose. The magician left me that and I never could kill it. By so much, he did change me.''

''Now you've spoken it,'' Carbri said, ''and that kills it. Why should you want my gifts? You are the champion, strength and honor of the Danans, nor have you ever sullied it. Others envy you.''

''Brother! I know well that I've never met my better with weapons. What gnaws is that I'm good for nothing else. Magic? Song? Any art or craft in the smallest degree? Ask those who tried to teach me.''

''This matters to you so much?''

''Indeed,'' Oghmal said, as though the word had been wrenched from him.

''Then we'll need to do something about it that does not involve kinslaying. Fire of the gods! Oghmal, I take it hard that you never uttered a word of this until now. A man would think you had no family to aid you.''

''You were too proud to let us try,'' Cena said. ''Too *proud*! You are the champion; it must always be you who defends and aids.''

"I was ashamed."

"What's that but pride? You were ashamed—to say you felt a lack. You'd go in secret to a dark magician, but you'd not speak to Loredan, me, or Carbri when we're somewhat skilled in magic ourselves, and of a cleaner kind. That makes no sense, brother."

"We will do something about it once we are clear of this land," Carbri promised. "Win clear we will, too."

"Yes," Alinet said. "That false prince is wrong if he thinks he has seen the last of us." Taking Carbri's hand and slipping her arm about Lygi's waist, she drew them into a circle with the others for a short, fivefold embrace. "We'll pay whatever price is needed, and stand together until we see the amazement in his foxy eyes."

"So we will, lady," Lygi endorsed, sounding more ardent than he knew.

In the morning, clouds pressed low upon the mountains, and snow fell softly. The swineherd had become a four-legged creature, not unlike a bear with a human face. Justice this might be, but if so it was not Danan justice. Cena had misgivings about the great Antlered Rhi, lord of death and rebirth. She did not care how noble the swineherd proclaimed him to be. He probably said those things for fear the god would do worse to him.

"If you are determined," the ever-changing being said, "then follow yonder valley to its end. You will find a sharp ridge on your left, with a cruel wind howling about it, ready always to pluck the unwary from their feet. Rope yourselves together and stand fast. Should you attain to the end of the ridge, you will see the Antlered Rhi's castle. Rather, you will not see it, except by the snow which has gathered on its ledges, for it is invisible from the outside. Easy you will find it to enter; I cannot promise that you will come out again. Of this, though, I'm sure. It's your sole hope of leaving this land."

"Friend, maybe you cannot help being so repetitiously cheerful," Carbri said, "but you have begun to weary me. For your hospitality and for your directions, many thanks, and may your fate be better than it was before. We will not forget you."

The gateway of the Antlered Rhi's castle had no gate in it, no hinge or bolt to indicate that there ever had been one, and opened into a paved courtyard of stone. Once they had entered,

it became visible in the normal way. Stone heads were carved
above windows and archways; as the Danans crossed the yard,
they turned on their stone necks to look, or blinked their stone
lids. One opened its dry mouth and intoned:

"*Welcome. Enter freely, by your own unfettered choice.*"

"We have," Cena said.

A door carved from a substance like ivory opened of itself.
Cena looked at it closely in passing, and told herself that it could
not be ivory, not when it was formed from one unbroken piece.
Could it? As she passed into the castle behind Carbri, she saw
what was hardly less shocking; that none of the walls or floors
had joints in them either. There were no cracks even so fine as a
hair.

"It's one piece," she whispered. "The entire place must have
been hewn from the top of the crag, or—"

She chose not to voice whatever alternatives came to her
mind.

They passed through corridors and chambers with smoothly
vaulted roofs. Whites and greys of various shades blended in
cool harmony. Pale crystals glimmered, and hangings of snowy
fabric rippled on the walls, though no breath of wind penetrated
the castle. Arctic furs made a luxurious softness under their feet,
and the place was deliciously warm—at least, compared with the
ridge they had traversed to arrive. But the silence, the whiteness,
and the emptiness worked upon their nerves. Oghmal handled his
axe with greater readiness, while Carbri's hand never strayed far
from his sword. Alinet, in human shape once again, stayed close
to him.

With never a hint of warning, they found themselves on
the threshold of a hall that, for all its enormous extent,
gave the impression of being a cellar. Its flat stone ceiling cleared the heads of the tall twins by less than a cubit,
and white pillars upheld it in even rows. At the center of the hall
blazed the first real color (aside from those they wore) the
Danans had seen in the castle. A stately chair of a pure, stark
crimson stood near a hearth where carmine embers glowed. Once
in a while a yellow flame peeped forth.

The crimson throne stood empty. Beside it, no smaller or less
magnificently simple, was a silver one, and this had an occu-
pant. She watched them approach, while the retinue of grey-
skinned, white-haired people behind her uttered no more sound

than their lady. Pillar by pillar, the Danans drew nearer and saw her more clearly.

Black hair, straight, smooth, and gleaming, framed a tranquil face—which had last known surprise—if ever—a long time before, even as immortals reckon. Oval, pure, and perfect, dominated by dark eyes which saw to the center of each of them, it was a visage neither man nor woman could forget. The dead throng behind her moved in a haze of silvery phosphorescence, their silence eerie. At least four of the Danans had seen such beings before, at the Battle of the Waste, when they had summoned their dead ancestors to fight on their side. Oghmal could not help remembering that they had had no luck at the Battle of the Waste.

"Welcome, Cena, Rhi of the Tirtangir Danans," the lady on the silver throne said. In this realm of the dead, her voice was mellowly alive, cadenced like a song. "Welcome to your brothers, the bard and the champion. Welcome, Alinet, child of the living sun. Welcome, Lygi the warrior."

"Very well, lady. You know us all." Cena did not intend to be overawed. "How far have you watched us while we approached this castle? Did you perchance see us through the eyes of two dead skulls in the hills?"

"Before that I saw you, from the place you entered Anuven." The dark lady did not smile or frown. "Did you intrude by your own will?"

"Scarcely." Cena faced her, a tall woman with tousled redgold hair, travel-stained, battle-stained, one who had suffered hardships and looked the part, as much the opposite of the lady on the throne as anybody of the same sex could be. "We were tricked by a man who had tricked us once already—Prince Nemed, who will be remembered as Nemed the False if fate is just. He has something which is not his, nor ours either, but which we must take back to its owner if war is not to devastate our land again. And then—Nemed will answer to me for the dishonor he has brought on me!"

"You are weary," the dark woman said. "No matter what you hear of the horrors of Anuven, we are as hospitable as any Danan, and you will find no horrors within my lord's castle. You must bathe and rest."

"That would be dear to us all," Cena admitted. "Yet what will happen if we do? How long has passed on the earth we know while we have tarried in Anuven for these days? We have all heard stories of men who sojourned a little while in some Otherworld, and came home to find that three lifetimes had passed."

"If that has happened, it has already happened," the lady said. "One day more in Anuven will not add to your toll of years by a number which matters. Can you let go of your fear sufficiently to believe what I tell you? Be assured, Cena, I do not lie."

"Then tell me your name!" Cena challenged. "You are free with mine!"

"More fear. I have no name. I am who I am. The days you spend here are neither longer nor shorter than the time which has passed in Alba, and if you return there, you will not be too late to settle your debt." The dark lady bent forward a little, resting her elbow on her knee and her chin in her palm, a gesture of pensiveness so human that Cena's misgivings lessened. "Or will you eat before you rest? The guest is free to choose."

"I'll bathe, and rest," Cena said. Despite her having slept at the swineherd's house, the journey into the mountains had worn her cruelly. She wondered again if she was growing old so soon. "My thanks, lady."

The castle's baths were sunken tubs in a marble floor. Three seals could have wallowed contentedly in the same one, and the water steamed, so hot that one could barely endure it at first. Cena floated, soaking the cold and exhaustion out of her bones, while the lady's servants brought cloths, towels, and perfume. Soon Cena forgot that foolish thought of growing old.

The grey-skinned servants led her to a room where vapor rippled in a heavy layer above the floor. When they made signs that she should lie down upon it, she found that it supported her weight, and that was the last thing she remembered for some hours. When she awoke, her clothes had been folded upon a stand beside her, clean and sweet-smelling. The mute servants brought ewers and basins, with all else she required, and began to brush her hair.

While she could not fault their ministrations, their fragile, hollow touch disconcerted her. She dismissed them in order to make her own toilet. Later, she followed a tall, silver-haired fetch to the lady's hall. Her kindred and Lygi entered at the same time, through another door, looking refreshed and clean, like her.

The Antlered Rhi's consort sat on her silver throne as before. She might never have left it, save that she now wore different garments. Perhaps even that proved nothing. In her simple richness she looked so exquisite that Cena felt merely gaudy before her, but only for a moment. Then she remembered what a bloodless, hueless place Anuven was, for the most part, and stood proudly in her human tinting.

Oh, green leaves, blue skies, bright flowers, and you my children, I swear I'll see you again yet! I'd rather live in a hut on a mountain with you than possess every tall castle in this land! Wait for me. And you, Nemed, wait too!

"You seem stronger," the dark lady said, "in all ways. Will you eat?"

"I am ravenous," Cena said. She glanced at the crimson throne, significantly empty yet. "Your lord remains away."

"He's absent a good deal," the lady said, "and when he is gone I rule this land for him. Have no doubt that my word suffices to return you to your own green earth. Eat, I pray you. Then we can discuss it."

A cauldron steamed on the sculptured fireside, a silver cauldron of graceful shape, its rim encrusted with pearls. At the dark lady's invitation, they served themselves, using the ladle which stood in the shining vessel. Silver should have heated readily, but though the food itself was smoking hot the cauldron proved barely warm. Servants were many in the wide, low hall, yet none of the Danans asked why they had not been attended as befitted their rank. So much in Anuven was strange that they accepted most of it, by now, as though in a dream.

When their bowls were filled, the dark lady called for wine. She poured it for them with her own hands. Lygi was startled, and even Cena thanked her hostess with a puzzled note in her voice.

"Is it fitting that you should do this for us?" she asked.

"It is fitting," the dark lady answered. "You do not know the test you have just passed. The cauldron yonder is one of my lord's treasures, and it has this quality. A coward or a breaker of oaths cannot eat from it. The food will slip from the ladle however frantically he dips. By filling your bellies here, you have shown yourselves to be people of honor—and I assure you that if you had not, there would be no chance of your leaving this land."

"But now that we have?" Oghmal asked, seemingly un-moved. "Are there further tests to pass?"

If there were, and he failed them, he would not tamely submit to detention in the White Land. A large number of these fragile courtiers would be shattered by his earth-born might if it came to that; so Oghmal promised himself.

"There may indeed be more," he was answered from the silver throne. "Yet I will not set them. I said that after you ate we should discuss the manner of your leaving. If you did not know how much depended on your eating, why, still you have done so, and successfully. Would you depart? If you would, whither?"

Cena looked at her companions. "Are you all content that I should speak for us?"

They were, even Carbri.

"We'd depart, lady. I've nothing but good to say of your hospitality." That wasn't precisely true; Cena liked her feasts wilder. "But we have oaths to keep at home. I do not want to starve when I return to your land by the road of death. None of us belong here now."

"One of you at least could come to belong here while he still breathes air," the dark lady said cryptically. "See you to that. Live while you may."

It seemed to Oghmal that she looked directly at him.

"We cannot live rightly but on what you call our own green earth," Cena said. "Nor can we reach it unless you tell us how."

"I will do more than tell you," the dark lady promised. "You shall have a guide to the Gate which leads to your world. Once you reach it, your own magic must take you through, to the place you left—and you will find it deserted by all but the dead. These things I know."

Cena did not doubt it.

"You are free to go," the dark lady went on. "That is my judgment, which only one has the power to gainsay or reverse. Who that is, you know. Now, I will describe the path you must take and the destination you must reach, so that you will know your guide is not deceiving you. When you leave this castle by the Onyx Gate and make for the single peak to the east, you will meet him." She told them in detail of the trek they must make then, and what they would find at the end of it. Then she made a request.

"Before you leave, I would have a tale from you, Carbri the bard. Your name is known here. Will you give of your art to my lord's swineherd, and yet withhold it from me?"

"Decidedly I will not, lady," Carbri said. "My tales, and the full fund of them, are yours to hear, though I do not know how fitting they may be for this company. They have to do with the things of life—battles, voyages, wooings, elopements, births, enchantments."

"And with deaths," the dark lady said. "None the less, choose any story which pleases you, son of Siala. They are not inappropriate here." She smiled a little. "All of them lead to this land in the end."

Carbri met the gaze of those tranquil, inexorable eyes for a long moment. Then he bent his head above his harp and struck a few notes while he considered. The dark lady waited in patience.

"For the Antlered Rhi's consort, who needs no name with her distinctions of beauty, grace, and wisdom, the tale of Liain the starsmith's daughter, whose cloak was the sky and who led the Danans back to earth."

To his harp's music, Carbri told the heroic, tragic story of the band who lost the star fields in finding their true home, and of Liain who watched the sky for her estranged lover all her days afterward. The dark lady listened with her whole attention, and once her throat moved as though it quivered a little with the emotions of a mortal woman—but that might have been a trick of the light. Yet Carbri did not imagine the silver bracelet she gave him. Its craftsmanship was worth a thousand times the metal, and Danans knew craftsmanship.

"Remember the White Land of Anuven by that," she said.

They left by the Onyx Gate, which like the other was an empty gateway. The single peak to the east stood forth so sharply conspicuous that no other could have been meant, a spike of rock driven into the sky. The five Danans passed among creamy ferns by the side of one of Anuven's streams, which bubbled and fumed yet numbed unwary flesh in an instant. Leaping across, one after the other, they ascended a long rocky slope.

At the top, a wild goat with smoke-grey hide and arching black horns waited for them. When they saw it, it stamped sable hoofs and bounded three leaps before pausing to look back.

"This is our guide," Alinet said. "He will be surefooted enough. Let's hope he makes allowances for us."

"Let's hope he is not some ill-worker being punished, like the swineherd," Oghmal said. "He might think it fine sport to lead us astray, and abandon us in the midst of something like that endless battle."

"Kinsman, you're gloomy!" Alinet cried. "If the lady's to be trusted, her guide is too; few would dare disobey her. We've been fed, rested, supplied, told how to go home, given a pathfinder in case we miss our way—and you're not pleased! Aren't our fortunes running well enough for you?"

"It's a little too good," Oghmal said stubbornly. "I'm going to shout for joy when I touch earthy ground again. Not before."

"Well then, be quiet and let the rest of us enjoy some hope!" Cena snapped.

Oghmal stared at the nimble goat, now poised against the skyline ahead for them to see. Its great black horns made it conspicuous against the endless whiteness, and even its grey coat stood out. Because he did not like to follow anything blindly, he set himself to remembering the trail and landmarks the dark lady had described. Her hint that he might belong here even though he had not died echoed disturbingly in his mind.

Oghmal fell to the rear in this bleak humor, and watched the white landscape behind them lest something disturbing should appear. After all, the lady had not promised them safety. She had said that only one power could overrule her. Neither that nor any other would take him without a fight.

Carbri did not have to glance back to sense his brother's grim mood. He knew these dark broodings better than anybody, and could tell when the champion hid them behind a merry face at celebration or feast, as he knew when Oghmal was genuinely merry. It came as an evil surprise, though, that his unfitness with anything but weapons had eaten into him so deeply. Kill his brother and eat his heart! That was a foulness no Danan had ever committed. And he'd considered it.

Brother, brother, we have to do something for you.

Even the weather of Anuven now favored them. The sky cleared, as it had never done before. No vivid blueness showed; not that they expected it. The pale sun shone with little warmth from a heaven wan as water, while trees rustled their frosty leaves and the goat alone moved in the rocks.

"What a country," Lygi groused. "If you are not climbing a precipice or crossing a scarp, you are descending into a chasm. I reckon it became the land of the dead by default. Nobody else would have it!''

"The Antlered Rhi and his lady must find some delight here," Carbri answered. "I wonder, now. Maybe the place is not so hueless to them. If they see colors in Anuven that we do not, it could be a fair, brilliant place for them to dwell in."

"As the sea is for Manahu a flowering plain where he drives with his chariot?" Alinet asked. "I hope it for their sakes. Or maybe they see this land just as we do, and still like it. Maybe, even, the whole realm is just a semblance, and none sees it as it really is until he dies."

"What do you mean, lady?" Lygi looked away from the goat for a moment. "That none of this is real? That everlasting battle was real!"

"The swineherd's predicament was too real for my liking," Oghmal added. "As for that monster, had we treated it as a dream we'd have filled its belly. You were there with us, and you ate its flesh with us after we slew it."

"Yes. And I still think none of this is what it seems. It's too much like the stories they tell of what Anuven is like. Certainly it is real enough to bruise my feet! I don't care for this hiking any more than you do, Lygi, but—I wonder if we are even really here."

"You can always fly aloft and see." Carbri laughed. "It would ease your feet, at least, whether they tread on real stones now or not."

"I'd rather stay close to the rest of you," Alinet said frankly. "This is the last part of our journey, if the dark lady spoke true, and I believe her when she says she doesn't lie. Ah! There he goes!"

The lean goat sprang ahead, bounding through a dark notch in the crags, vanishing from sight in a moment. His sudden burst of speed seemed significant, and the Danans increased their own pace to reach that narrow gap. Oghmal particularly wanted to be through it before the strange night of Anuven began. In his own world, he would have thought such a narrow defile the perfect place for an ambush, and he did not care to relax his caution here, even though the place's rulers had small need to skulk in wait for their victims. Some of the dead, newly come from Alba or Tirtangir, might have failed to learn such things as yet. From what the swineherd had said, this was a place where lessons were taught. Oghmal did not wish any to be learned at his expense.

From guarding their rear, he moved forward, into the black gap through the white rocks. He found nothing there but echoes. The lady's word remained good, and he felt somewhat ashamed for doubting it.

At the far end, a boulder-littered fell, sparsely grown with grass and bushes, descended to a heath of broad extent. This was their destination, the place the lady had described, and in the distance he beheld the stones of the Gate. His dark heart lifted at the sight. He raised an exultant shout, already smelling the airs of earth.

"Cena! We have arrived, we're here! It's as the lady told us! Come quickly, while there is still light to see."

They spilled excitedly from the dark gap to follow the line of his arm, pointing across the moor. Anuven's pale twilight glimmered on the triple circle of white stones, their configuration very like that of the temple in Alba, desecrated by the Firbolgs; but these stone rings were complete. Lygi let out a whoop.

"Body of the Mother! We're as good as home!"

"We are!" Cena said joyfully. "Once we reach the stones, we are indeed, my dear." Then she sobered in a moment. "We cannot go that far tonight. This fell is sheltered, and there are bushes."

"It's as good a place as any," Oghmal agreed. "I'm for chancing a fire. We'll stand guard, we men, and no matter what happens, you must get back, sister. You are more important to the work that has to be done. Without us, you can still do it, but we without you—"

"—could succeed," Cena said defiantly, "and will have to, if I am slain or otherwise taken from you. That it would be harder then, I'm aware, but by those stones yonder, if you fail because it is difficult, I'll lead a troop from Anuven to haunt you."

They made a small blaze, using the white-leaved bushes as fuel, and the flames cheered them greatly. Even when the fire sank to a tiny bed of coals in the night, its glow was pleasant to see among the shielding rocks. None of the land's fantastic beings came near them.

In the morning, they set out with the sunrise, their bundles strapped securely on their backs for the last stage of their journey. Alinet pointed to the goat, standing on a jut of rock above the defile, watching them. It turned on its rock-gripping hoofs and trotted away with an air of final departure.

"Farewell," the Sunwitch called after it. "You were a good guide."

"It won't lead us across this open ground, though. We had better cross it ourselves as swiftly as we can."

The ground which had appeared so blessedly level from the mouth of the pass proved rocky and uneven. Tough plants with tiny leaves hugged its surface closely, forever shaved by the razor of the wind. They filled every hollow which offered a little shelter, and the occasional trees were all bent, their branches reaching away from the prevailing blast as though begging for surcease. The Danans toiled across the moor, and by midday the stones seemed little closer. They rested beside a frozen pool. Carbri tossed a stone to the surface and watched it slide.

"Must be natural water. Whatever the other springs in this place are made of, they don't freeze as they should. It's a sign."

"Of what?" Oghmal asked, standing while the rest squatted or sat. His breath plumed white. The great axe gleamed like grey ice in his hands, and his eyes held a similar glint.

"That we're closer to our own world where things are right, brother. What else?" Carbri jumped to his feet. "But those stones are more distant than they seem. Let's get on."

Alinet groaned. "We just sat down! A little longer, kinsman. My legs are not as long as yours."

They were not. The tiny Sunwitch did not travel afoot with the same hardihood as the rest of them, younger though she was, and it made small sense for her to fly ahead when their goal was in sight. None of the Danans wanted to separate now.

Then it came. The winding of a horn sounded across the blanched heath, seeming to come from all places at once. It shook the brain. Even minds like three of those there, trained to sorcery, reeled at the sound, while Oghmal's plunged as though battered with clubs. Fiercely he took control of himself, using the resistant toughness which existed marrow-deep in him. He focused his vision on the stones ahead. Perhaps they offered some protection, but they were so far away.

"Move," he said. "*He* will not stop us now."

Bravado, and yet Cena felt grateful for it. They dropped their supplies and possessions, all but Cena's small bag of sorcerous objects and their weapons, and ran across the moor. The terrible horn dinned in their heads until they did not know east from west, and scarcely saw clearly before them. Now a wild, avid baying formed a counterpoint to the horn's notes. The Antlered One was hunting.

It was so unfair as to be monstrous, when they were so close. Alinet had that outraged, childlike thought even as she ran, desperately trying to stay level with her longer-legged kindred. Lygi dropped back to protect her. It puzzled him that she did not change, for it was full daylight.

"Can't you get aloft and fly?" he demanded. "Lady, don't heed us! You'd not be deserting us. The stones are so near for you."

It was all a senseless babble in Alinet's tortured ears.

"I can't will the change!" she screamed. "I can't even recall how!"

Lygi knew what she meant. In the daunting, confusing noise of that horn the most familiar things became impossibly difficult. Offered a sword, then, he might easily have gripped it by the wrong end. Then Cena was beside them.

"You can do it," she said. "Stop running a moment, little one. Stop. There, that's it." She took Alinet's face between her hands like a mother with a frightened child, wildly though her own heart hammered, unreal though all things appeared to her. "Remember how warm feathers are, how free it is in the void sky. It's yours by right of birth. No harder than breathing, Alinet."

She covered the Sunwitch's ears with her hands and pressed gently, hoping to shut out the worst of the horn's paralyzing sound. Alinet closed her eyes, drew a few deep, steadying breaths, and altered her form within Cena's reassuring arms. Her burning feathers scorched the Rhi's garment and she flew upward, wings fanning, trailing golden sparks.

The dogs raved their disappointment. Lygi snarled, drawing his knife. If they were close enough to see what had just happened, they were too close. He spurted, running over the rocky ground beside Cena, catching the twins as they slowed to allow him to overtake them.

"Where are they?" Lygi panted. "The rider and the pack? Gods! They sound almost on top of us! I cannot see them."

"Hope that you don't," Carbri advised from a raw throat, and continued taking long strides. "Hope that you don't. Keep your eyes on the stones. They seem—within reach—at last."

High above them, the sunbird beheld movement on the heath. White hounds against white vegetation could scarcely be seen, except as a flowing tide of motion, but horror emanated from them. Alinet felt it through fathoms of air. Although nearly a league from their prey, they ran so swiftly that she feared they would intercept her kindred short of the stones. And there was nothing she could do.

The four earthbound Danans ran on, pain tracing its course through every fiber of their bodies. Hearts and lungs worked like bellows in a dilapidated smithy. Oghmal, the battle-champion at the top of his prowess, lasted best, with Lygi close behind him. Carbri, a bard before he was a warrior, fonder of cup than of sword, puffed desperately while death itself bayed for him. Cena fled beside him, feeling the cost of each child she had carried, and each long day of judgments administered from a chair.

The white stones loomed above them. Perfect rectangles, each surface smooth as ice on a lake, they stood in their ordained circles as they had done for unknown years. The Danans ran between them to stand at the center, back to back, gasping. Alinet flew down to join them as the dogs of Anuvin flowed in a clamoring mass to the edge of the first circle.

The pack recoiled from it, breaking apart, its individual beasts loping around the outer ring seeking to enter. They howled terribly, lunging as though against an unseen wall. Alinet stared at them, appalled yet fascinated.

"They are dreadful," she said, "more than mad wolves!"

The hunting pack was handsome in its way. Each hound stood tall as a calf, with muscles like heavy ropes under a dazzling white hide, the white of annihilation. Carbri thought of the killing white snow which covers everything, and in which nothing can grow. Their pricking, forward-turned ears, though, were as crimson as the empty throne in the castle where they had guested; crimson as the dogs' eyes and the deep caverns of their mouths. They howled and howled.

"Make them stop!" Alinet screamed, covering her ears.

"Tell their master that, not me," Oghmal answered roughly. He lacked the breath to say more. The dogs bayed on every side of them now. Unless the Danans left these circles by sorcery, they were doomed not to leave them at all, for none of them supposed that the white, red-eared dogs would lose interest and go away.

The sky darkened as their master approached. He rode at a leisurely pace, fitting to one who knew that all living things were his quarry in the end. His horse, greater than any the Danans had seen, was all grey, smoke grey, shadow grey . . . corpse grey. It reduced the demon hounds to the dimensions of puppies as it passed between them. They moved aside with never a growl.

Its rider was mantled to the throat and collared to the ears in the same grey as his steed. The Danans saw only his booted feet and the dark hands on the reins. His face they did not more than partly see, and still they found it hard to remain on their feet. Except that they were Danans, and most of them royal, they would have sunk to their knees and buried their faces in the enchanted ground.

A royal stag's antlers rose from the hunter's head, tined and lethal. He wore them as if they were weightless, nor were they an assumed ornament, a mere badge of rank. They grew from his head. Blue flames ran over them.

"Strangers," he said in a voice like the hiss of lightning. "Intruders."

"Not by our own will, lord," Cena answered for them all. "We never presumed to come here. Another presumed to send us, by trickery. The quarrel between us was wholly an earthly matter, and he chose to involve your realm by sending us through a Gate we never knew was there."

She heard herself beginning to repeat, to excuse their presence, and she stopped talking. She was Rhi of the Danans, a mistress of sorcery, a better queen than they had had in generations; she would not grovel even to the lord of death and rebirth. Nor would begging help if she were so inclined.

"I see that you speak truth," came the elemental voice from beneath the burning antlers. "Some of the truth. Also, you are alive, and therefore do not belong in Anuven, though that might be changed. But you have intruded, by your own choice or not. What amends will you make?"

"Your lady guested us," Cena said. "You may come and be my guest at Ridai in return. As for our trespass—name your own compensation for the offence, lord."

She gambled on the swineherd's assertion that the Antlered One was just. Half-seen eyes in the god's face looked into her, scanning the content of her heart and brain, seeing it all as of simple right, with a surety of power that enraged her. She shut her soul to his peering with her strength of sorceress's discipline, and resisted new incursions.

"None of that, however mighty you are," she blazed at him. "Get down from your nag and fight me if you mean to take such liberties as that! Can you not judge a matter so simple without pawing through my soul?"

The enormous grey horse stamped. Its rider never shifted a hair's width in his saddle. "Intrusion for intrusion. You do not like it? No more do I. Here is the compensation I will take from you. When you return to your own world—" Hope leaped like fire in all of them. "—you must find Prince Nemed, the man who dispatched you here, and send him to Anuven. Send him not living, but as men ordinarily come. You must slay him."

"Lord, that was always what I intended," Cena said, "nor have I changed my mind." She felt the familiar salt rush of fury when she thought of him. "He will answer, first to me and then to you. I have sworn it. Now I renew that oath, by the womb of the goddess who bore us both."

"I hold you to it, Danan," the Antlered One said. "Fail, and I will indeed visit you at Ridai, nor will you like it when I come. Remember what you have seen here; remember my hounds. Do not begin to say to yourself it was some dream or fancy. I hunt in your world as I please, I come and go as I please, and none hides his scent from my pack for long. Forget this, and you will be reminded when you least expect it."

"I am not forgetful in that way, lord."

"See that you are not."

Turning his horse, he rode away, and lifted a hunting horn jewelled with tiny black stars. A single blast upon it called his hounds after him. Cena watched the pack stream around the circles and unite at the far side. It flowed away, unanswerable death pouring over the ground, following its master towards his castle. Lygi shivered.

"They wouldn't come into this place by their own choice," he said huskily, "but one word of command from *him* and they would have rushed in to rip the spirits from our bodies. Earth of Tirtangir, but he was lenient!"

"Do not think it was any light charge he gave us," Oghmal warned. "So far Nemed has won each time we have crossed him. He took the cauldron, he kept it; he tricked us out of our own world, and by all reasonable chances we should have perished in this one. That we have another chance is not to our credit. If we miss this one—let's see that we don't.''

''We will not.'' Cena kindled a fire at the center of the circles. ''Nemed has had his share of luck, too. It's for us to make sure that it runs out. It's our right, our obligation, and it is going to be my rich pleasure. Think of what he has done to us!''

''We are all thinking, sister,'' Carbri said. ''It's needless to be reminding us.''

''No. There is need! Oghmal has it ever in mind, for he is used to carrying the tribe's honor on his weapon's edge. You, Carbri, are too easygoing for deep fury. I truly think your chief stake in this is the wonderful songs you can make about it.'' Carbri smiled and made no denial. ''Lygi, you follow your lord, and to you, little Sunwitch . . . I do not know, but I think to you all this is sport.''

''Sport! Being Nemed's dupe? Running before those death hounds? What sport is there in that?'' Alinet planted small hands on her hips. ''I come to save our honor and clip a war in the bud. Are you sure it is not you who finds this merry sport, after many a dull year holding your throne by Sixarms's grace? You were a fighter to reckon with in your time.''

''Thanks, infant,'' Cena said, amused against her will. ''In my time? But this is my time! The meat of this nut is that we *must* now take Nemed's head if we wish to keep our own. Yet that is still second to getting back the cauldron. If we must leave Nemed alive in order to take the Undry back to Sixarms, we will.'' She nearly choked on the words. ''If it means that the Antlered One comes to Ridai with his hounds in full cry, that too must be so. We accepted that our lives were less important than the Undry when we began this quest . . . or if any did not, they shouldn't be here.'' She gazed long at them. ''So look around you. Think well what that means. If one of you thinks the price too high, leave me when we have passed through. I'll not upbraid you. I am going on, no matter what befalls. Do not answer me now, but in Alba.''

The five of them linked hands. As they moved sunwise around the fire Cena had kindled, while odors of burning herbs rose to their nostrils, she sang a song which ranged through pitches a mortal voice should not have been able to encompass. At the close of each phase they stamped their right foot in unison, setting a kind of seal to its ending.

With their first stamp, the white stones began to whirl about them. At each succeeding one, they whirled faster, until the Danans moved at the heart of a shifting kaleidoscope of angled shapes. Vertigo made them dizzy. At Carbri's vehement urging, they stayed upright, for to fall would have meant their destruction with the song and the dance unfinished. Cena ended her song with her head threatening to split from the effort of forming it precisely aright.

The white vortex around them showed tiny rainbows by the thousand, as though some force had fractured it into the component hues. As its whirling slowed, the prism colors resolved into the greenery of forest and marsh, and the flowers of an earthly spring. Stone circles still surrounded them, but here the pattern was broken by scores of missing stones, while those that remained were smaller, more roughly fashioned, and bluish in shade. They had returned to the Circles of Heaven they knew.

Ugly proof lay about that this was truly their world. Bodies of many tall Danans lay pierced or hacked on the ground. The fetid smell of stale blood permeated the air, along with the buzzing of flies and the shrieks of carrion birds. Wolves watched green-eyed from the forest, waiting for the night. Oghmal scanned the scene with harsh impassivity.

"The Firbolgs won, and carried away their dead," he decided. "Our folk had no chance to do the same. The Firbolgs didn't trouble. I suppose they have taken a few more stones after this slaughter."

"Stones?" Lygi said in outrage. "Lord, who cares for all the stones in Alba? We left Arn and Tavasol with this same warhost! They lie among the dead for all we know!"

"I haven't forgotten them," Oghmal answered. "You needn't look so reproachful, Lygi. They were both wounded, remember? They are unlikely to have been in the fighting here, and Nemed has no reason to suspect them. Likely they are where he is, and as concerned for us as you are for them."

"Leave it!" Alinet burst out. "Can you not leave thinking and scheming for a while, even now? We are home, you men, back from the land of death! Let yourselves feel it!"

She dropped supply to her knees and grasped both hands full of moist spring earth. Her heart rejoiced at the feel of it. Holding it out with her eyes closed in bliss, the golden hair coiling against her flushed apricot skin, she made a picture so lovely that Lygi's heart slammed against his ribs. And if she had been plain as a starling, she was still the girl who had withstood the rigors

of their journey through Anuven, scouting for them, fighting
with them, keeping up gamely although the smallest and weakest
in the party, seldom complaining. The earthly sunlight seemed to
pour into her, invigorating her so that she glowed. It concen-
trated about her like a corona of tenuous flame.

Sunwitch.

For some while she stayed like that. After that first ravished
moment, Lygi looked away, feeling as though he had spied upon
Alinet by seeing her so unguarded. The image remained with
him, though, from the curve of her lips to the last fold of her
vividly colored skirt. Forever after he was to see it when he
thought of her.

She was right. There were no words for the way it felt to be
back. Even here, with Danan dead carpeting the ground for a
stark reminder of Alba's troubles and Tirtangir's, it gladdened
the spirit. Away from here, it would exhilarate—but at any time,
victorious Firbolgs might arrive, and add them to the corpses on
the torn soil.

"If they number at least thirty," he muttered.

"You spoke, Lygi?"

It was Carbri who asked. Lygi flushed a little. "I did, lord. I
was saying how many Firbolgs it will take to defeat us if any do
happen along."

"And you reckon a mere thirty could do it? Why, you deni-
grate us. For my part, I so honor your prowess that if thirty
Firbolgs do appear, I'll leave them all to you."

"You see why Carbri has the name of being the generous
one?" Oghmal asked.

Warriors could rally and jest in the midst of such carnage.
With the first ecstasy of her sunbath over, Alinet could not. She
asked sharply if anything delayed them at the Circles of Heaven.

"Just the risk of being cut down by Firbolgs if we leave as our
true selves," Cena said. "Little one, I can make no more magic
for the present. I'm fordone. Let you prepare an illusion which
will give us all the semblance of Firbolgs, and then we will walk
out of here. Yours convince better in full daylight than anyone's."

"My thanks for that," Alinet replied, pleased. To create a
convincing illusion demanded skill. "It won't make us talk their
foul language, though, nor will it last after sunset."

"By then we will be deep in the forest, and it will not
matter."

The five adventurers stood in a quincunx, with Alinet at the center. Shortly afterward, five dark, curly-haired Firbolgs with broad faces left the Circles of Heaven, unstrung bows in their hands and quivers on their backs. A day later, five Danans had rejoined Tringad and his seamen aboard the ship they had doubted they would see again.

Chapter
Eight

"You could say the foreigners won," Tringad allowed, spitting into the waves to show how reluctantly he admitted it. "They're saying it themselves, doubtless, and loudly. But Horvo's thunder! The prince made that victory so costly for them they won't dare afford another this year."

"By spending a few hundred desperate Danan lives," Carbri said sourly. "We beheld the remains."

"They spent their own lives, brother, and they knew what they were buying," Oghmal said. "None forced them into Nemed's host. Cena and I have both led warriors into battle. Isn't that spending lives?"

"Is Nemed your friend now?"

"Scarcely! I do but take issue with your condemning him for the wrong thing." Oghmal leaned against the ship's rail. "There is enough else to condemn him for."

"There is." Cena gazed over the glittering bay. "Where has he gone, Tringad? For wherever he is, the true Undry will be with him."

Tringad swung around on her, exasperated beneath his deference. "Lady, are you still chasing that accursed crock? Isn't it plain by now that Nemed is not about to give it up? I'm astonished from what you have told me of the White Land that your hair hasn't turned the same color! If you meddle with that man again, you do not know where he will send you next—and he seems hard to outwit."

"Hard. Not impossible." Cena looked into Tringad's face, which had always reminded her of salt-cured bacon. "You did a splendid thing for us, captain, waiting here when you knew from our comrades that we had vanished, none knew whither. You have my heart's thanks for that. But what now? Do you wish to leave us? *We* are not giving up. Nemed is not the only one who dislikes doing that."

"Who spoke of giving up?" Tringad growled. "You wouldn't ha' found me still here if it came easily to me either. As for Nemed, he retreated to his valley stronghold with the survivors of his host. You cannot seek him there."

"Will you wager?" Cena asked. "We have a large advantage now. Nemed thinks us trapped in the Otherworld, or slain there. A fresh attempt upon the Undry by us is the last thing he'd look for. Thus it's what I mean to do."

"He will be glum after his defeat, no matter how costly he made it for the Firbolgs," Carbri offered. "Suppose a traveling bard comes along to sing his praises? He might become reckless with what he promises. If he asks me to name my own reward— and I'll make him say it before all his followers and kin—I will ask for the Undry."

"No, brother," Oghmal objected. "No matter how cunning the glamor that was on you, he'd know you at the first harp-note you struck. You might as well stroll in as yourself, and ask for the cauldron because honor demands he yield it. You'd have the same chance."

"I'm playing with various notions to see which has the most promise," Carbri said. "What of this one? I'll gain entry as I said, and play his household the Three Strains—sorrow first, then joy, lastly sleep. While they slumber, I will open the hall doors and stroll out with the cauldron."

"Better," Cena owned. "Considerably better. The failing is the same one Oghmal spoke of before, brother. When you strike your first note he will recognize you. Didn't he share my hall with you for the whole of last winter? Then there is his wife, his first wife. Vivha the sorceress. After what has happened, she will be well on her guard, and one glance from her will reveal the truth behind any glamor.''

"That is like saying none of us can go, lady," protested Lygi. He scratched his auburn head. "The prince threw me out of his host for daring to touch the Undry, even though I made it a drunken joke. He told me not to come back on pain of death. My lord Oghmal he knows. You he knows. It seems we will have to depend on Tavasol and Arn, who are with him already. Tavasol's wound at any rate should have healed by now. It wasn't so bad.''

"And you may depend on me," Alinet said. She dimpled sweetly at Lygi. "Is it so easy to overlook me? Remember that I'm not well known to this prince. He saw me, yes, and had eyes of desire for me, but I suppose he might have forgotten me since, and I wasn't at any of his battles. Why, I am your best hope.''

"You may even be our last one," Cena admitted. "Yet I do not like sending you into that crafty weasel's lair while he is there. You cannot be sure he has forgotten. No man would.''

"The risk is less for me than for any of you.''

"Still, I'd rather he was out of there. It would make many things easier. Maybe we will not even have to find a way to dislodge him. Maybe he will take his ships of his own volition, and go to fight Firbolgs on Sabra.''

"If he doesn't, it will not take much to make him," Carbri said, out of a deep knowledge of princes' hunger for glory. "His defeat will rankle, and sea-fighting is what he does best. Remember how he levelled the Revolving Fortress?''

"Goddess, yes!" Cena replied. She looked sad. "I'm nigh ashamed that I sent him to do it, now. He wasn't good enough to triumph over Sixarms that way.''

"Sixarms isn't the wonder of pure nobility you paint him either, my sister," Oghmal reminded her. "Who unleashed those three worms of evil upon us, and forced us to raise the Blind Boar in response?''

"I won't dispute that," Cena said. "We both did unworthy things, and spread devastation across the land. We could yammer until the stars fall out of the sky anent who was first with it, or who did most of it. The weighty thing is that it must not begin again, though by the Mother's womb, it will, if the Undry is not returned!'' Her strong hands gripped the rail. "Yes . . . if the sea calls Nemed, I think he will go. We can arrange it. And pay my debt to him.'' She looked at Tringad. "Take us north, captain. Set us ashore in Nemed's country. This matter is far from finished, as he will discover.''

"Come," Rosgran said. "What weighs on you? There's reason for you to be cheerful, so. Not every man takes a wound in the thigh like yours and keeps his leg. Also, you do not need me for a nurse any longer, yet here I sit." She moved a piece on the game-board. "You and the dice will have to work well together to get you out of that."

"Now, let's see." Arn dropped the cubes through the top of the dice-box and watched them tumble to a stop. "That is not bad."

He moved his own pieces, while the sun shone on the grass around them and cloud-shadows passed across the valley. This rounded, brown-eyed girl was the pleasantest company he could have asked for, and she seemed to like him, but he could never quite forget that she was the sister of Prince Nemed's second wife. She could gain the ear of the first wife, Vivha, at any time she pleased. For more than one reason, it would have been good to believe that she fancied him and spent time with him only because of that, yet the knowledge of his own deception made him see deceit everywhere. He pondered the board with more concentration than the game really deserved, and made his next move without speaking.

That was the single thing Arn had to trouble his mind, now; the dread that he might carelessly give himself and his lords away. He knew too well how bad a dissembler and actor he was. Besides, he had been alone in Prince Nemed's household since Tavasol departed, with no comrade to share the tension and danger.

No matter. Things might be worse. They had seemed a thousand times worse in those long, dreadful days after Cena and her kindred—and Lygi!—had vanished from the world due to Nemed's trickery at the Circles of Heaven. Arn and Tavasol had almost become demented, waiting, hoping for the lost group's return, fighting despair through each endlessly dragging hour, while maintaining the pretence of being Nemed's cheerful followers. A red, almost overwhelming urge to murder the prince had assailed them both each time they saw his face, yet they had restrained themselves and waited—the hardest feat either of them had ever performed.

Their reward had come after several interminable days. Tavasol, riding out to hunt some troublesome robbers with a band of the prince's men, had been greeted by Cena's voice, speaking sorcerously from the void air to his ears alone. Before the hunt was over and the robbers they sought dangled from nooses, the Rhi had twice met Tavasol in secret to exchange news and devise plans. Arn remembered the astonishment, the delight, the wildly surging relief he'd known when Tavasol gave him the tidings. Their dark, taciturn lord had returned, and the Rhi with him, ready for a new attempt to lift the cauldron from Nemed's guileful clutches.

Better yet, Nemed himself had gone from his hereditary lands, taking his ships southward again to Sabra. The Firbolgs' successful counter-attack against him at the Circles of Heaven had stung his pride. For his reputation's sake, he had sworn to spend the rest of the summer clearing their crude leather boats from the water. Tavasol had gone with him, after fighting two contenders to earn a place aboard the prince's ship, for Cena had reckoned it imperative to have one of her brother's comrades beside Nemed, to watch his movements and slay him if it proved needful. It couldn't be helped that this left Arn without a friend immediately at his back.

There was sport in his position, though. The same danger which gnawed his nerves made each moment full. It was merry to watch the prince, his Rhi's betrayer, and relish his ignorance of what was passing in Arn's mind. It had been particularly merry for the last days before he sailed, when Arn had known that the Rhi had survived, and returned, and was close at hand. All he required now for life to be complete was two strong legs.

Who would carry the Undry away for Cena now?

"Where is your mind, stranger?" Rosgran asked.

"It was with Tavasol," he said, "though it shouldn't have been, when I am in your company. All our fights since we were foster-brothers have been fought together, and we were always lucky. I'm hoping his luck holds."

"If offerings for victory and Vivha's spells can ensure it, he will return. His own prowess will have something to do with it, also, and that's not lacking, is it? Besides, he sails with a good leader."

So far as craft and experience went, Arn had to agree with

that. Nemed's seven years as an exiled pirate had taught him all a man could know of sea-fighting. If Tavasol made his aim to survive, not to do deeds worthy of a song, he should come back whole, but if he forgot himself and caught the battle-madness, his chances were slim. Well, men of the champion's war-band could not expect long lives; their achievements were a debt owned by death and the tribe.

Nonetheless, it would be sweet to see Tirtangir again. To return with the cauldron would be glorious.

"Aye," Arn said, to Rosgran's last statement. "He's about the best to be had, on blue water." He would not concede even by implication that Oghmal had any match on land. Even at sea, *about* the best was not the same as saying the best. "If he contains them on Sabra, he will at least keep them out of the western mountains."

"Enough of that," Rosgran decreed. "Talking of it is making you moody. What will you do, Arn, when the fighting is over and your leg reasonably healed? When Tavasol comes back?"

"I haven't thought," Arn said slowly. He lied. "I reckon we will do the same as the others, and wander. North, maybe, to a place where the ravagers haven't set foot. More likely east, to fight them again. I shouldn't like to settle somewhere and live my whole life wondering when they would come—when I would see their black bows flexing once more."

That he could say with conviction because he knew it was how he would feel, if he belonged to Alba and had lost place and kin to the Firbolgs as he claimed.

"You would not stay here?" Rosgran asked. "If fighting is all that matters, you would not lack Firbolgs to blunt your sword's edge. They raid our shores often, and when they do not, my sister's man goes seeking them. As he's just done."

"That isn't all that matters. There are other things, even for a man with revenge to take." Arn knew he was looking at Rosgran too ardently, and blushed bright red—not because he was such an innocent as that, but because he had no right to let her imagine he might stay. "That debt should be paid first, though. It will be."

"No one is asking you to promise all your days, or even a year," Rosgran said evenly, while her own face turned pink. She threw the dice and made her move, a less shrewd one than usual. Looking at the new positions on the board, she saw her mistake. Her blush receding, she said, "I think you win."

Arn ignored the game; at least the one on the board between them. He kissed her. Although she allowed it, and even returned it with liking, she went no further, slipping out of his arms with a laugh when he felt a stab of pain from his injured leg. She remarked that he must indeed have recovered.

"I have so. You need not treat me any longer as though I am made of brittle glass, Rosgran, neither as frail nor as cold."

"No. And neither am I. Nor am I playing with your desires, Arn. Yet that wound of yours should be less prone to open and bleed anew before you kiss too hotly." She pressed her lips lightly to his, a gentle way of saying, "Until another time."

Then she called her servant to help Arn back to the barrack-house, where men were quartered when Nemed mustered a war-host. Thoughtful, she returned to the manor. Soon she was chattering to her sister, the prince's second and younger wife. They looked so much alike that the least observant man would have recognized their kinship.

"How does your wounded warrior today?" Siranal asked.

"Oh, well enough," Rosgran answered carelessly. She did not intend to be drawn into discussion, for something nagged her like twinges of warning from a seemingly sound tooth where Arn was concerned. Her instincts told her he was honest by nature, and not much of a boaster in sober moments, yet he had boasted wildly of his kinship and descent in lands now overrun by the Firbolgs. Why? He plainly came of good stock, and had been reared in a good household. For a man of his plain nature that should be sufficient to claim.

"Oh, well enough?" her sister teased. "Your lips did not swell like that from eating hot cakes."

"Try a cleverer trick than that if you want to catch me," Rosgran told her, "and pick a matter in which there *is* something to catch me. I like the man well. So far, there is nothing more. If ever there is and I want someone to hear of it, you will probably be the first. Confess, you want to be entertained now that Nemed is gone. Well, I'll tell you all the fine salacious stories you want, sister, but no true ones."

"Too much sharpness there," Siranal adjudged. "I wonder why. And entertained? Why, by the paps of the goddess, I would like to be! First Nemed is exiled soon after I wed him. Then, directly his term is over, he rushes back to Tirtangir and steals a treasure which seems to be worth more to him than Vivha and I combined, and last of all, he leaves again for the seaways. That the Firbolgs are a fanged menace, I know, but he might spend one summer at home in a decade. Never link fates with a prince, Rosgran. It's to vow faith to his empty high-seat."

"Sister, I'm not likely to, unless I travel north. Anyhow, I no more dream of a prince than you did, before you caught Nemed's eye. Unless I loved him deeply, I'd not consider one. Rather would I have a fine craftsman than a warrior, or maybe a jurist, though a man who deals in words might have little else to commend him. Still, he'd be useful if ever we had litigious neighbors. He could argue his own case."

"He'd quite wear you down when he argued with you."

"Yes. That would be the greatest drawback. I'll stand by my first choice, then. A craftsman skilled with his hands. A good taciturn bronze-worker or carpenter, with the strength of a bear." Rosgran closed her eyes and smiled.

"Yonder man Arn looks strong, and good-humored with it."

"Oh, sister. Go to the lake if you want to fish. To be sure he is! I wouldn't seek his company if it wasn't pleasing. But all he seems to know is cattle and fighting, nor does he seek very hard for a place of his own. Either he cares no longer, or he has obligations somewhere else. It doesn't matter. My feeling is that once he can walk, he will disappear."

"You know best about that. He might also come back."

"Now, why would he?"

"To serve a lord like Nemed, I should think." Siranal stuck her tongue in her cheek. "If you want a better reason, ask your mirror. And you accused me of fishing? Come, this man interests you. Tell me more of him."

"I would I knew more. He's quiet and steady—most of the time—yet when he talks of his past he utters such foolish brags I have to discount it all."

"That is nothing unusual in a man. Sister, have you thought that he may be homeless because of trouble with his own folk and not with the Firbolgs?"

"I have. I'd still like to know the truth."

"Then ask him for it, or else let be. You are not the custodian of his spirit. All men lie, as much as they have to, or more. Half the men in the war-host must have fabricated pasts."

The matter still nagged at Rosgran. She spoke to one or two other warriors, one of whom came from the same region of Alba that Arn claimed as his home. She asked him about the royal clan of that tribe, its descent and branches. What he told her did

not agree with what Arn had said. She wasn't surprised; she had
known that his boasts of belonging to a princely line now
scattered were only vaunting. But he had not even a similar
accent to the man she had been quizzing, yet he was supposed to
come from the same parts. Rosgran could not place it. She
wondered if it was worth investigating further.

She caught herself suddenly. She was thinking of Arn as
though he might be a spy, an enemy. She had gone behind his
back, hinting, comparing, verifying. That was no way to treat
the friend she considered him. Siranal had been right; if it
mattered so much to her, she should ask Arn himself. Besides, if
he were a spy, whose might he be—the Firbolgs'? That was
impossible, when he had fought them and taken a wound which
might easily have caused his death.

She walked pensively up the valley. Glancing at the balcony
of Nemed's manor, built to receive the rays of the summer sun,
she saw the senior wife standing there, basking in the light.
Vivha had not fretted too much over her man's exile, those long
years before. Instead she had settled to ruling the land for him,
holding it against all comers, including some of his own brothers. Maybe she had ruled it more for herself and less for him.
Seven years was a long time, and now it had stretched to almost
nine, in which Nemed had been present for a single winter. He'd
be like a stranger to her, nor would Vivha especially like giving
back the powers of governance she had held. Growing from
child to woman in the long valley, Rosgran had realized long ago
that Nemed's senior wife liked the responsibility and the power
both. She hadn't gone without the strong assuagements of a man
in all those years Nemed had been missing, either. One glance at
her body, her carriage, her haughty, passionate face, made nonsense of that idea. For that matter, it was nonsense to think it of
Siranal. Neither woman had ever been timid or bloodless, and
Danan women enjoyed great freedom.

Nemed would not believe it, either. He wasn't so stupid.
However, he would not accept the presence of lovers now that he
had returned—if, so far, it could be called returning. Maybe that
too irked Vivha. Maybe she had a man she preferred, and would
not grieve too deeply if a Firbolg arrow ended the prince's life.
Maybe, even—

Rosgran forbade herself what she had been about to think.

Because she happened to be looking upward, she saw the fiery
blaze in the sky, like another, smaller, sun. It arrowed over the

mountain, and passed directly above Vivha, who followed it with an astounded gaze. The resplendent bird with its thirty-foot wingspread, body large as a child's, long tail plumes and slim neck, flashed like burning gold. Arn saw it too. It filled his heart with hope, for he knew who that flaming bird was. With its appearance, the first move in the real game had been made.

Vivha, standing transfixed on the great sun-balcony, also felt a great upwelling of hope. She knew well the sort of omen a sunbird was said to be, and the magnificence they conferred on the places they graced with their presence. They brought more than luck. They brought riches, power, generosity, strength, and pride.

The possibilities filled her mind. She went indoors and summoned the chief herald. Among other duties, he bore messages and spoke for his prince by proxy—or, as now, his prince's lady. Ycharn was his name.

Attending Vivha in her solar, he received the full impact of her personal strength, for which her spectacular appearance was only the vessel. She curled on a fringed purple coverlet, and let her confident power spill over him. Ycharn could guess what she wanted. He too had seen the sunbird's passage. The entire valley had.

"Send the word to every farm, steading, and hut in the land, worthy Ycharn," she said. "If the sunbird is seen again, I must be told. If it nests in our land, I must know where. For the man or woman who tells me truthfully where it is to be found, rich rewards; for the one who harms it, even a feather or the least claw of its foot, my displeasure and vengeance. It is to be treated as a guest of the land. None may offend it."

Ycharn bowed, and went forth to do he bidding.

Vivha rose, strode about the solar, threw her arms wide to send the blood moving more strongly in her body, and considered all she must do on the morrow. Any malingerers living on the valley's bounty should be sent on their way; genuine heroes who had fought well in the Danan cause must be helped, and some at least should be adopted into the clan—or married into it—for the greater fighting strength they would give. Goddess, but her valley needed strength, and while Nemed kept the Firbolgs at bay she seemed the only one able to provide it! The appearance of a sunbird was the best of signs.

Another sign too, or the lack of it, gave her the best of reasons to be happy. She was almost certain now that she carried a child.

It would not be Nemed's heir; like the Danans of Tirtangir, the Albans reckoned descent through the mother, and the prince's heirs, the children closest to him, were his sister's offspring. Vivha's child would be her own, and of great interest to her several brothers, since boy or girl it would be eligible for the position of Rhi, which at present went unfilled. The Firbolgs had shattered it, robbed the title of meaning. For a Danan Rhi to preside in Alba again as anything more than an empty show, the Firbolg power had to be broken—and Vivha relied on Nemed to do it.

"When you are grown," she whispered, hands on her lower belly, "the invaders will have been brought low, little one. They will serve you and our clan. I—Nemed—my brothers—we will ensure it. You will be inaugurated in a throne and temple at the heart of Alba, which will again be ours."

Her dream was interrupted. With a knock and a perfunctory announcement, a man walked into the solar as though it was his unquestioned right. Vivha colored with anger. She knew exactly as he did what his self-assured presence implied, and he was mistaken. She regretted having to mar her mood to tell him so.

"Pechorid, you are not the lord here. Even if you were, I would have you approach me with more courtesy than this. Can you remember what I said to you when Nemed returned?"

"I can indeed, lady. Yet now he has gone again, as a hero should, and I am still here. If he neglects you, light of beauty, that is not your fault or mine."

Vivha's eyes blazed. "You may not sneer at him, little man! You could never survive what he has, or do what he has done. Were you courageous, you would be with him this day, not lounging here at your ease hoping to smooth your way back into my bed. I tell you, the winter of his return saw the best loving I have known in seven years. If you imagine you can continue as you have done, far into the future, you are wrong."

"Vivha, we have been bedmates seven years—"

"And seven years could well be enough." The tawny woman walked with her smooth stride to the balcony and looked down the valley again, the home she loved and defended. "Nemed is no fool. He knows. That won't offend him, but your continued presence will. You'd have gone home with the coming of spring, if you were wise. Stay on your family's lands and learn to work, Pechorid. That would do you more good than being here. It's time you left. Smirk in the prince's sight as you just did, and he's likely to throw you over a treetop.''

She was discarding him, Pechorid realized, standing there handsome in the finery she had given him. And what had he of his own to take home? He crimsoned to the ears, with anger because his pride was hurt, not because he had lived on a woman for so long.

''You do not care so much for Nemed,'' he accused. ''It didn't take you long to find another when he went into exile.''

''Several others, Pechorid, from time to time, and so did he, doubtless. One day we'll tell each other about them and there will be no heart-burning over it. That is between him and me. Between you and me . . . you have got into the habit of thinking all these lands are yours and that I am the same, often as I have told you differently. I believe you truly imagined you were the prince.'' She refrained from laughing, yet it showed that she refrained. ''That was to your own harm, my dear. You are not.''

''Your prince is not such a glorious fellow as you think,'' the dandy snarled. ''His paths of theft led him at last to stealing the cauldron in Tirtangir; the tale he told didn't approach within hurling distance of the truth.''

''I know he stole it.'' Vivha was amused. ''Now you are hurling mud. It isn't important, what he may have done to a tribe of hairy Freths. He'd have betrayed *us* if he had not obtained it. No.'' She forestalled Pechorid as he opened his mouth. ''Do not say it. Whether you mean to ask pardon or traduce him more, it is not worth hearing. Come. We have at least been companions for a long time, and the times were merry. We should be able to part better than this. For parting it must be.''

''Why?'' her lover asked. ''You were willing that he should take a second wife, once you found that you could get along with her.''

''What has that to do with anything?''

''This. If Nemed can do that, you can have another man.''

''I daresay I could. But, Pechorid, I do not want two men at once. As for Siranal, we share the duties and we agree well together, as you remark. Do you think that you could ever do the same with Nemed? Your jealousy shows each time you hear his name. You cannot abide him. Besides, you fear him, though you will never say it, and fearing him would be nothing but wisdom if you make him your enemy. There are no grounds in that for working together.''

"You forget I am a jurist with the law at my fingertips," he said. "Haven't I been of use in that way, until you can scarcely do without me at a judgment? Who else stands by your seat when you give your decisions?"

"Again," Vivha said, "you pretend I am helpless, which is a lie. That you're a jurist of ability none is denying, but the judgments I give are mine. Pechorid, none of this bibble-babble is to the purpose."

"The purpose. And what's that?"

"You were telling me I cannot do without you. Nonsense. I said to you plainly, always, that this would end. You didn't listen, and if it finds you unprepared, you are to blame."

Hurt pride bubbled thickly in Pechorid, and pain from the mangling of something he would have called love. Anger gave him the spirit to stand, compose his face, and say to the prince's lady:

"Indeed I will go. My family can also do with the services of a lawman. I'll send them word to expect me at Midsummer, and—"

"Pechorid! I care not. Send them any message you please. I'll agree to Midsummer, though few men would have stayed another day after hearing what I have told you. Besides reading hearts, I can see a measure of the future, as you may have forgotten. It's in your mind that much may happen before Midsummer, which is a few nine-nights away; that we might even hear that Nemed has been slain." Her full mouth shaped the words with a brimming serve of scorn. "As if that would be comforting news for you! But you never did see farther than the end of your own nose. There, I'll do a last thing for you, to help your vision. I will look into your future, all the branching roads which lead from *now* to *then*, and tell you which are the brightest."

"Keep your counsel!" Pechorid snapped. "You cast me off like a jewel you are tired of wearing, and would soothe me by telling my fortune like a star-gazer at a fair? If that is how you read hearts, you are less skilled at it than you think. I want no such drool. Wait for your prince, then! And may your bed long be cold."

It surprised Vivha that he had the backbone to walk out on her. She liked him the better for it. Still, he must leave. His trouble was that he had quite lost his head over her, while hers remained on her shoulders.

"Even if I picked an ill time, you should have let me read the promises and threats of your future, my friend," she mused. "You are in a humor to follow a course anybody could tell you leads to disaster. Well, I will scan as best I can while you are not here." She closed her eyes. "That much is your due."

Breathing deeply and slowly, she let her spirit slip the confines of her body, and soar to other realms. With Pechorid's image in her heart, she ranged ahead of the present, searching through the many possible events which might become real. Only one would eventuate, and which one depended on Pechorid more than anyone.

She saw him remaining in the long valley. That led to further quarrels, and finally to his death at the hands of an adversity-hardened warrior who did not like his manners. Then she saw him riding back to his clan, no longer the prince's man or the lady's, choking on humiliation. But humiliation was not smoke; it never burned out a man's eyes. On that path he learned something, and grew too wise to grasp beyond the length of his arm.

There was a third major path for the jurist, which Vivha could not clearly perceive. It led like a mountain trail up treacherous heights, with murky passions obscuring his progress, and finally into darkness. Beyond that, Vivha's perception failed in a confusion of too many possibilities, too far removed in time. She had no doubt, though, of what Pechorid should do for his own sake. She closed the eyes of her spirit and opened those of her body.

"Would I could see my own future," she murmured, "and the fruits of my own desires."

No seer could do that. Those very concerns led to wishfulness and error. Scanning her own future was like trying to lift herself by her own shoulders. Certainly, she had spent time enough trying to aid Pechorid, when he did not even want it, and the fate of the valley was her concern; the valley, and all her people beyond it, and the tiny life within her which had such a mighty heritage to be made secure. She could not predict its pitfalls and chances either, since its life was so intimately mingled with hers, therefore she must do whatever else she could. Ycharn must take a message to her brothers when he returned from carrying his present message. Vivha thought again of the sunbird, omen of glory.

She did not ask herself whose glory.

Watching from a crag beyond the valley, Carbri saw Ycharn ride away. He knew the look of a messenger, and if this man was not a herald riding with news, Carbri was a trout. The sunbird's appearance would be known the length of the peninsula in a day.

He had seen Arn as well, moving with the support of a crutch, accompanied by a young woman who seemed most friendly to him. Already Carbri's head swarmed with ideas for taking the Undry out of the manor, since Arn could no longer help them, and for getting Arn away too. If Diancet, their physician, had only been there, he would have had the lad leaping in the air, clicking his heels, within a day. Since he wasn't, they would have to wait a little longer.

He saw Pechorid, too, though he did not know the man by name, and merely saw the fine raiment, the angry, forceful gait. Ignorant that he was watched from afar, Pechorid halted to glance around the high-sided vale, remembering how he had dreamed of ruling it, with all the lands around, by Vivha's side. Fool. Triple fool!

But he did not blame himself for being a fool. Instead, he blamed her for not making his dreams come true. Blacker and more twisted grew his resentment, and there was nothing he could do about it, nothing to gain satisfaction. It would make no difference if Nemed died on the sea. Vivha would never be his.

Still she had no right to dismiss him as she had done, no right! Not when he had served her seven years. The more he brooded, the stronger grew his need to strike back, to avenge himself, and the less he was able to imagine how. To murder her was unthinkable, while Nemed was far out of reach, and would have defended himself against any attempt of Pechorid's with one hand. Although he had trained with weapons like any other young Danan, the jurist possessed average skills or less.

In more balanced moments Pechorid thought of returning to his clan as Vivha advised—no, as she had commanded. Then his bitterness refused to think of it. He would not face them like a beaten man. He would have retribution for this treatment. Again he thought longingly of the manor burning, Vivha's treasured balcony and solar a mass of flames, collapsing into a pit of fire which the lower storey of the house had become—and taking Vivha with it. One sudden shriek, and that resolute, haughty face would never torment him again. Yet he hadn't the ruthlessness to do it, and besides, he knew that he would see Vivha's face when he lay dying.

Distracted, hardly knowing where he was, Pechorid heard

Arn's voice by merest chance. Rosgran had not been able to know a Tirtangir accent, but the jurist did. He stiffened, and then relaxed. Danans from all parts had joined the war-host. A Tirtangir man was nothing extraordinary. Still he gave Arn a glance of casual interest, and recognized the warrior Rosgran had nursed, the crutch outthrust before him where he sat. Involved in his own unhappiness, Pechorid gave the matter no thought then.

When he saw Arn the next day, exercising in a stand of trees while Rosgran watched him with sewing in her lap, his interest quickened. Bidding them good-day, he let his face smile, speak, and question for him, while his thoughts followed their own paths. When, in answer to some casual, natural query about his kindred and place, Arn replied that he had been bred in Alba, Pechorid gave a silent howl of triumph. This man lied!

Nor was Pechorid like Rosgran, to place innocent interpretations on things like that. If one aspect was false, then so was much else. Nemed had stolen the cauldron of plenty in Tirtangir; this fellow came from Tirtangir, and said otherwise. Pechorid went away, talked to some of the other fighting veterans and made a comment or two concerning Arn.

"Broad man, you know; he looks strong, and uses a crutch. He might be the man I hold a cloak-pin to give. Vakor said before he died that he owed a debt, but didn't make it clear to whom—''

Since Pechorid had always been a busybody, this seemed strange to none. He learned a number of things from talkative men without having to suspiciously inquire. What had begun as a game rapidly became more.

"Arn! Yes, it's too bad about his leg. No matter, he's alive, and he's kept it to throw over many a horse again. I do not know him well; he doesn't say much.''

"He used to have two friends here. One left with the prince, and the other—I seem to remember the prince himself ordered him to go far and not come back. Yet I cannot recall why.''

"He laid hands on the Undry for a drunken bet. He was fortunate to keep them. His hands, I mean.''

Once more the Undry was concerned. Pechorid felt that he had something real, unsure though he was of its precise shape. He might go to Vivha with his suspicions. She would require only a little speech with Arn to know his heart's secrets, and any evil he might be planning would soon be revealed.

That first impulse died. He, Pechorid, would not run to Vivha with a half-suspected plot. He would not run to Vivha at all. He would uncover the evil himself, if there was any, and if there was not, he would be saved from looking a fool. Below the surface, something whispered that he would even be pleased if any plot against Vivha's tranquility met with success.

He set out to cultivate Arn's acquaintance.

He barely succeeded. Arn spoke to him readily enough, but was not encouraging after the first few exchanges. Pechorid grew more suspicious. He noticed, for one thing, that Arn slipped into a Tirtangir accent only sometimes. It showed that he had been tutored with care to imitate the Alban tongues, but that his response to the training had not been perfect. In the event, it was worse than leaving his speech uncorrected, since it showed that he was trying to hide something. What but his origins?

Many a one of the prince's men had been to Tirtangir, and would have recognized an accent of that isle as readily as Pechorid. Arn must have stayed very silent until now, when the prince was absent and most of his travelled veterans with him. It had taken Pechorid to discover the trick.

While he luxuriated in his cleverness, he wondered if Rosgran knew. He couldn't see her as a traitress. Hugging his knowledge to himself was pleasant for a while, but sooner or later he must do something.

While he vacillated, the sunbird flew again. Alinet displayed herself in her candescent plummage above the mountains, and farmers dropped their tools to gape. Word went back to the valley almost as swiftly as the sunbird flew. Vivha rewarded those who brought the news as richly as she had promised.

"It must be nesting in our mountains," she said. Her eyes glowed. "A sunbird, Siranal! Those creatures are talismans of force and greatness for any who are lucky enough to possess one. With it for my familiar, I could confound all the Firbolg swarms. My powers would become tenfold what they are!"

Siranal frowned. "You did forbid any to harm or offend it, on pain of dire punishment. Are you going to molest it now?"

"Molest?" Vivha looked astonished. "I did not want it frightened away! Now that it has nested here, I mean to own the powers it can grant to its mistress."

"You mean to have too much." Siranal's face was troubled. She knew Vivha in this mood. "I've always heard that a sunbird brings great luck and prosperity to a land only if respected to fly free. Will you bring a curse on us?"

"Give me credit for knowing what I am about. I'll lure the creature, tempt it, coax it. Nothing shall be too good for it. Loved it will be, honored greatly—and some of the strength of the very sun will be ours!"

"Is this not to be talked about? Though you are the first lady, I have a voice, and, Vivha, meseems you go much too fast. The strength of the very sun is a lot to presume to capture. It's the beauty and splendor you want, not so? The glory of owning what no other does. But you reach for what no mortal can truly own. What if our valley is burned by its fires? I'm opposed. Put the question to our people and see how they take it; they will be as doubtful."

"I won't offer this for debate at an assembly. It would take too long. Meanwhile, some ambitious upstart from the mainland could well come sneaking in to catch our sunbird."

"*Our* sunbird, already!"

"Yes. This is where rule belongs; the blood of the Great Rhi is here."

"The blood of the Great Rhi," Siranal repeated. She looked at Vivha closely, realized something, and embraced her with a sudden laugh. "Now I see! It is wonderful, but funny. This ringing talk of sorcery beyond my understanding, and the royal mysteries, all because you want your babe to have the sun to play with. Will you burn down a forest to cook his porridge?" She shook her head. "It's not wise."

"You still do not understand," Vivha told her. "I've born one child; not as many as I'd wish to, yet I know something about it. You have just called me an idiot who hears nothing beyond the wails from the cradle, do you know? I have bigger concerns than that, Siranal. The future of us all is bound up in this."

"It's still a change of tune since yesterday. Vivha, can you not wait, and see how the land fares with your wonder bird as its guest? Jewelled cage and diet of cake though you offer, you are still making it a prisoner instead. The sunbird may reckon it a poor bargain."

While the two disputed, Cena stood on a windy peak in her sorceress's cloak and shouted into the wind. When she had ended her incantation, she turned about to climb down. Rain had streaked her face. When she had descended to safety, alone, as the ritual demanded, she swayed in a way not due to the physical work of climbing.

"I'll not do that for a year or two again," she declared.

"What was it?" Oghmal asked, concerned.

"A cantrip of influence. I've sent a dream to find Vivha and fill her sleep. She's a sorceress, used to paying attention to her dreams, and I made this one magnificent. She and her descendants were enthroned in the temple the Firbolgs are building at the heart of Alba, while the Firbolgs themselves stood humbly outside, disarmed and bowing. Add that to the powerful wanting Vivha has for you, cousin, just because you are beautiful, and I am sure she will be chasing you before a nine-night has passed. Sadly, she is not going to trap you until you are ready to be captured."

"And then, when she is eager past words, we give her her desire—at our own price." Alinet laughed, savoring in advance what would happen. "I know the plan."

"Yes. Do not be too sure it will go as we have made it," Cena warned. "Few plans do. Let it only go well enough for Vivha to bring the Undry from wherever she has it hidden, guarded no doubt by spells and ugly little monsters, and I'll not complain."

"Will she want the sunbird sufficiently?" Oghmal asked. "All depends on that."

"She loves costly, beautiful things very greatly," Cena answered. "When a thing is unique, she desires it even more. Sorceress or not, wise or not, she holds the Undry a poor thing in her heart, because it is not beautiful."

"It's as ugly a piece of misshapen pottery as ever man's eyes, or woman's, beheld," Carbri corrected. "I agree with her there. Yet power comes out of it with the power to feed your people; would she trace beauty for that? With the responsibility she has upon her? She must be a fool in some ways if she would."

"She sees it as a source of power too. Withal, for her it is not enough to have the power without splendor and show; the sunbird is the key to all three. And when next she sleeps, she will see it in her dreams, will she not? Even a sorceress can find what meaning she wishes to find."

"I'd say especially a sorceress," Oghmal said unguardedly. He mistrusted magic, so slippery and many-formed, so easy to miss, so apt to twist against the user.

Alinet and Cena looked at each other. The former said coolly, "Has it eluded you, kinsman, that two such are with you now? And that you are depending on us to accomplish this thing? We may be hiding like outlaws, yet a Danan lord need not forget his manners on that account.''

"We're depending on each other," Oghmal answered. "Can you swear you have never deceived yourself while working sorcery? All I know of it is that it's a tricky art, and perilous as juggling with knives and vipers together. I include sorcerers in that," he added, turning to Carbri. "Recall the time you and your friend turned the Cave of Ruarga inside out?"

"The clothes on our bodies, too." The bard hacked a piece of stone-hard bread. "Lucky we were not to do it to ourselves. Still, be fair, brother. It's raw youngsters we were at the time."

"And grown magicians like Sixarms loose deathworms on the land, to which a Sanhu replies with worse," Oghmal growled. "No, I like this plan. It's elegant, at least, and will not leave the whole land wasted. Not a single life will be destroyed if we have luck, and are careful."

"And if Vivha runs true to sorceresses' fashion, a self-deceiving fool," Alinet added. "You said it, kinsman. I will not let you forget it. How is this for deceit?"

Staring into his eyes, she became a cat-headed demon with a body from the foulest pit in Anuven. Hissing, she reached for him. Oghmal sat calmly, used to illusion. So many tricks had been played on him as a child and youth that he had learned to know by instinct when something was real. She dug her nails—which looked like filthy claws—into his neck, just hard enough to sting, then drew them back. Dispelling the illusion, she sat as before, young, golden, and demure.

"As deceit, it was nothing," Oghmal said, "for you told me to expect it. Your fancy in monsters is fearful, though. How many of your clan have you terrified with that one?"

"None. I imagined it for you, Oghmal, but as you say, you knew. Watch Vivha's henchmen squeal if I have to frighten them!"

"It's sad to spoil your fun, but I'm hoping you do not. The perfect end to this would be for us all to depart, none knowing we had been here."

In the afternoon, the sunbird winged through the changeable sky again, to pass over the valley, this time coming and vanishing in a swift flash, so that only the alert or fortunate glimpsed her. Arn wasn't among them. However, he heard of her appearance, and dragged himself to the lake on his crutch, listening to the excited tales of those he met. One and all, they were convinced that its sighting meant felicity for them and their rulers. Arn felt rather low for deceiving them, although the feeling passed when he remembered how gleeful these same folk had been to hear that their prince had stolen the Undry from Tirtangir.

Meeting Rosgran's honest brown eyes caused him a pang when next he walked with her, though. She was not just any woman, or a foe to despoil. She was the one who had healed him, very likely saving his leg, and he felt more than a debt of gratitude. He liked her as herself.

"What think you of this marvelous bird?" he asked. "Is it true that the lady Vivha plans to catch it, and make it a pet eating from her hand?"

"She has wider plans than that, from what my sister tells me," Rosgran said, then bit her lip. She should not have said so much. "I hope it is true, what they are said to presage: luck and victory. The Freths are a curse."

"Freths?" Arn repeated.

"I mean Firbolgs," Rosgran said. She had not missed his unguarded look when she mentioned that name. "If the sunbird truly means triumph for us—oh, goddess, let it be so! The black bows must never sing here as they did on your doorstep, Arn." She laid a small hand on his shoulder. "Maybe the day is near when they will be driven out of your home."

"I'll believe that when we win a battle against them instead of losing, no matter how gloriously," Arn said. He couldn't resist his next question. "What made you say Freths? They are the brood your lord fought against in Tirtangir, and a hard gang by all accounts, though I doubt they could be worse than the Firbolgs. Anyhow, he defeated them."

"Yes. That's what I have heard." Rosgran's voice was steady, her look candid. "We're nowhere free from trouble, we Danans. I must have had the battles over there in my mind. I've heard so much of them from our singers I may utter the word Freth in my sleep! Did you ever see one, Arn? Are they as ugly as the songs make them? With horses' heads, or one arm, one leg, and half a head each? It's difficult they would find it to fight, if that be true."

"I have seen one," Arn said. "Far from home he was, working on a farm for his keep, and ugly enough, but no monster. Were he taller and darker, he could have passed for a Firbolg. I will say that he looked strong enough to break an ordinary mortal like a twig."

"What of your strength? How does the leg?"

"I could run and leap hurdles," Arn said cheerfully, "but I wish to stay here awhile yet, so I am pretending it is weak. Also, I plan to steal you when I go, so naturally I want to be at my fittest."

"Oh, naturally. It doesn't occur to you to ask me, rather than carry me off by force? Who knows, Arn? I wouldn't go with you, in the wilderness Alba has become, but I might just wait awhile to see if you grew tired of tramping like a vagabond and came back."

He wouldn't be able to come back, that was certain. He said, "Best not, Rosgran. That wilderness has swallowed greater men than me. If I'm gone more than a single change of the moon it is unlikely I shall ever be back."

"You look gloomy! It isn't so serious, is it, except that I mislike the thought of your leg failing you somewhere if you have no kindred to help you. There's your comrade Tavasol, but he won't return before the summer's end."

"Aye, and I had another, Lygi, but he left the host and might be anywhere now. Those two are the nearest thing to brothers I still have. I'll seek out Lygi, for I know a place where he will have left a message. Then we will meet with Tavasol again, if he comes back."

All this sounded very cool, flat, and distant in his own ears when he burned to take Rosgran in his arms. No twinges from his wound were dire enough to restrain him. Not any longer. Yet he owed her kindness, and he had a selfish interest too. If he played with her feelings he risked more than a surface scrape to his own.

"So you are determined to go?"

"I—yes, when my leg mends. I've earned that long a stay. Then I will go and fight Firbolgs with Lygi, under any good war-leader who will have us. We're worth our keep.'"

"So long as you stay honest." Rosgran blinked. "Never sink to a bandit, Arn, or a scavenger preying on Danans. Other good men have done that. Our prince is no god, he has his faults. But this is a land where a man can plant a crop and expect to reap it. Nemed has kept it that way. Even while he was in exile he sent metal and trusty, helpful men here, when he could find them."

Arn felt uncomfortable. She was virtually defending Nemed to him. He had said nothing against the man. It made little sense, unless she knew Arn's purpose here was inimical, and the same applied to her question about Freths. If she really accepted Arn as Alban, she would not expect him to know. He must not blind himself; she was suspicious and probing, though she might care for him besides.

When she left him, he watched her move out of sight. Then he hopped along by a different way to intercept her, halting between the buttery and a storehouse. Though his leg throbbed and he felt short of breath, he remained fit to handle any trouble which might arrive. He was spying on Rosgran and he admitted it freely to himself. If he was caught he would give the obvious reason. Yes, there she was, by the brewing-house, and the smoothly surreptitious way she entered said that she had some furtiveness to regret, too.

Arn didn't go there at once to listen. Someone might be coming to meet her. Not caring for his own position, he waited, leaning against the wall in his shadowed corner as though resting. He decided against trying to eavesdrop. He wasn't an experienced sneak and would surely bungle it. Rosgran wasn't, either—he would have bet his sword on that—but still, she had more than common alertness.

After a short while, someone came out. Arn recognized him even while the man's upper body remained shadowed in the doorway. The stance, the posture, the well-shaped legs, all belonged to Pechorid the jurist. Arn felt certain the meeting had not been one of desire. Arn had spoken to the man—more often than he wished to, lately—and he did not think Rosgran would want him. It had seemed almost as though Pechorid was trailing him about.

Pechorid and Rosgran seemed unlikely partners in anything. The jurist *was* an experienced sneak, or Arn had no perception. Arn watched him depart, then waited until he saw the brown girl emerge and look about her. She walked off in the opposite direction.

Arn went on his own way, not a little worried. He was the last of Oghmal's men in the long vale. If Rosgran wondered about him, and Pechorid the nuisance had become suspicious, then Arn's usefulness had ended. He felt a ludicrous indignation that she should suspect him, as if she would not be right to do so, and then began thinking of what he should do about it.

Vivha, it was said, could read the inner passions of a man's heart by standing close and speaking to him. Certainly she could tell lies from truth, and if she searched him for falsehood with

her powers, she would expose him in moments. After that he
would be tortured to rags for all he knew, then cast on a midden.

He could not run while the chance remained that he might
serve the tribe, or its Rhi, or his own lord. Thus he must stay
and risk being caught. If he *was* caught, he could not betray the
others, and that meant it would be necessary for him to die with
his mouth sealed. He couldn't do that under torments of wood,
stone, and fire, therefore—if he was taken—he must slay himself
and hope that the others could finish the work somehow. He
rather thought they would manage.

He hid a small knife in his sleeve, and practiced letting it fall
into his hand with a quick jerk of his arm. That was easy, but he
didn't know whether he had the nerve to slash his own throat
deeply, upon the instant, should the worst eventuate. Bleakly he
contemplated that. Never had he believed he was the sort to
suicide, nor was it a Danan custom. A man was expected to die
in battle, though, should it be needful, and this in its way was no
different.

Be it so.

Arn made his peace and left the corner where he had stood
concealed, the knife growing warm against his flesh. Not until
he lay in his cot that night, listening to other men snore and talk,
did it occur to him that he might slay others beside himself, and
make his secret safe that way. His eyes flickered open the instant
he pictured it.

A fool's thought. He'd have to slay both Rosgran and
Pechorid—and on merest suspicion—and possibly Vivha too.
To a Danan, slaying women was about as acceptable as eating
human flesh. Not to consider the fact that he was the first one
anybody would suspect if Rosgran were harmed. He couldn't
even put the jurist out of his way so cold-bloodedly. This wasn't
a predicament he could escape by spearing his way out of it.

He shut his eyes again. The thoughts marched like ants around
the inside of his skull before they settled down, and the steady
throb of his wounded leg kept him awake a little longer, but Arn
was by no means highly strung, and he slept at last.

Chapter
Nine

Oghmal watched the small band of riders canter past. Vivha
kept sharp vigilance. While smaller than the horses he rode at
home, these mountain steeds looked tougher, too, with eyes in
their feet and flame in their blood. Nemed's men carried long
lances, not the short saddle-javelins for casting from horseback
which Cena's folk principally used. Oghmal had smiled at the
length of the Alban lances, the first time he had seen them. No
man, he had declared, could prick from the saddle with such a
thing. He'd go backward over his horse's tail directly he drove
his lance-tip home.

Then he had observed the riders at home on their own crags,
scarps, and forest slopes. Oghmal had long since stopped laughing. Men who could spear fish from a mountain stream while
fording it were not risible. They could guide their lance-tips
through an enemy's throat at a full gallop just as skillfully, and
do it without falling off their horses. The champion stayed
hidden and watched them with respect. He was no less ready for
that to fight and kill them all if he must.

They passed from sight with a clop and jingle. They were careless in that; his own men would have uttered spells to make their passage wholly silent. He needn't fear that they would surprise Cena.

Time was passing, though. Each day increased their risk of discovery by someone. Vivha sent out such groups of horsemen at random, in daylight or dark. They could not be everywhere, and she used her best men to watch the shore, now that Nemed was away with his remaining ships. Still, there was always the chance that they would find one of the Danans, which meant finding all.

Oghmal moved on with care. His garments blended with the summer growth, and he used the cover well. His goal was the valley. The semblance of one of the warriors who lived there hid his real appearance, he and Cena having decided it was worth the risk to speak with Arn. If Vivha or one of her magicians should look at him closely, his imposture would be over at once; that had to be accepted. It was time to act.

He approached through an oakwood whose holy trees would never feel an axe, and paid his respects to the tree spirits as he passed. Oghmal seldom did such things save when he felt the need for luck; many thought he gave too little heed to the goddess and the lesser powers of earth, but he believed it was better to depend on himself. Just now, though, he would not willingly have offended the tiniest of sprites.

He walked boldly down into the community beside the lake. Thatch shone golden or black with age under the sky; carved door-posts and beam-ends showed brightly painted. Oghmal walked on, neither slowing nor quickening his pace. He pictured the amazement of the warrior whose form Cena had given him, should they come face to face. The man would think he had met his own fetch in daylight, and turn pale.

The champion spoke to none, save when he was greeted, and then he responded gruffly. Knowing no one, aware of the few names, he must come and go before someone who knew his double trapped him in conversation. He watched constantly for a broad figure walking upon a crutch.

Striding into the barrack-yard, he saw his man seated on a bench, enjoying the sun while he massaged his leg. The red, twisted scar ran deep into the tissue, and Oghmal's own body-scars ached in sympathy when he saw it. Arn looked healthy, though some signs of his convalescence were still upon him, and he was talking with acquaintances. Oghmal went straight to the grindstone in the center of the yard, told a menial to help him turn it as though he ruled the valley, and began sharpening his axe. A busy man was less likely to be questioned.

He finished the work and caught Arn's eye. Although it was risky to confront strangers, he didn't care to stand about. Boldness was always better. He crossed the yard after dismissing the servant, and sat beside Arn. Giving a nod and a curt word of greeting to the other men—who for all he knew were supposed to be cronies of his—he addressed Arn by name and asked how his leg was mending.

"Say something else," Arn requested. "I'm tired of talking about this damaged shank that I was foolish enough to get in the way of a weapon."

"As you like, boy. Remember when Mahon came to the red house after that trouble with his kin, and we made the drink go round for him? A pity he didn't come on this war-trail. He'd be hardened by now."

Arn closed his hands tight on his own thigh. The red house might have been anywhere, the way Oghmal spoke of it, but it happened to be the champion's own hall in his house at Dar, across the sea, while Mahon was a youth he had befriended. Arn knew who sat beside him now. He made some responses he never clearly remembered, afterward, and set his mind to protecting his lord from a slip which might betray him. He must not do too much talking, which left that up to Arn. Then another forestalled him.

"What are you talking about, Hieth? This war-trail hasn't been so hard. Why, the fighting there was at—"

He named places and events where, to hear him describe them, the world had almost ended. Oghmal, as Hieth, gave short answers, and Arn talked volubly to cover his silence, for the real Hieth was not a reticent man. Before long the two warriors left to get a meal, since they were departing that day and could not be sure when their next chance to eat would come. Oghmal swung his axe, exercising his oak-tough body while Arn watched him, and when he felt limber, the blood tingling throughout his body, he sat again beside his henchman.

"Yes, it's Oghmal," he said. "when I leave, what's the best way for me to go, and where is this Hieth whose face I have borrowed?"

"Hieth could be anywhere. The safest way to leave is by the

shore road past the lake, on the north side, then slip away by the
path that leads past the shaking aspen there. See it? You chose
the right man to personate, lord. He's leaving today, like that
pair who talked to us, and any mistakes which might give you
away will depart with them.''

"But you look at me as though I'm stark mad." The slurred
voice of Hieth came from Hieth's own oft-broken lips, past a
wide gap of missing teeth, with Oghmal's lean face buried
somewhere behind the illusion. "Come, be merry; make a joke.
Then tell me what I have to know.''

"You are mad," Arn said with conviction. "Why didn't you send
Lygi? Cena could have placed a glamor on him as easily as you.''

"More easily; I resist such magics hard, even when I'm trying
to accept them. Lygi would be slain if he was caught, though.
Maybe I would, too, but only if Nemed's weapon-men grew
over-eager. Did I survive to confront Vivha, I'd be ransomed—
and I'd die seeking to escape rather than impoverish the tribe
further by one cow. That's me. What of you?''

"I'm suspected. A girl who nursed me, a jurist who'd be
better fitted to muck out stables, with whoever they have told.
Rosgran and Pechorid, their names are; she's Nemed's sister
through his second wife.''

"You select your company wisely, don't you?" Oghmal lifted
his glamor-masked head and laughed aloud. "You wish to leave?"
That was asked in a low tone. "I'll take you out if you do.''

"I stay, lord, until this is finished. Never insult me like that
again.''

Oghmal nodded, satisfied. "No insult; a reasonable question.
But you said what I thought you'd say. Still I will remember
those names. Rosgran and Pechorid? Is there any chance that
you're wrong? That they suspect nothing, and you are fretting
without cause?''

"I am not fretting, and think the chance is small. Vivha is
ready to begin hunting the sunbird. She has made enchanted traps
and lures, and there's a reward for the man or woman who procures
her the creature, though not high enough. It's in mere gold.''

"She'll raise it when she is desperate, won't she? How badly
does she want our shining dear one?''

"I'm not privy to her confidences, but she reckons it the most
desired prize on the ridge of the earth, by what Rosgran says—
and she hasn't given away the tenth part of the lady's craving.''

"She doesn't know it to give away," Oghmal said. "From

Vivha to Siranal to Rosgran to you is a long chain of hearsay, Arn. Much could change on the way. No matter, the affair's well started. Can you ride yet?''

"At a walk, I can. A trot would shake this leg loose at the hip.''

"A walk will do. Ride as far as that stand of ash on the mountain's shoulder, where the soil is deep. Go each day for exercise, and let Rosgran come with you if she likes—but come alone sometimes. Maybe you'll be met, maybe not.''

"When they see that I can ride, they will send me away. Vivha doesn't wish an over-supply of homeless warriors in the valley to cause trouble. You know that, Hieth.''

Arn spoke the last words for the benefit of some house warriors who chose that time to come by. One heard, and glanced casually at the lamed man. There was a certain impersonal sympathy in the look, but no deep regret.

The other hadn't even that much concern. "True, wanderer,'' he said. "We do not need your kind. Be ready to part soon.''

"You'll wish you had my kind in plenty, if ever the Firbolgs come howling to your home,'' Arn retorted. "Then you'll be placeless your own self, if you're not prone with a black arrow in your gizzard—and I doubt that you'll be too proud to come to my campfire, scrounging a dry leg of rabbit.''

"Some would say that called for a challenge. You may well be glad of your injury, but do not trade too hard upon it, boy.''

He strutted on his way, not knowing why he felt suddenly cold, or whose sword-gray eyes watched him from within Hieth's battered face.

"Too many of Nemed's men are like that,'' Oghmal said. "I should have known what it meant from the first. Put off your departure all you can. After the sunbird begins to be hunted, Vivha won't allow you to leave. You will be her last hope. Aught else?''

"No, lord. Not yet.''

Oghmal rose, apparently to Hieth's full stretch of limb, which was considerably less than his own. Had some belligerent rover tried to hit Hieth's mouth, he would have landed his fist in Oghmal's upper chest instead, and rued it instantly afterward. The champion gripped arms with Arn, who warned him to go quickly, before someone became aware that there were two Hieths about the valley. His own grip said how much he appreciated Oghmal's risk.

"Abandon any thought of slaying yourself to avoid betraying us," Oghmal said, astonishing Arn with his knowledge, "and if you become certain you are discovered, run. There will be no use then in your staying anyhow. But only if you are certain, Arn. Be at the ash grove each day."

"I remember. Farewell—Hieth."

Nemed's lady came from her bower with dark rings beneath her eyes and stains on her hands. Behind her she left a great cage of wicker shaped in rising courses, its weaving intricate and sorcerous. It shone like ivory, with gold wire twisted in endless knots at the crucial junctions. Powerful spells against fire lay upon it.

Three nets like circular spiderwebs hung from frames, flimsy in appearance, fit to restrain a bear in fact. Various cords, missiles, and coils of supple twine which Vivha had twisted herself from strange materials lay on an ivory table. The work had made cruel demands on her eyesight and fingers for sleepless days and nights, but she was pleased by the results, she who was not readily pleased and judged her own handiwork most strictly. Vivha slept for a full day before she began her hunt.

She rode forth on a tall black gelding whose coat shone, while the gold wire braided into his mane supported thirteen golden bells on every lock. His blue saddle-cloth had been fringed with gold and sewn with blazing golden wheels. Vivha wore combs, rings, and bracelets of the sun's metal, a white and orange skirt, a blouse embroidered with the ships which represented the sun, and a round bronze mirror at her belt which flashed as she rode.

Before her went twenty warriors, armed and resplendent; behind her, twenty more. Harpers, drummers, pipers, and jugglers followed, dancers gay with flowers, two big men in kilts bearing the cage she had made, others with nets, more with her enchanted cords, and finally men with weighted darts for stunning in case all other measures failed.

One of the latter grumbled from the corner of his mouth, "Were I a bird, I'd see this procession and fly fifty leagues! Does *she* reckon it will be stunned by the display and fall into her lap?"

"You know nothing of it," the other told him. "Neither do I, but I'm prepared to say so! Take care your hand and eye are sure if we're called upon to throw, and leave the rest to *her*."

Vivha, riding side-saddle, fixed her sight on the rock spire where the sunbird was said to nest. Impossible to climb in the estimation of any sane man, it showed a spearhead outline against the summer sky, with a flash of dazzling light at its point. Vivha knew that brilliance. She drew a deep breath, anticipating triumph. Lowly men who knew little of sorcery might think her methods foolish, but she had not come hunting a sparrow. To capture a sunbird, one had to hunt in a fashion which honored the quarry. Had she possessed the wealth of Egypt's rulers, she would not have thought it too much for her purpose.

"Now, my darling," she whispered to the budding life within her, "now you will have the sign of your mastery, Rhi of Alba."

The harpers played a song to the rising sun, born from the Earth-Mother's dark womb to give life to her many other children. The drums and pipes played rousingly. Riding in a circle, Vivha lifted her mirror, flashing the summer daylight toward the peak. The bells in her horse's mane and tail jingled clearly.

"Bird of the bright sun, come to your mother's people," Vivha said. "Stay with us. Be our honored guest. Lend us your magnificence, grant us luck in war, grant us triumph and dominion over the Firbolg demons. Grant . . . us . . . *power*."

On the high, inaccessible peak, great wings spread. The sunbird launched itself into blue air, riding the wind, its flaming tail plumes thrice the length of its body, its wings banners of golden fire. Circling, it descended, a child of the sun coming to the mirror, as round and bright as the sun. Vivha's heart hammered between her ribs.

Now she saw the creature in detail, the slender neck and long, curving bill, the delicate plumes and crest, a bird as gorgeous as potent, coming to make her tribe masters of Alba, her offspring its ruler. The sunbird hovered. Vivha held forth the mirror, her craving naked and fierce in her countenance. The sunbird touched the earth with a flutter of huge wings. It stepped toward her.

Vivha retreated, moving behind the cage of ivory-white wicker, thrusting her hand through the bars so that the mirror tempted from within. The sunbird stopped at the cage's open door. None dared stir.

"Come, bird of fire, bird of greatness, giver of luck," Vivha coaxed, the flatteries spilling from her lips in profusion, along with promises. "Come. Is this not your second self you see here? Is this not a fair home for your beauty? Come."

Alinet entered the cage, whisking her intricate tail like the train of a gown, posing exquisitely as though about to dance. Vivha shuddered with the joy of capture.

"Enclose now, penfold! Enclose and contain!"

The cage door moved shut. Its gold latch fastened, and the thick gold wire twisted itself about the hasp in the serpentine coils, complex and endless, a copy of the golden knot Vivha wore about her neck on a chain. She drew back her arm to stand prudently far from the cage, gloating outright.

The sunbird looked at her. That long meeting of gazes left Vivha doubting somehow, wondering if she had misunderstood this being's nature from the beginning. It lifted its head. The wings ruffled, and fire surrounded the bird in a searing mist. Vivha blinked in the heat, but never flinched. The wicker cage showed no sign of burning. Vivha had wrought well, and her enchantments held. A tiny, ecstatic sound broke from her throat.

The sunbird called on a piercing, angry note, its bill stabbing skyward. Fire answered, fire from the sky in brilliant streams, raining upon the cage. Its ribs were consumed in an aureate flare, while the bindings of gold wire ran molten. The mirror Vivha held suddenly blistered her palm. With a cry, she dropped it.

Her captive broke out of the half-consumed cage with one outthrust of its wings. Beyond thought, Vivha ran forward to clasp it in her arms, calling on the netmen. The bird rose through the blazing wicker, scattering the fragments over Vivha, setting her clothes afire.

Her warriors showed the presence of mind to leap upon her, wrap her in their cloaks and roll her on the ground. They beat out the flames with their hands. She might otherwise have suffered greatly, but that comforted her not at all. Singed, dishevelled, reft of dignity and her prize together, she gazed at the smoking remnant of the cage she had fashioned.

Alinet heard her scream of frustration from far off in the sky.

"She's in a state to gnaw stones," she reported to Cena, happily. "Oh, she was so sure she had me! I do not like that woman, cousin, at all."

"What do you think of her?"

Alinet considered. "She *wants*, and that is all she knows. She wants her sunbird even more now; I made a fool of her, disappointed her, and she cannot bear that. All her retinue saw. I think she would kill them all if she could. Imagine it! She thinks I can give her the power to conquer Alba. Me! Is she mad?''

"No," Cena said. "She believes what she has heard because it's her heart's wish. And who can say she's wrong? If you led them against the Firbolg hosts like a living standard you might do that, giving them the unity they need. Never as Vivha's personal emblem, though. Were she to rule, Alba might come to prefer the Firbolgs."

"You cannot mean that! Vivha at least is a Danan."

"Think you she would bungle if she gained that rulership, then?" Carbri asked. "Deal so badly?"

"Maybe not at first," Cena said. "She's done well enough ruling here while Nemed was away. With time, though, she would grasp at more power than a Rhi is allowed. None she got would satisfy her. Nor would she think it enough for Nemed. Any Rhi of her making would have to be deposed in the end. Maybe I'm unjust, for I saw her but once and have only her actions this summer for guide, but that's my reckoning."

"She's said to be wise, though."

"We must see how wise. Not sufficiently to trace us here, let's hope. And brother, it's time you went to meet Arn. He'll begin to think his daily rides gain him nothing but exercise."

Carbri went forth by starlight, taking a long, careful way to the ash grove on the mountain and finding a position below it wherein to await the morning. He slept in snatches, kept warm by his cloak, sword in his hand. The surly yammering of one of Vivha's prowling dragon-guardians, had it reached his ears, would have sent him climbing a tree more swiftly than any man had ever done. He wasn't his brother. Oghmal could kill such a thing in darkness with two well-directed blows. Carbri might impale it on his sword, but it would chew him to rags afterward, and then might not even die itself.

Carbri welcomed the dawn. It showed him a stable, flourishing world with no snuffling demons in it. He settled to await Arn, and to see if the spy was followed. Arn wouldn't like that word spy, he reflected, yet like it or not it described him. Truly, they were all spies on this venture, and would become thieves if it succeeded, lurking, hiding, and scheming. Carbri wondered if any man ever acted in such a fashion because he liked it.

He was about to see one.

Remaining where he was until after midday, he merged with the brush in his cloak of subdued colors. His only movements

were an occasional slight shifting of a limb to forestall cramp. At
last he heard the soft nicker of a horse. Arn appeared, riding
slowly, his weak leg poking stiffly ahead while he whistled and
sang as though he had no cares in life. Carbri smiled appreciatively.

Arn passed without seeing him, moving on toward the grove.
The horse failed to sense him as well. Carbri relaxed into more
thorough stillness yet. Arn had said that he was suspected, and
he was probably right; he had never struck Carbri as the sort to
panic or leap to conclusions. He waited, until one leg went to
sleep, and then he waited longer. It would not hurt Arn to keep a
fruitless vigil once more.

Carbri heard someone else approach, then, and felt the heady
satisfaction of being right. Shortly the man came into view,
moving furtively along the trail between walls of tangled brush.
Carbri might have sprung out with a ghostly cry and frightened
the fellow through the treetops; it would have been fun and was
the least he deserved. Carbri would have enjoyed doing it, too,
save that he would have had to kill the man afterward. He
contented himself with marking the pale visage and muscular,
well-knit body. That should have been an outstandingly handsome man, and would have been but for a certain air of sulky
weakness about him. The expression of his face now that he
thought none saw him gave away much.

Two people suspected him, Arn had said; Rosgran and Pechorid
the jurist. This had to be the latter, and because he tracked Arn
himself, wearing the garb of his profession, Carbri guessed that
he was acting alone. Had he authority or spare time, he would
have sent someone else, or at the least changed his clothes. It
followed that Vivha did not know what her lawman was about.

Carbri smiled among the leaves. Doubtless he wanted proof
before he approached her. After what had happened, her mood
must be less than tolerant. Although that didn't seem like the
whole answer, it would suffice.

Carbri reflected. He did not have to meet Arn or speak to him.
There was nothing truly urgent to impart, or, most likely, to
hear. All he could do was assure Oghmal's henchman that all
was well—a thing he would know after hearing of Vivha's
disastrous hunt. Pechorid could watch Arn while the harper
watched him, and then, having seen nothing suspicious, he could
go home dissatisfied.

Carbri departed quietly. Returning to the corrie, he told the
others what he had seen, and they agreed he had acted rightly.

Pechorid must have other demands on his time. If his vigils and surveillances proved useless, he would either give them up or entrust them to someone else.

"He'd have sent another by now, if he meant to do that," Oghmal said.

"So think I. He's more apt to give up."

"Unless he's stubborn beyond reason." Cena shrugged. "He may hate to concede that he's wrong. Making away with him or bringing him here in bonds would draw too much attention. Now that we know, perhaps we can gain some advantage through him."

"This girl, Rosgran, may have more wit and be more perilous," Oghmal said. "Arn likes her. He'd make errors with her he would not make with the jurist, even if he has been forewarned."

Carbri hooted. "You're judging him by yourself, brother! Arn has had enough to do with women to guard his tongue when it's needful. One with an understanding heart and plenty of wit would do you immensities of good, so."

"That requires an equal exchange," the champion answered.

"Surely. It may be late for you to learn to make one. Never will it grow any earlier, though. The best weaver in Ridai will not wait endlessly."

"When the Undry is back with Sixarms it will be time to think on that! We should be preparing for Vivha's next hunt."

Vivha was stubborn. The next hunt came. Goaded by the dream Cena had sent her, she gathered a smaller band and tried by stealth what she had failed to achieve with display. Planting a cake of new copper alloyed with gold, she watered it from her body and trod a triple circle of footprints around it, singing a chant of fecundity as she walked. From the ground where the copper cake lay seeded sprang a copper tree with golden leaves and fruit, flashing in the summer light. With eyesight far keener than an eagle's, the sunbird would see that from afar, and be drawn to the double pleasure of gold and enchantment. This was Vivha's second lure.

She waited from dawn until noon, her fowlers with her, nets and cords ready in skilled hands. When the sun stood highest, Alinet appeared, swooping through the sky in joyful spirals. Vivha forgot to breathe while the bird alighted in the copper tree's branches, pecked discriminatingly at several fruits so that they dropped to the ground, and then descended after them. She bent her head over the richly scented golden pears, spreading her tail behind her like a fan on the grass.

The first net whirled and spread, cast unerringly to fall over her and whip around her, its folds tightening as the weights at its edges whirled together. The second and then the third covered Alinet, so that she lay entangled, struggling feebly under the copper branches. Vivha stepped from cover, a golden chain in her hand. She approached, forcing herself to be calm.

Cena's protecting sorceries now had their effect. The enveloping nets slipped from Alinet like raindrops from a leaf, to lie on the ground, flaccid and weak. Alinet whirled upward with a stormy thrashing of wings, through the branches of Vivha's enchanted tree. Fruit fell softly ripe as she went, spattering Vivha with decay. A shower of the golden leaves drifted down in their wake, lifeless and brown.

Vivha's face turned dangerously white. The fowlers studied the grass and waited for her to excoriate their ears.

The outburst did not come. Vivha returned to her manor with her white teeth clenched hard. She refrained from grinding them through a lifetime's habit of discipline where her beauty was concerned. The story sped through the valley in whispers, and spread beyond with every visitor who came and went. The lady Vivha was rapidly losing prestige in this matter of the sunbird.

When Pechorid heard of the second fiasco, he felt a certain mean satisfaction, yet he was even less inclined to go to her with his suspicions of Arn. He had nothing definite to say. All the warrior had done was brag a little, and take a daily ride for exercise. Although Pechorid had a perfect opportunity to speak when Vivha called him again to her bed, he did not do so, and that night proved long and torrid, but loveless. When Pechorid left her chamber in the hour before dawn, he knew that if he did not depart the valley at once he had neither pride nor manhood. His suspicions no doubt were wrong; so he told himself.

He confided some of this to Rosgran, though by no means all. Having shared his misgivings about Arn with her and made her his ally, he now told her his new belief that his suspicions were unfounded. She surmised much of what he was not saying. Little though she cared for the man, Rosgran did not dislike him so deeply that it pleased her to see him downcast.

"It does seem you were wrong," she said, "yet having listened to you, I owe it to Arn to be sure." She remembered that startled, guilty-seeming glance of his too well for comfort. "Suppose I ask him straight whether he is from Tirtangir? If he lies, I will know. That will show he is hiding something, whatever it may be, and if you do not dare go to the lady with that, then by the strength of the oak spirits, I do!"

"I believed you were fond of the rogue," Pechorid said sourly.

"Fond enough to want him cleared of suspicion."

"Then I hope he is, lady," Pechorid said, insincerely. He wanted to be proved right, yet in his unhappiness he no longer cared greatly whether he was or not. Rosgran had a tougher spirit in her.

When next she dallied with Arn, she leaned against him and said, "Is it true that Alba's your birthplace, wanderer? There are times when I hear an accent of Tirtangir so plainly in your voice that I seem to be standing on its earth. Why is that?"

"Do you know the accents of Tirtangir so well?" Arn had prepared a tale for such an eventuality. Still, he was flustered by Rosgran's direct question. "Born in Alba I was, indeed. In the house where I was fostered a leather-worker from Tirtangir taught me the craft, and some of his way of speaking rubbed into me with the wax. You're not the first to mark it."

He uttered the lie in a nicely offhand fashion, then changed the subject. Although Rosgran allowed him to do so, she felt by instinct that he was lying. He had delayed his answer with another question, and then been a little too long-winded, too earnest, with his explanation. The innocence she had wanted him to prove seemed further away than before. Now she was obliged by an oath to carry tales to Vivha.

Gaining an audience with the tawny-haired sorceress, she explained her suspicions. She did not mention Pechorid, since nothing he had done made the case against Arn a whit more substantial. Vivha, with two humiliating failures burning her heart and the mastery of Alba at stake, as she believed, was not inclined to pay attention to such a flimsy likelihood.

"I think you have quarrelled with your lover and are making trouble like a bondmaid," she declared, raking Rosgran from brow to shoes with a haughty look. Recalling how sour her dealings with her own lover had become, she felt the more eager to believe it. "He's done nothing, by your own word, except fight in Alba's cause and receive a wound. I'll want firmer proof than that before I so much as query him!"

Rosgran left, more relieved than displeased. She had done as her obligation demanded, and it had caused no trouble for Arn. She knew she could have made a better case for questioning him, and chosen a better time. She hadn't wanted to; it was that simple. Vivha had received a warning which she had decided it was beneath her to heed. In Nemed's absence, she ruled. Rosgran's heart felt light as she stepped from the manor. Pechorid waited for her, anxious creases in his forehead.

"She would not listen," Rosgran said succinctly.

The creases eased, leaving only the faintest of lines behind. Pechorid spread his hands in a disclaiming gesture. "So? That ends it."

"Maybe not. You planted this worm in my mind, friend, and it has not done gnawing yet. I won't make trouble for Arn. Still, if he—"

"If he does anything he should not?" the jurist suggested, when Rosgran did not complete her sentence.

"It would have to be something large. I'm not for throwing spears at gnats again. I feel petty enough! And yet trust is hard to win back once suspicion is sown. I know Arn has told me some lies. Well. What do you intend to do, Pechorid?"

"About this man? Nothing any longer. I've followed him and found no harm. At Midsummer I'll be going back to my clan in any case."

The jurist's tone was glum. His erstwhile smugness had quite gone. His self-pity was obvious, and Rosgran did not find that an improvement, yet a brief irked sympathy touched her.

"Belike those lies of his mean nothing," Pechorid added, in a belated effort to seem fair. "They swarm like bees in every war-camp."

The next day, tidings came to the valley that the sunbird had saved a life. A farmer, ill with a sickness of the lungs, had been sitting outside his house in the sunlight. The wonderful bird had appeared from the sky, hazed in golden light, and breathed into his face. Drawing in that coruscating air, the man had felt his lungs ease in a moment, and by nightfall they had healed so much that he scarcely coughed.

"I've used pomp, and I've used enchantment," Vivha declared. Her chin came forward in stubborn resolve. "Now I will use pity, if that's all that is left. Bring Nerild."

"Nerild isn't sick," her companion objected. "There has

never been a sounder girl, lady. It's exceptional if she coughs in the winter.''

''That I know.'' Vivha felt proud of that in her daughter; she did not like folk who were constantly ailing. ''Yet is she going to seem so desperately ill that even the sky will weep for her. Deathly pale she will lie abed, with I, my women, and kindred sobbing softly about her. Through my enchantments she will scarcely even breathe. Her condition will bring tears from a stone. If the sunbird reckons it worthwhile to give a gnarled farmer back his life, how much more will it do for a descendant of the chief dragons?''*

''Lady,'' her companion protested, ''the sunbird is more powerful than any dragon, and you have tried to deceive it twice, now . . .''

Her voice trailed into silence as she met Vivha's look.

''Do not bring sorrow on yourself by speaking of that.''

The woman grew very prudent indeed. Reminding Vivha of her two humiliating reverses had been unwise. She did not compound the error. Siranal, though, was less easy to intimidate, even if she was Prince Nemed's second wife, and could be put aside if Nemed and Vivha together decided she should go. She came to Vivha's chamber with indignation warming her hair roots, yet she spoke calmly.

''Senior woman in this house, may the second woman question you?''

Vivha lifted an eyebrow. ''We're alone, my dear. Why be so correct? You are not so formal in public, so you may as well use middle speech now. Question me you may, though I will not promise to answer; a sorceress has her treasured secrets.'' She smiled like a cat replete with cream. ''More than other mortals.''

''Goddess, but you are self-satisfied!'' Siranal said. She sat on a cushion as though about to bounce off it again with contained energy. Her brown hair gleamed. ''Why, I cannot tell. Are you truly about to use our daughter to arouse the sunbird's pity, and enspell her besides?''

''Nothing harmful.'' Vivha stretched on her green-fringed couch, watching with an opponent's eyes a woman she did not underestimate. The people might boast of Vivha, but they loved Siranal more. ''She is *my* daughter, after all. She can take her part in bringing that bird to our hall and our people.'' Vivha

*High kings or queens.

almost spat the words *that bird*. "Then we will drive the Firbolgs back."

"Then we will mend Vivha's damaged pride, you mean. In the beginning, the sunbird was to be treated with honor as a guest from the goddess. You said that. Any offence given to it would be followed by your displeasure. Now it is to be captured at any cost, is it? Any at all? Because that which Vivha wants may not commit the offence of rejecting her?"

"Siranal, you are wearisome already. Never mind my reasons. You know enough of magic to know what the sunbird means to all Danans in Alba. You are wholly aware of it."

"Yes, wholly," Rosgran's elder sister agreed, "but you are not the one it will consent to have bind it, seemingly, and it cannot be bound unless it consents. Let others try. Can you not endure the thought that one might succeed?"

"It would be bitter," Vivha owned. "Twice and three times bitter. Still, I would see it happen rather than lose the victory-bearer to some other tribe. Do you think that another could succeed where I have failed?"

"That would depend on the sunbird, not on you."

"So, then. If I do not capture it this time, they shall have their chance, any and all. But *I* must try again first, Siranal. I shall."

The other woman stared at her. "Risking Nerild? She so adores you that she will play any game you devise. Suppose, when the glorious one sees that her illness is false, it grows angry and smites her with a real one—some fiery infection to devour her alive? You of all women must know the powers can be cruel."

Vivha sat silent. She had considered only the means of bringing her quarry within range of her fowlers' darts and cords yet again. What Siranal feared was too likely. If the risk had to be taken, better that it should be taken with someone else's child, and one genuinely ill unto death, so that there should be no insult. Vivha no sooner formed that idea than she rejected it. Just anybody would not do. The sunbird had healed the farmer on a whim; so Vivha reasoned. She wished to be certain of attracting it, and only the blood of Alba's great Rhis would serve that purpose.

Nerild did not deserve to be used so. Vivha wrestled in silence with the fierceness of her desire. Using her daughter as a lure was one thing; making of her a sacrificial victim was another. If plague or famine had ruined the land, then, perhaps, she could have done it, to win her tribe relief from the angry powers. But were the Firbolgs not plague, famine, and storm in one catastrophe? Even with the cauldron of plenty to feed his warriors, Nemed had lost to them; it did not matter how close he had come to winning. The sunbird represented a new hope. Vivha gripped her own arms violently above the elbows.

Do this thing yourself, said her inner voice.

She thought at once of the growing life within her. That would be placed at risk with her if she carried through this trick. Yet it was right if the thing was to be done at all. Not right as men used the word in their tiny judgments, but right by the elemental laws of magic, it stood forth as inevitable now in Vivha's mind. This affair of the sunbird was hers, no other's—yet.

Siranal waited quietly, seeing that much was passing with her fellow wife, and leaving her to resolve it.

"Be proud and strong, little one," Vivha told that budding life. "You take the greatest risk in the greatest cause before you have even moved. This will bring the rulership of Alba to you, if I succeed."

With Siranal present, though, she said none of that audibly.

"You are right," she admitted. "I must not use Nerild so. The powers would eat her and leave a husk. Vivha, though, is less easily eaten. I'll be the one who feigns illness—and the cries of grief had best be convincing, or I will give them cause to lament!"

Siranal expostulated, demanded, coaxed, and reasoned. Vivha could not be swayed, and in Nemed's absence she ruled. Nor had she ever required a granted authority to do what she intended. She was her own law, always.

Thus she staged her final attempt. In the terraced garden behind the manor, she lay unmoving on a bier, surrounded by flowers and cordials. Twenty young women wailed over her, lashing their faces and arms with roses so that blood mixed with their tears. A high, sustained keening rose to the sky. It went on for three days and nights without stopping.

Alba's red dragons appeared in the sky, flying in intersecting circles as they were said to do when the highest blood in the island ran to a halt in someone's veins. They might have come for that. Equally, they might have come for the carcasses of several royal stags impaled on high poles, and the "dragon call" shrieking from pipers' instruments on the roof of the manor. Only the wise, deadly forms drifting on ribbed wings through the

sky properly knew. Perhaps they had not come to any such facile
lures, but because they sensed a developing joke to tickle their
reptilian humor. Men glanced uneasily skyward, gripping amu-
lets in one hand and weapons in the other. None could predict
the dragons, but their presence was seldom a good omen, and
now it seemed that none could predict Vivha, either.

The sunbird did not arrive on its wings. Leaving the sky to the
wheeling terrors there, it came walking lightly through the flowers, through the ranks of lacerated, crying women, who grew
silent one by one as the shining visitor approached the bier. It
sprang atop Vivha's body and stood there. She felt no heat in the
deep trance she had imposed upon herself, and Alinet did not
burn her. She turned her avian head to survey the ragged,
tormented throng, and her posture cried aloud of scorn.

Two men disguised in women's cloaks threw off their mantles
then. One hurled a weighted fowler's dart at the sunbird's leg
joint, the other at the base of its wing. Both missiles wobbled in
flight, to strike Vivha instead, on the knee and shoulder. When
she emerged from her trance she found herself bruised in both
places, her leg and arm troubling her for many chagrined days.

The fowlers cast their cords. Enspelled by Vivha so that they
should move like things alive, they unravelled uselessly in the
fowlers' hands, trailing their separate, limp fibers on the grass,
all their supple obedience to their masters' fingers gone. Standing with one gilded foot on Vivha's face, the sunbird flexed its
talons very slightly. Not one drop of blood was drawn from the
woman who had ordered twenty others to scourge themselves
with roses for a convincing wake. Only four red marks were left,
gradually fading.

Alinet departed at her own pace. Brilliant in fiery plumage,
she hopped from terrace to terrace, once flapping up a low rock
face, to reach at last the top of the bluff behind Nemed's manor.
There she was far out of range of anything less than a Firbolg's
bow. Spreading her wings, she glided away southward, over the
sea, to mislead those who saw her disappear.

Vivha came mazed out of her scarcely breathing state, to
know again the taste of failure. She felt the slight sting of
Alinet's print on her face, and called for a mirror. In it she
beheld the tiny dints with a redness of pressure about them,
harmless, but warning reminders of what the sunbird might have
done. Vivha did not take the implied rebuke gracefully. With her
head high and ashes in her mouth, she returned to the manor,

seeing nobody all that night, digesting her third fiasco. The digestion proved hard, to judge by the cries of fury and sounds of objects shattering which awakened her people now and again.

"She has gone mad," a woman said, while a friend smoothed unguent into her deeply scratched arms. "She wishes to capture the sunbird, and instead it has stolen her wits. I'd joyfully wring the head from its neck! Do you know what I believe? It's no true sunbird at all, but a sprite of mischief haunting us, bad luck to it."

"Be still," her friend said absently. "You have a thorn in you here—no, two." She nipped them out with her fingernails. "I'd not say such things with too free a tongue, Lis. The lady has been generally just, until now, but as you say she is changing. *Hau!* Listen to that!"

Something in the room above was violently overturned, to the utterance of a panted malediction. Lis raised her head from her cushion and gazed hatefully at the ceiling.

"Three days pretending she was dead, beneath a sky filled with devils," she said, "while she had a long, easy rest—and *she* is furious."

The morning came at last. Vivha's fury had cooled, though her determination remained as hot as ever. Looking around her, attuned now to the feelings of her people, she became aware that the manor was a bubbling pot of ill-will, most of it directed against her. Enough remained over for petty jealousies, quarrels, and slacking to mar the running of a great household which had always been well managed before.

"Could you do nothing?" she demanded of Siranal.

"I?" The second wife stared, flabbergasted. Then she replied as the question deserved. "This is due to you! While you feigned near-death with twenty women lacerating themselves over you—and having to be relieved now and again so that they didn't faint with weariness—it's a marvel that food has been cooked hereabouts! Maybe the sunbird can give wealth, prosperity, and power, and you are the knowing one where magic is concerned, yet all you have done in three trials is make yourself look foolish. We'll be a laughing matter to our friends and seem an easy prey to our foes if this continues, Vivha."

"So I've concluded too. You need not tell me."

"Good," Siranal said, still angry. "For the disorder in this house is of your making, and when you blame me you are unjust. Few could have held it in check better than I, while you lay in your deep slumber looking beautiful.''

"I'm awake now.'' Having worked out her rage in her chamber—which now looked as though a whirlwind had roamed there—she was prepared to go forward again. The people she needed most must be won to her support, if they had drifted from her.

"It would have been worthwhile had it worked,'' she went on. "Then, belike, I'd have been so joyful that I'd have forgotten your part while I ordered games and celebrations. My sorrow, Siranal! I did wrong to blame you when you deserve high praise, but I will make amends.''

"Will there be more extravagant chasing of the sunbird?'' Siranal asked, doubting Vivha's ability to stop. She had seen the sorceress set upon a purpose before, and never had she conceived a stronger one than this.

"Not by me, I promise you on my magician's pact with nature,'' Vivha swore. "I cannot catch it. That is hard bread to chew and swallow, yet I have done it now. I'll offer rewards to any who can bring the sunbird here, unharmed and uncoerced, but punishment for any who offends it further. I'll own my fault and say that I want no others to commit it.''

"Doubtless there will be tears and forgiveness for you,'' Siranal said dryly, "and all will remember how good a ruler you have been in the past. Perhaps the sunbird will make no such allowances, Vivha, and we will have to do without it. Having it here in the land would be luck enough to content most. If it *is* still here. Will you now send every fortune-hunter and bandit in the peninsula to trouble it? How will they succeed when you failed? Have sense, my dear. They will go about it more clumsily than you did. You still cling to any faint hope of catching that dream of fire.''

"Poetry from you, now!'' Vivha exclaimed. "But you speak the truth. I would not have any beggar meddling with that elemental! They might drive it away altogether. Strange, but I have been close to it several times now, and I sense that it is mortal as well as a manifestation of the sun. How could that be?''

"Are you asking me? You know more of sorcery than I ever will, and you are baffled. Forget the sunbird, Vivha. Make it an offering to show that you're contrite—if you truly are—and then leave it alone. You have just been telling me how you accept at last that you can never own it.''

''I did not say *that*, Siranal.''

''Goddess! Then what are you saying?''

''All my craft cannot capture this being. So, then. I will let others try, for I cannot give up completely, yet neither can I leave the contest open to any idle fool. This forfeit I will set upon the attempt. Anyone may try, but failure means death.''

Siranal shook her head. ''Then the desperate men will come, those who have nothing to lose. The Firbolgs have created plenty of those. The wise ones will not try.''

''Have you a better plan?''

''No! I do not wish you to pursue this thing at all. You have heard all I want to say. Now it's time for you to decide what you will do. You know you already have. So long as you give more of your time to ruling the land, I'll be content.''

''I thought you wished me to give less to making a very ruin of this household! The land hasn't fallen into decay yet.'' Vivha breathed slowly, aware of a great desire throbbing in her heart. It almost slew her that the sacred bird had rejected her. How could it dare? She wanted to see at least that it would accept nobody else. That, had she chosen to understand it, was why she wanted others to try, and insisted on death if they failed. Also, she would not miss even a small chance that anyone could procure what she desired for her.

Looking to a future without the sunbird, Vivha saw it as dismal and hopeless. Endless, inconclusive struggle with the Firbolgs would fill her life and those of her children. At last it would bury them. Future generations would have more of the same to suffer, until the dark Iberians conquered Alba and the children of the goddess were only a memory.

The sunbird could change that. Every tribe and clan would follow it. None would hang back. Vivha would lead that war herself if her prince did not.

Chapter
Ten

Arn rode at greater speed than before through the summer trees. None of the Danans had met him on the mountain as yet. There had been no need. Now, though, he had matters to discuss, and he hoped that one of his companions would be waiting. He ducked beneath a dipping branch which by now was as familiar to him as the spoon with which he ate porridge, and urged his horse out across a stretch of open ground at a canter. Each pace jolted his leg uncomfortably, but he could endure it, and his leg grew stronger each day. It no longer poked out from the horse's side at such a stiff, awkward angle.

Arn felt concern about what was to come. Although he had mended considerably, riding for his life would still show him at a disadvantage, while running would be impossible. Oghmal had said he would not abandon Arn, and the warrior knew his lord too well to suppose he would forget that—yet it had not been a realistic promise, and surely the tribe came first.

Riding into the grove where the ashes grew tall in their deep mountain soil, he sat his horse idly, like a man in a daydream, thinking of Tirtangir. Then he dismounted, looped the horse's bridle over a limb, and walked about the grove. He could do that now without a crutch, though he moved stiffly. At times the world tilted and there was a roaring in his ears. He leaned against a trunk, crushing willow herbs and meadowsweet beneath his feet. Farther away, ground ivy crawled over the earth. Arn recovered his full senses and listened through a faint, dizzy humming for any sound which might show that he was not alone.

"You were not followed today," Carbri said, "except by me. It seems your law-expounding friend has given up."

Arn whirled, stumbled, and righted himself. Carbri wore the appearance of a huntsman in greasy buckskins. None would ever have taken him for a lord of Tirtangir, and his harp appeared to be a sack of dripping meat. Although his face remained essentially the same, his hair had turned black and a beard masked his cheeks. Arn knew him by his voice.

"Lord, good it is to see you! How is it with you all?"

"We're safe and hale. I see that you can stand and walk now, but say no more just yet. I might be a sending of Vivha's for all you know, and this voice you hear the one illusory thing about me."

"I'll chance it. If she's that suspicious, I have no hope of leaving here anyhow." Arn dismissed that possibility. "I'd swear she has been too occupied of late, to watch me or think of it. Hasn't the Sunwitch told you?"

"Ah, yes." Carbri sat on a tuffet of tall grasses. "She's told us everything, and laughed at the joke till her dimples nigh fell out."

"It is a good joke." Arn grinned. "She performed her part right well, and Vivha has given up. She means to have the bird yet, but by the hand of another. All are free to try; failure means death. The lady made a fine speech in which she did all but promise the sun itself. She has kept some wisdom, though. A man must name his preferred reward in advance. When I say that I want the Undry, Pechorid will know that he was right about me, whatever the lady may think."

"She may think and do a great deal—to you," Carbri agreed, "though not until you give her the sunbird. In the excitement of that event we will enter the hall, Arn. It's easy for a crowd to become larger than it should. We will be on hand to help you leave should you need it. And I'm thinking you will."

Arn thought so too. The feathery leafage of the trees around them seemed to rustle agreement, but he went back to the valley more determined than ever to carry the business through.

He told Rosgran so, the next time they were together. "I'm going to try for the sunbird."

She stared at him. "You cannot! Oh no, you have nothing which can hold that creature! Arn, get away from here. Run before ambition traps you. Vivha failed with every resource she had, and she—how can you succeed?"

"You are all making the same mistake in this valley," Arn said. "Vivha tried to catch the sunbird in all the wrong ways. I shall be simple."

From that, Rosgran could not budge him. His strong, limping figure came before Vivha as she sat in the hall, a cloak of emerald silk falling from her shoulders over a white gown. Hearing his name, she recalled something she had been told about a warrior named Arn, and not in a pleasant context. The details eluded her, but she was rendered a little wary even before he spoke.

"Lady, I crave your leave to bring you the sunbird," he said.

Vivha looked him over slowly, from the broad, unremarkable face to the damaged leg. Though her own face showed no softness, she answered him fairly. A man who has served her lord like this one deserved a chance.

"Weapon-man, I will not refuse, as you well know—but do you not think you have suffered enough? How can you obtain the beautiful one for me?"

"We worshipped them at a shrine where I was born, lady, the spirits of the sun. That is the whole of what you did amiss, that you think I or any man can *obtain* one, or *give* it. They will dwell with you, or they will not. Now I need no enchanted nets or anything of that sort. All I require is a few witnesses." He paused. "If I fail, it's not likely that you will be able to punish me. The sunbird will do that, for they do not like presumption."

"No more do I. Should it omit to punish you, be certain you will receive it from me. And there is another thing, weapon-man. Why should you take this risk? I know that you have nothing." Her eyes narrowed like those of a cat sighting a bird as she said that, watching for any response, the least tension of muscles. Nothing showed but a certain drawn gauntness about the mouth and cheeks. His wound accounted for that. "Are you so desperate that you feel any risk is worth having gold and a place? If that is so, I forbid you to try. I would not give the sunbird additional offence because you have nothing to lose."

"No, lady." Arn straightened his stance. "A rich reward means something to me, especially since I must offer my life at hazard. That much is true. Chiefly I want to do something against the Firbolgs. Maybe I'm wrong to hope this is the way; the sun shines on them as well as on us, after all. But it is the one way I have still left untried."

"You talk to my liking, Arn," Vivha said, "yet words are easy. Since you want none of my assistance, how will you entice this being to you?"

"With this, lady." Arn held up a simple flute. "And I'll bind it with this, if it consents to be bound." With his other hand he produced a plain leather thong, weighted at one end with a wooden ball. "Do not laugh. I cannot do worse than has been done, can I?"

For an instant Vivha's eyes appeared to seethe. Then she decided to let it pass. She said, "You may have talked your way to riches—or a hard death. Now tell me the reward you desire."

"For the sunbird, lady, I can take nothing less than the cauldron of plenty, the Undry." Arn's voice could be heard throughout the hall. He wanted his terms heard clearly by everyone. "There is no other treasure here which equals it, or begins to be worth a spirit of the sun. Neither should I chance my life for less."

A babble of astonishment and outrage filled the hall. Pechorid looked stunned, then richly satisfied. The expression shaping his features said mutely, *I knew it.* Rosgran sighed, and lowered her sight to the floor in understanding and regret. So this was it. This was why Arn had come to Alba, fought in the battle, done all he had done.

Vivha looked at Arn for a long time, and not simply at him, but into him. She scanned his soul. The thoughts passing through his mind were not open to her; still, his feelings and passions were hers to share, though she searched him only for flaws, for weaknesses, for untruth. When her long silence ended she knew far more about the warrior than he would have wanted her to know.

An old kinsman of Nemed's shouldered unceremoniously toward Arn. White hair surrounded his head like a dandelion puff, and his voice reverberated with anger. He remembered days when the Firbolgs had come to Alba only as traders. He stabbed a gnarled finger in the young man's direction.

"Who do you take yourself for, pup? Who? My sister's son came near his death, getting that cauldron from the desert of Tirtangir, and you—you—would trade a singing bird for it with a gamble of your silly life added in! Vivha, you know what Nemed would say to that if he were here. Your faith with him demands that you throw this jackdaw out!"

"My faith with Nemed demands that I help him against the Firbolgs and uphold his honor," Vivha corrected. "With the cauldron, he has lost one battle. With the sun in his hands, he can win them all. Think of the rain of fire which consumed my cage, falling on a host of the dark ones. Yes, Arn. Succeed, and I will give you the cauldron. You may take it and go."

"I'll slay him first!" the old man declared, and others supported him. Arn suddenly found himself protected by a group of Vivha's men, loyal to her before anyone else, who surrounded him and fended off his attackers. She commanded them to desist, and with some of their number bleeding, they eventually did.

"My thanks, lady," Arn said sincerely.

Vivha's eyes held a disconcerting glint as they looked at him. "Do not thank me yet. You and I have not wholly made our bargain, Arn."

They settled the pact, there in Nemed's hall, with the prince far distant. He would doubtless have spat blood had he known of it. Arn asked for (and received) sureties that his reward would be given when he performed his side of the bargain, as was always done in an agreement between a weaker party and a stranger. Vivha stipulated the conditions again, and most clearly. Arn accepted them, giving his oath to that. All was straightforward and true—to outward seeming.

Arn remembered that deeply searching look of Vivha's, though, and the glint in her eyes as she had accepted his terms. *I will give you the cauldron*, she had said. *You may take it and go.*

She had not specified how far she would let him go. She had not told him how long he would keep it after she had given it to him. All of those things were for learning, yet, and Vivha unquestionably knew more than she had disclosed. She would not be much of a sorceress else. She must fulfill her bargain to the letter, though, even if she violated the spirit, and that meant producing the Undry from wherever it lay hidden, and placing it in his hands. Arn burned with impatience for that hour.

*   *   *

"So that is your scheme," Rosgran said to him later, confronting him within the hearing of some who had wanted to eviscerate Arn for his daring. "You desire the Undry, to take it home to Tirtangir. A theft for a theft. Were your two comrades a part of it also? I wonder what Tavasol is doing now, aboard the prince's ship?"

Arn declared that he would not take the Undry anywhere. Men were not backward about assuring him that he was completely right. He claimed that he wanted the cauldron of plenty for himself, and was prepared to give a fair price to possess it. As for Tavasol, had she been a man and suggested such a thing about him in his absence, Arn would have fought her.

"What I said of Tavasol is true," Rosgran said.

"I'll not answer that, since you have decided not to believe."

"Of course I cannot believe! You lied too much. You lied to me only now, when you said you will not take the Undry anywhere. Can you imagine that Nemed will allow you to remain here and own it when he has returned? Your only slight hope of that would be if he did *not* return. And many a man here would challenge and kill you in that case."

Arn knew it. He did not need the hostile, vehement glances around him for reminders. Yet he had been truthful when he said he would take the cauldron nowhere. Oghmal would do that, since Arn was disabled. Before the scowls of the warriors yearning for his blood, the young man was calm; they would not draw blades on him until after he tamed the sunbird. There was no profit in fretting before then.

Vivha did not wait long to test him. Next morning at daybreak, he was on his way to the white peak where Alinet roosted, out of reach of anything which could not fly. The old man rode as straight-backed as any youth, never looking at Arn but yearning to see him fail. Vivha had remained at the manor, keeping her promise to Siranal to share the work of governing the land for a while, sending her most trusted warriors to guard Arn in all senses of the word. Riding across the ridges and scarps of Nemed's country, looking down on woods of ash, beech, and yew, Arn thought of the trick he was going to play on his escort and not of their intentions.

The white peak loomed above them, impossible to climb. Only Danan horses could have ridden up the steep rocky slope which led to the base of that final, vertiginous crag. No citron-gold beacon sparkled at the top, for the bird of wonder was not at home. Dismounting, Arn folded his cloak on the broad ledge to sit in comfort. He played his flute and watched the scene around him.

"You are mighty at ease and sure of yourself," a warrior in a three-colored cloak said to him. "What if the one you seek does not come?"

"Then I'll have to look for her, or wait here each day until she returns," Arn replied. "That's plain. It would be rare if your mistress had driven the sunbird away when she wishes so greatly to have it."

"Rarer for you," grinned the other. "Your head would pay."

"I think not. The lady Vivha is just, so they say, and it's not just to slay a man for failing a task he has had no chance even to attempt."

Alinet never appeared. Arn had known she would not. It would have been too perfect for him to find her on his first search and bring her home to Vivha. He and Carbri had agreed that success on the second day was the least the sorceress would believe. Thus he returned empty-handed, faced Vivha's recriminations and threats, and waited for the morrow.

They rode to the mountain again, his escort grimmer than they had been the previous day. Their faces changed when they saw the hot aureate dazzle atop the peak, and heard the sweet cry of the shape-turner. Some looked glad, some troubled, but they all turned to Arn. The old man, Nemed's uncle, spoke to him at last. He could ride with any of the younger men; now he flung a challenge in a few curt words.

"There you are," he said. "Make good your boasts."

Arn smiled, and drew forth his flute. Every high-born Danan was expected to have an art and a trade as well as the skills of battle. Arn's trade was leather-working, his art, music. Sweet and sparkling as clear water, the notes cascaded from his flute, a melody that even these men who disliked him nodded to hear. He might not be Carbri; he could not work sorcery with his harmonies, but he could pretend, and the song rose toward Alinet's roost.

She too pretended, throwing herself into the air, cleaving it with her shining breast. While the men below watched spellbound, she circled the peak, dropping lower with each gyration. Arn's fluting grew sweeter, more alluring. It wasn't so surpassingly wonderful that a child of the sun would come to it, drawn

helplessly like a cat to the scent of valerain, yet many a man
swore afterward that it was, and vied with the others in adding
details. The urge to improve a story was one no Danan could
resist, even where his enemies were concerned, and to these men
Arn was an enemy, a worker of trickery against their prince
behind his back.

Silent as stones, they watched the bird drift toward him on the
golden tapestries of its wings, tawny where the long flight-
feathers slashed the air, creamy at the base, and sulfur-colored in
between, shading together through a haze of subtle fire. Pechorid
was also there, having asked to ride with the party and having
been moody all the way. Now he wondered if he dared make a
noise to startle the sunbird away, and decided that he dared not.
There were witnesses; Vivha would know at once that he had
done it deliberately, and change him into a midden cur. Jaw
clamped, Pechorid looked on.

Alinet touched the ground, folding up her great wings like a
poem, and faced Arn across a yard of bare rock, with the crag
above and summer woodland below. Arn felt a sudden conviction that this was real, no foreplanned pretence, and that if he
failed to prove worthy Alinet would be gone with a disdainful
buffet of her wings.

Bending his head to her in grave welcome, he put away his
flute without haste, and drew the thong from his belt. One light
cast, and it had coiled around Alinet's bright-scaled leg. She
accepted it. What an enchanted cage, nets, and fowling-weapons
had failed to achieve was now done with a thin line the sunbird
could snap with a tug. Sighing breaths of disbelief came from the
witnesses.

They had brought a drum-shaped block for a perch, with
Vivha's golden chain attached, but they left the plain thong on
Alinet's leg as well, knowing it was that which held her, because
she permitted it. Once the block had been strapped to Arn's
saddle, and he had been helped to mount, with the prized bird
beside him, the party felt free to show its pleasure. Men laughed
and sang. They admitted frankly to Arn that they had not thought
he could do it, and felicitated him. Nor was it false; for human,
generous reasons, they were glad of his success and wanted him
to know it. Besides being elated for their own sakes, and sharing
the triumph, they liked him for winning. Arn knew this would
not last. By tomorrow they would remember what his success
meant, and detest him again. Still, he enjoyed it while it lasted.

Pechorid rode slowly, lagging behind. There was no spirit of congratulation in him, not even a transient one. Darkly, he dreamed of how he might have been the one riding home with that living treasure beside him, if only he had dared try to capture it. He might have been Vivha's favorite again, more so than before, not this outland spy who thought he had won over them all. Well, he was to receive a surprise or two yet. Pechorid savored in advance what would happen to the fellow, after he received his reward according to Vivha's witnessed promise. There were things he did not know.

Pechorid received a surprise of his own in the next moment. Hands of incredible strength plucked him from his horse, took him by the throat, silencing the outcry he tried to make, and slammed him against the earth. Dazed, he looked into a wholly shaven face, lean and grey-eyed, which was the last thing he saw before the sinewy hands at his windpipe choked him senseless. The jurist struggled frantically, his head bursting, believing this was death. He might as well have struggled against time. When he recovered, he found himself in a stuffy leather sack bound to a tree-limb, judging by the way it dangled and turned. His limbs were bound and his mouth gagged. Glimmers of light showed where slits had been cut in the bag at the level of his face, so that he could at least breathe.

When he eventually thought about it in that light, the gag seemed reassuring too. It meant that if he could make any noise, someone who mattered might hear him. He began to struggle, and was still struggling by nightfall, when he fell into a furious, exhausted sleep.

Long before then, Carbri had assumed the unconscious jurist's appearance and mounted his horse. He rejoined the party as it made its way back to the valley. There were facetious questions about what had delayed him and whether he had become lost. He answered them grumpily. For him to look as morose as Pechorid was difficult, especially with laughter bubbling in him as it was, but he attempted it bravely and came to the long vale with his countenance dour.

None paid much attention to Pechorid's brief disappearance. As Arn rode through the valley with his shining prize perched by his saddle, the perspiration spilling from him because of her heat, men and women came running from all directions to gape at the sunbird. At victory. At power and joy wrapped in a feathered skin and delivered to them. Few gave any thought to what the sunbird might feel or want. Maybe the disappointment they were due to suffer was mere justice.

Vivha came to meet them, proud and dignified, very much the aloof lady, but with astounded delight behind the mask. She would have danced and cried out with her revelling people, but the defence of her pride was firmly in place before this secret enemy. Her gates were closed and barred, the stakes were set at angles in the outer ditch, and the points were sharpened to piercing needles. Yet none of this unfriendly preparedness showed in her manner.

"Warrior Arn, you have done what I could not," she said. "You have kept your part of our bargain, and by the powers of earth, mine shall be kept tonight! After we feast from the Undry, it shall be given to you."

"I'd expect no less from so mighty and honest a lady," said Arn. "Thus I'll take what I have earned, and I thank you, Vivha and sorceress, because no power in this land can compel you to pay."

"That is only the truth," she said. "Remember it still, my friend, when you receive your full due."

Arn bowed from the saddle, slid awkwardly to the ground, and allowed men to take charge of the sunbird. He went away to stable his horse.

As he rubbed it down, thinking of the events to come, a stable-boy came to him. Taking the saddle, the youth said quietly, "I'm Lygi, my comrade. I had thought you might know me even in this glamor."

"You are whom?"

"Lygi, cautious one. A warrior like you, of the champion's war-band. You know what is to happen tonight?"

"Some of it. The rest it's best I should not know, in case I am asked. If we're feasting tonight, and I am to receive the Undry then, it will mean that Alinet has returned to human shape; she cannot remain the sunbird after dark."

"Or work any kind of sorcery. I know that as well as you. Therefore Carbri will buy you a little extra time. I'll be without, preparing a—never mind, for as you say you may be questioned. Just be ready to leave at the right moment, which you will know by the confusion. First the Undry must be brought out and placed in your hands. Hold Vivha to her promise to allow you to leave with it."

"At night, alone, my leg in this condition? Never will she

credit that. A woman called Rosgran will be piqued enough to denounce me.''

''If you must dally with girls at times like these, you take that risk. No harm done. Vivha will never let you go with the cauldron anyhow, as we all know. So long as we see it and place our hands on it, you will have done your part. And this time we will be sure it is the right one before we take it.''

''We'll be feasting from it tonight.''

''Aye, that's what I meant. Enjoy your last day here. Make a decent farewell to this Rosgran, if you wish.''

''How?'' Arn inquired caustically. ''By telling her all? No, there is nothing more to be said in that quarter, I fear.''

''As you like. Now, you'll be told at some time in the evening how to get clear of this place. Be ready, and don't fear to go alone if it comes to that. You know where we are to meet.''

''I do indeed. Luck be with you.''

''And with you.''

Lygi went away, to fork dung unnoticed in the stable-yard for the remainder of the day. He neither slacked nor worked too industriously, and by that simple means he went unremarked. So the time passed, and at sunset he faded into hiding, to make preparations against the coming hour.

Arn had not asked where Cena was. He supposed it was best for him to remain ingorant. In fact she had made a long flight in her eagle's form, to find Tringad and bid him return to Nemed's land as swiftly as he might. Then she had returned herself, and rested three full days in preparation for a last feat of sorcery which should see them all free of Nemed's country—if they were fortunate.

Carbri's preparations were also made. Vivha, not a gullible woman, had looked at the sunbird with her enchantress's sight, to be sure Arn had not attempted a deception with glamor, for some men might have been so foolish. Now she knew the creature was real.

In his guise of Pechorid the jurist, Carbri entered the great hall where Alinet had been taken. She was no longer there. Carbri slipped behind a tapestried hanging and mounted the stairs as though he had all the right in the world to do so. Coming to a curtained doorway, he heard Vivha's rich voice speaking behind it.

''Child of the sun, if you find us worthy we will burn the goat-adoring Firbolgs from Alba's shores, and build such temples to your brightness as have never been seen before. Sun's blood* will run molten in every royal fortress to make your adornment, and your food shall be grain reaped with swords. Milk of the red lowland cows shall be your drink. First of your rights will be that Alba's people bow before you on Summer's Eve, worshipping.''

Carbri shook his head, listening. Vivha was betraying what she would most like to receive, in these large promises. She did not understand even yet that the sunbird could fly on its way tomorrow if it wished, and would not be held in one place by gold or worship. When such became a burden or a duty rather than freely offered gifts, their meaning failed and such beings departed.

If Vivha remained in that chamber after sundown, she would see her prize depart in a most unexpected way. Carbri took the simplest means of bringing her out. He coughed and said in a phlegmy voice:

"Lady, it is Pechorid. The hour grows late. Shall I have your women attend you before the feast?"

Vivha flung aside the curtain, puzzled and angry.

"Are you struck witless, Pechorid? Will any excuse do now to approach me, no matter the time? None enters here but me. My women can prepare me downstairs, and they know it; go tell them I will soon arrive. No! Wait."

He waited, wondering what lay between the lady and her jurist for her to address him in those terms, and making some guesses. In a moment she emerged again, wrapped in a cloak.

"I will go down now," she said. "Warriors will be here soon, to guard this chamber so that a mouse could not approach it. Meanwhile, you must watch it instead, Pechorid, for my sake— and watch closely. But on no account enter." She stroked his cheek regretfully. "Those days are over."

Carbri would have snatched a kiss in other circumstances, and done his best to make Vivha forget she was a ruler. This time he murmured sycophantic assent, and watched her walk away with a new appreciation of the hardships of Nemed's exile.

No sooner had she vanished than he stepped within her chamber. His risk was calculated; if she meant to post guards of flesh and blood, it was likely she had set no sorcerous wards yet. Besides, the sun was setting.

---

*Gold.

The shining, long-feathered bird became a girl in bright garments almost as he entered. Quickly, he told her who he was, made his preparations, and performed the cantrip necessary to deck her again in a sunbird's appearance. This time it was false. No bodily change took place, but with luck Vivha would not assure herself of that a second time. Carbri had already formed the opinion that she was careless in small things. He embraced Alinet for luck, and was out of the chamber with her whispered encouragement in his ears a bare moment before the warriors arrived. Descending the stairs, he thought of what might have happened, beginning with Vivha's looking closer and harder at him instead of accepting him at face value. The back of his neck turned cold.

From this time, anything could happen. His own pose as a jurist was reasonably congruent with his true calling; a trained bard knew a deal of law. Oghmal, of course, wore the appearance of a warrior, and with it a silent, forbidding demeanor. When they passed there was not so much as a glance of collusion between them. They were a competent pair.

The champion positioned himself by a pillar near the door, with two broad-headed hunting spears crossed on the wall within easy reach. Danans did not wear or carry weapons at a feast, or for that matter indoors, unless they had a special responsibility like the men outside Vivha's chamber. Oghmal wanted to have the choice of arming himself at once. He studied the people within the hall, estimated angles and distances, and waited.

Wine and honey-liquor had already been drunk. In the partitioned booths around the sides of the hall, separated by fretted, carved wooden screens, the various ranks and trades of folk awaited their lady at the tables. All were brilliant in their Danan fabrics and dyes, unique upon the earth, like Danan horses, ships, and sorcerers. Harp-music chimed and rippled. Two dancers in kilts leapt like harbucks between flung, hissing swords that flashed repeatedly close to them, thrown and thrown again. They laughed as the blades spun by.

As the dance ended, silver triangles chimed. Vivha entered, her hair built high in an intricate structure with combs and jewels, her gown the month's labor of her people's most skilled weavers. Beside her, two men carried the sunbird on its wooden drum-block, its feathers outshining her garments, filling the hall with light. Carbri felt justly proud of that illusion. It could scarcely have been better if he had hours to create it.

There must be twenty folk or more at this feast with the sight which pierced glamor, though. If one of them thought to turn their trained vision on Vivha's great hope, before the Undry appeared, it meant farewell for Arn and all of them. Carbri, too, marked the nearest weapons and estimated how quickly he could reach them.

"Greetings, lady," Arn called. He had drunk enough to be merry. Vivha returned his greeting, pledged him in her own cup, and made a speech concerning his feat in capturing the great bird now watching them with hot topaz eyes. Then it tucked its elegant head beneath a wing.

"As all may see, you have what I promised," Arn said, standing. "Now I would see what you vowed to me—the cauldron of plenty, the Undry."

"You needn't look far, my friend," Vivha replied, smiling with no more than the edges of her teeth. "I promised we should feast from it tonight. Yonder it comes, filled and ready. View to your soul's content."

Arn was not the only one who looked. Ugly and ill-shaped, a monstrosity to the artistic Danans, the Undry was placed on its ledge of flat stones above a fire. Which was more desirable, the lumpy clay pot or the supernatural child of the sun, was a matter of taste, Carbri supposed. Even which one could do more to sway the course of a battle was open to debate. Vivha must think she was making a good exchange—except, of course, that she did not intend to make it.

Cena and her band had been fooled once. This time they waited, while the cauldron simmered. The rubbish which filled it soon changed to rich food, giving a tempting aroma, and bowls were heaped with its contents, a new dish each time the ladles went in.

"Now, warrior, are you content?" Vivha asked.

"Not I, lady. Having seen, smelled, and tasted, I would claim my reward and go, for indeed I have far to travel."

"Indeed you have, and I will speed you on your way when the time is suitable. I would not hold an unwilling guest." Vivha almost purred. "However, the night is for revels and sleeping. Wise men travel by day. Depart in the morning with your reward, warrior."

"Lady, I would if I might, but I have too far to go, and not by mortal roads. Unless I take the cauldron with me now, I will not arrive.''

Arn made his voice deep and resounding. It could do no harm to imply that he was more than human, or came from another realm. Some might take the notion seriously for a moment. After all, he had delivered the sunbird.

The laugh which had been tugging at Vivha's lips since she entered the hall now peeled free. "Yes, you say the truth there, and I think for the first time! Do you think that I, stranger, that *Vivha* cannot recognize an accent of Tirtangir? Did you imagine that I would not read your heart when we met, and you made your lying bargain? Shall I go on, poor fool? Is it necessary? Your guilt is plain in your face!''

"My part of the bargain was kept, lady.'' Arn faced it out, keeping his voice sonorous. "What you read in my heart was only what you wished to find there. It cannot be read that easily. Do you seek now to cheat me of what you vowed to give? Who would trust you thereafter? It should make no difference to our pact whether I come from Tirtangir or the White Land. The powers hate a perjurer.''

"My word is true,'' she said. "I vowed you might take the cauldron and go. Accuse me of oath-breaking once more and I will have you boiled piecemeal in the pot you so covet, *stranger*. Take it, then. Go. Nothing was said of how far you might bear it.''

"Lady,'' Arn said, using the word with an edge honed thereon, "I thought of that too.''

Standing, he moved toward the cauldron with his unsteady step, pads of cloth in his hands. Straining, he lifted it from the hearth and began moving inchmeal toward the door. Vivha watched with a cruel, interested smile.

"He had better be what he implies, for assuredly in no other way will he leave my land with that cauldron,'' she said. "Hmmmm. How far should we allow him, Pechorid?''

"A little beyond the door,'' answered the supposed jurist, with a smirk Carbri did not like to feel on his mouth. "Then none can say you were ungenerous to him.''

Arn struggled on. He possessed the power to carry anything a pack pony could carry, and bear it unseen by any, besides, but that had been before he was wounded. He passed Oghmal, who stood listening to the laughter of Vivha's folk as Arn struggled like a crippled ant, and the champion's eyes were cold as winter's ice.

Arn passed beyond the doors, through the foreroom and the main portal. Then Vivha tired of her game. With a snap of her fingers, she said, "Slay him."

The sunbird attacked her.

Most of those who glimpsed the incident beheld a buffet of thrashing wings and the gleam of a swordlike bill. Only a few, who had the magician's sight and thought to use it, saw a ravishing young girl snatch a drinking-vessel and strike. Vivha fell backward on her rear, and the next parts of her to strike the floor were her sumptuously clad shoulders, after which she sprawled senseless. Alinet stared at what she had done, proud but a little horrified. Then she recovered her wits, and hurled the vessel at the head of the nearest man moving in pursuit of Arn. It missed by a yard.

The sunbird was struggling in its chain, to the perceptions of most. Two warriors sought to carry it out again, block and all, while Vivha's women lifted her to bear her up the stairs. Men had hesitated to carry out her last order and slay Arn, especially when they saw how the sunbird reacted to that; but at last a few surged purposefully after him.

They never reached the door.

Oghmal snatched the spears he had been watching all night, and flung one entirely through the first of the warriors. Then he rushed the others, killing two before they realized their easy task had turned to a death sentence. Carbri added his own share to the chaos by shouting, "We're under attack! The Firbolgs are here!"

Some repeated the cry, for outside Lygi had set a number of fires and let out the cattle, which milled about aimlessly. Men wasted time driving them back to the byres. Other men were hindered in their work of putting out Lygi's fires; they cursed the scatterbrains attending to the cattle, and demanded their reasons for trying to fit the impossible-to-insult beasts back into sheds that were burning anyhow.

Most of them were not. The fires made a danger, though, and might spread, so Vivha's men left the cattle to wander while they fought the flames. Some used wet sacks, some magic. The fires began to die.

Lurking in shadows after his feats of arson, Lygi had seen Arn emerge, staggering with the Undry. At once he joined him. The pair spilled its contents before the door so that men who fol-

lowed would slip in the mess of food. The inexhaustible cauldron poured forth a stream of curds, venison, and broth until
they wished it would stop. Their immediate purpose had been
achieved, and the Undry's weight was no less. None followed
them from within the hall, and hearing the sounds of ferocious
death, they could guess why. They carried the cauldron into
shadows, where Lygi touched it with his fingertips and spoke a
brief incantation Cena had taught him. They spilled the last of the
food, and this time the Undry remained empty, though still hot,
and still heavy as a stone. Lygi wrapped his cloak around it and
did not complain.

Within, Oghmal had gained the stairs. Carbri joined the warriors who rushed after him, yelling. Pechorid the jurist was not
usually in the van of such actions, but Carbri no longer worried
about acting as Pechorid would. He thrust and shoved his way to
the front, crying, "Rescue the lady!" Even as he yelled, he
thrust other men backward or tripped them out of his way,
making it impossible for them to do as he said. Men's general
opinion of Pechorid was not raised that night.

Carbri reached his brother's side. The pair went through the
upper rooms like wolves through a sheepfold. Warriors and
women alike resisted them, fighting with weapons or anything
else they found. Stools flew; shears flashed. Vivha still lay
unconscious, with blood caking her brow. Alinet had hit her
forcefully. Both brothers were glad of it, less from hatred than
because they knew what sorceries she could have worked against
them, awake and concentrating.

Oghmal roared, *"Tir-tan-giir!"* and did slaughter among the
warriors who faced him. In their last moments, they knew they
were dealing with a champion, and died more proudly for it.
Still, they died. Bronze flashed red and blood gleamed redder,
looking silky in its first spurt.

Oghmal spun his weapon, striking with butt and point in the
same heartbeat. He drove it at fullest reach through a man's ribs
and lung, with a cracking of bone heard around the room. Carbri
killed a man himself, taking a wound he never noticed until
later. He hurled a woman aside, for she was trying to remove his
eyes with a smashed glass vessel. Then they had all fled but
Alinet.

Removing the glamor he had cast himself was easy, just as
destroying a garment is easier than weaving it. The sunbird
vanished. Alinet appeared as one young girl in what had been a

chamber filled with them. None should ask her who she was in
the uproar.

"Go downstairs and get out," Carbri said swiftly. "You
know where to go? The stables? The horses?"

"Yes! What of *her*?" Alinet pointed to Vivha.

"What of her?"

"Hostage!"

"No," Oghmal said. "More danger than she's worth. You go
downstairs like the others. Don't forget to scream."

"Like a specter from Anuvin!" she promised, her face alight.

Then she was gone, a child playing the most exciting game
she had ever known. Oghmal slammed and bolted a door he had
not noticed before, and ran back to his brother as Alinet's
promised shrieks faded below.

"She's enjoying this finely," Carbri said.

"I suppose you are not? This is no fun to you at all, hey,
brother? Now let's leave, for they will have that excuse for a
door in splinters with one blow."

"I'm not the one who is standing still to blab."

Carbri led the way to Vivha's sun-balcony. There were two
ways to leave it, apart from back through her solar; up to the
roof, or down to the ground. Oghmal took the latter. Throwing
his spear into the earth, he stepped to the balustrade and jumped
after it. The drop was seventeen feet. He rebounded, his tough
body absorbing the shock, and shook his brain clear of the
effects of impact. Carbri landed beside him, splashing blooddrops
from the cut he had taken, still wearing the appearance of
Pechorid. Oblivious to these things, he grasped his own spear
and raced into smoky darkness beside his twin.

"Vivha didn't look well," he muttered. "Alinet may have hit
too hard. I didn't tell her, but yon sorceress may die."

"So may we." Oghmal too was a Danan, to whom women
were sacrosanct, yet he would shed no tears for Vivha. "Away
and meet the others."

Ten warriors with swords and shields burst upon them, sure
they could overwhelm the pair. Oghmal met the first with a
ferocious kick to the lower rim of his shield, which flew up and
smashed his jaw. The champion leapt atop the shield before his
victim could collapse, and sent his spear downward into the neck
of a second warrior. As the first man crumpled beneath his
weight, he wrenched his spearhead out of flesh, touched the
ground with his feet and one hand, then lunged for the dead

man's sword. His ears had registered where it fell, even as he struck and leapt.

His free hand closed on the blade. Coming smoothly upright, he tossed the weapon a little, to catch it by the hilt. Carbri had engaged three men at once, and they had driven him back toward the manor's wall of trellised timber. Oghmal left him for the present; the three who pressed him were wholly occupied, and the champion had no intention of turning his back on the others.

He faced a stocky, long-armed axe-man over a shield painted with a black seal. The axe leapt downward as though to take a bite out of his thigh. Oghmal shifted slightly, and then sprang straight upward to escape the expected crippling blow from the shield. He landed in a cat's crouch and smote straight across in front of him, opening the axe-man's throat. That wight's eyes bulged in horror as gore bubbled down his chest.

Oghmal trod past the jerking body, his pale eyes aglare. Going to his twin's assistance, he found that Carbri had drawn blood from two of his assailants. Oghmal called to the rearmost of them to turn around. When he did, he received a spearhead among his vital organs, and Carbri opened the throat of one of his companions. The third ran. With such an example to follow, and so many of their fellows having met with death so suddenly, the others fled likewise. Their opinion of the sport to be had with these strangers had altered.

The twins raced into the sheltering dark. Lygi's fires were all extinguished by now, and Nemed's uncle, with a few others like the warrior Brasc, had brought some order out of the confusion. This was no place to stay. They found Alinet waiting at the stables, cloaked for concealment, her distinctive hair covered, but no sign of Lygi. Carbri gave their bird-call signal and hoped for the best. Lygi responded from behind a byre to the west.

"Ah, good man!" Oghmal said fervently. With a wild drumming of hooves Lygi came out of the dark, Arn beside him, leading a string of five other mounts. They were the best he had been able to find. Only two were saddled, but the twins were not minded to be particular. They flung themselves astride, bareback, as they had often ridden when they were youths. Now, as grown men, they gritted their teeth in the first couple of moments; then they forgot the discomfort, and brought their rearing horses under control, grateful at least for bridles. Alinet mounted one of the saddled horses while Lygi held its reins for her. Arn whooped at them.

"The Undry?" Carbri panted.

"It's here."

"No mistakes this time, eh? Then out of here!"

Oghmal clamped his gelding's sides between thighs like seasoned oak, and kicked it forward. A flying spear missed him, to sink into the side of the animal beneath him. It screamed in agony, almost as a child would scream that cannot understand why it has been hurt. Still it gathered its strength, to carry him through the gaping, smoke-obscured space between the buildings. Then he was riding beneath the stars, Alinet and Arn behind him, Lygi and his brother bringing up the rear.

As they galloped onward, their hooves drumming beside the lake, Oghmal reached downward to hack through the ash shaft protruding from his horse's flank. The vanished weight relieved the beast a little, but as they came to the southern end of the lake it foundered, gushing pink foam from its mouth and nostrils. Oghmal, holding its head while it died, cursed the hand which had thrown the weapon, and himself for riding the beast into peril. This hadn't been a quarrel of the horse's. Then he heard the sound of pursuit in the night behind him.

"Get along," he said. "It seems we're too early for Cena's timing. How she avoided hearing all this I don't know, and it's of no use to wonder. I'll hide in the rushes, then swim to the lake's end."

"Mount behind me!" Alinet urged. There was little of the child about her now. "I'm the lightest. We can ride double."

"I'm the heaviest. No. You may win clear as you are. You just may. Try, girl, and so will I."

"Lord, that lake is bottomless, so they say." It was Arn protesting. "Do not risk it. Come with me; my horse is the best."

"Then make full use of his goodness, and keep him safe. As for the lake's depth, it doesn't matter. I'll be swimming in the top foot of water only. Now stop wasting your time. Get on, I command you."

"Listen!" Carbri snapped.

From the mountains around the valley, a strident foreign war-cry sounded on every side. Hundreds of throats uttered it. Broken echoes gave it back from many a granite crag. The Albans thundering in pursuit reined their horses, disconcerted, as the war-cry sounded again. Then torches flared in many hands as the foeman's host came down from the mountains. Groups of them bellowed a war-chant in their Iberian tongue.

"Firbolgs!" Alinet said. "They really are here to sack the valley. Let's away; this is luck."

"And you a witch in your own right!" Carbri bantered. "Eu-hai, a witch you may be, but it will be some time before you rank as a sorceress, at this rate. It's not luck. That is illusion, raised by Cena—the illusion of a Firbolg horde, and it's lucky for us all Vivha is not conscious to dispel it! But she may recover at any moment. Our friends may decide to make us their first concern. A real Firbolg host may come, though that isn't likely."

"Then let's ride," Arn said harshly, his leg giving him pain. "Whither, though? I know none of your plans."

"First, to the marsh," Oghmal ruled, his quiet, somber voice silencing all lighter talk, "and go without speaking. Your voices fill the night. I'll swim, as I said."

They made the brief ride, and dismounted to lead their stolen horses into the tiny marsh. As they entered, Alinet's foot slipped from a clump of sedges. She began to sink. Sucking in a scared, whistling breath, she made no outcry, only said with soft urgency, "Help me!" Carbri seized her hand, lifted her back to dry ground with a heave, and set her on her feet. She went on, squelching. Arn also missed his footing once, and had to be dragged free of mire. Lygi carried the cauldron.

They reached a minute island, no more than a hummock of raised ground among the alders. It accommodated the four of them with room for their horses and two more Danans, if they crowded close. Then Oghmal arrived, announcing himself with their bird-call, and towards morning Cena appeared. Even for a sorceress, it was no small feat to find a group in the darkness, in such a place, with mounted warriors searching the valley like a crisscross of swords. The searchers should know by now precisely whom they were hunting. They must be fools, Lygi thought, if they did not.

"Sister, you've done as well as I thought you would," Carbri greeted her, "and that means none could have done better. What did they say when they discovered your Firbolg attack was illusion? Did it take them long?"

"They were slow," Cena said, "but they have known for hours now. Your compliments please me, brother—they do—but we have no time for pretty speeches. You should all know where we stand.''

"I found Tringad. He is coming, but when depends on wind and tide. He should arrive by tomorrow night; it's for us to remain alive so long, and meet him. Oh, it gladdens my heart to find you living, all! I dared not hope. But I'm past working more sorceries now. That means you must do it, Carbri, and Alinet when daylight comes . . . Before the goddess, I can scarcely think. You and Oghmal must lead now.''

"Gladly, so long as it's away from here.'' Carbri slapped a mosquito, though the thin, monotonous whine of its myriad cousins went on unchanged. Frogs said contentedly, *full-gob, full-gob.* "Arn was just asking where we could go. Well, they will search this entire valley and all the woods down to the shore by next sunset, so we must not be anywhere they are apt to look for us—nor can we lug the Undry about. Why don't we sink it here and come back for it later? Have you a better plan, any of you?''

They had not. They enclosed the Undry most firmly in a net of rope which Carbri conjured out of sedges and bark, then lowered it into the water at the end of a line whose other end they tied to a tree-root.

Barely had they finished this when a band of men came by. Dismounting, they led their horses into the tiny marsh, their weapons shining as they walked. Cena's party held the mouths of their own steeds and waited. They knew they must kill.

Sudden and ugly, the fray began. The rearmost man never had a chance as Oghmal struck him down, nor did the next in line, and when the others turned about to deal with him, Oghmal's companions fell upon them from the direction they least expected. Cena fought, despite her exhaustion. They all fought save Alinet, and she would have joined them had she been competent in battle. There were fewer and fewer searchers standing upright, then, finally, none at all. But Carbri had received another wound, and Arn lay in the mud with a dead man beneath him.

"Catch their horses,'' Oghmal said. He lifted Arn. When the warrior breathed, air whistled in and out of a wound in his chest. Familiar with all battle-hurts, the champion made a pad and pressed it over the sucking hole. Arn coughed foam which smelled of blood.

"You might as well have saved your shirt," he rasped. "This one is not going . . . to heal . . . for any lesser physician than Diancet."

"About that, you could be wrong," Carbri said, "and if you last another day you will be sailing home. Diancet himself will attend you once we're there."

"Oghmal?" Arn said weakly. "You speak to me. The lord Carbri means well, but—" He arched in pain. Spasms of coughing shook him again and again.

"He does mean well," Oghmal agreed, "and he's right."

"No. He's wrong. The only medicine I need . . . cures living."

Arn still held his knife. Now he drove it at his own throat, but Oghmal moved like a burnt marten to catch his hand. They struggled for a moment, until Oghmal took the blade away from his henchman like a chisel from a careless child. The pad had become disarranged; air whistled from the lung wound again. Oghmal pressed it back in place.

"You're a fool," he said. "I told you you'd get no leave to do that, and I meant it. Carbri will sing you asleep if being insensible is the only way you'll submit to sense. Won't you, brother?"

"I will. We are not abandoning you, boy. Make up your mind to that."

Arn jerked for the last time. His noisy breathing stopped.

"His life's gone," Oghmal said at last. "The goddess commend you to her antlered son, the lord of death, and may his lady pass you nobly as you deserve through the cauldron of rebirth. May your enemies serve you in Anuven, my warrior Arn."

He covered the young man's eyes. "Now we can go."

"Go?" Alinet repeated. "He was your man. He was our friend! How can you be such a spire of ice? Do we leave him here unburied?"

"No. We sink him in the marsh and I raise a stone for him at home. Do not think I lack grief for him, but we cannot stay. As you must not stay if I fall."

They weighted the bodies and hid them in the mire. Then Carbri effected another change in the appearance of himself and his companions, and of the horses, too. They could not keep the semblance they had worn before. It was known. Leaving the spare horses in the marsh, they mounted and joined the hunt. Until an hour after dawn they helped search for themselves, and then rode back to the manor. Stabling their horses and caring for them, they lay low in a barn which Lygi had attempted to burn.

"With luck, none will look closely at us here," Carbri murmured. "At any rate, we'd have no chance at all in the valley or the mountains. This is *their* land. When they fail to track us, then they may begin to suspect we are lurking here—but not before. Who would?"

"Vivha would," Alinet answered. "That hard old uncle of Nemed's could guess it, too."

"There is danger whatever we do," Cena said. "Let us stop troubling our heads about it. *I* am going to sleep. If we are caught, we should be accused of naught worse than slacking, and sent out again, which is what we want."

"We're here while they seek us outside, and outside again while they seek us here," the Sunwitch said. "But Arn won't be with us." She shivered. "Why did he have to die?"

Tears began to fall. She did not howl or sob, but sat there with the drops pouring down her illusory face, incongruous against the weapon-man's scars. Oghmal took her hands. She wrenched them angrily away.

"You think of nothing but getting safely home!"

"Yes. With the cauldron Arn died to obtain. What should I do? Have my sorrow now, and waste what he did? Cena is wise to sleep while she can. Do the same, Alinet, or feign it if you must, but do not show your face, or someone may wonder why a seasoned fighter is sobbing."

Alinet flung herself facedown in the hay beside her Rhi. The tears flowed for some time, then faded to an occasional gulp. Oghmal moved into the shadows, lay on his back, and gazed at the dark roof, hands linked behind his head. What passed through his mind he did not share. Carbri sat with Lygi, caressing his harp slowly, while the younger man gripped his sword-hilt until the pattern of the binding was impressed on his skin. Neither of them slept.

Nemed's riders came and went like shadows through the cloudy day. Rain began to fall heavily, which pleased Cena's band. Oghmal roused his sister with the suggestion that they ride out again, losing their tracks in the downpour. From him the suggestion had the force of an order, and Cena, who could not be ordered by any man, accepted it because it made sense. They departed as quietly as they had returned.

Hours later, it was still raining. The horses they had aban-

doned had long since found their own way out of the marsh, and
been taken home by Nemed's riders. No doubt they had drawn
conclusions from that, but not the right ones, Cena hoped.

Oghmal went alone to regain the Undry. The tree-roots lay
under water by this time. He found the right one at last, and
dragged up the cauldron. Lifting it to the sodden land required
all his strength, before he emptied it of water and mire. When
the rain had washed it clean, he carried it into the dripping
woods, alert for ambush from men who knew these trees far
better than he. None had been laid. Vivha had only so many
warriors, after all.

"Tringad had better arrive tonight," Alinet said, "as expected. You should have taken Vivha for a hostage when you
had the chance."

"Too late now to think of what we should have done," Carbri
said, rain running down his face from his rats' tails of red hair.
"The cauldron makes as good a hostage, if it comes to that, and
it won't change us all into trees as yon sorceress would."

"If she were here now, I couldn't stop her," Cena admitted.
"Nor could you, little flame."

Alinet bristled. "I'm more powerful than that fortune-telling
hag! She couldn't even protect herself from a blow with a
flagon." Smugly, she added, "I can still feel it hitting her."

"You did well," Carbri said, meaning it, "but you had great
luck that she was distracted at the time. How hard hit was she?"

"Are you afraid that I killed her?"

"No. Not any longer. I'm afraid that you may have struck too
lightly. It's my hope she will be senseless for some time to
come. We'd be foolish to bide here relying on it, though. Bigger
fools to hope we can just board Tringad's ship and sail away.
I'm for stealing one of Nemed's boats, and meeting Tringad
where we choose."

"I'm against it," Cena declared. "Suppose it were you,
brother. Wouldn't you have every boat you possess dragged far
up the beach, and well guarded too, no matter how your men
complained of the wet? Besides, we're none of us seafarers. Best
we wait for him to arrive. As for getting aboard, the simplest
ways are best. We cannot be wetter than we are."

She explained her plan. When she had finished, Carbri embraced her and swore she was the cleverest of them all. The
sky continued to drizzle, yet for them it seemed to lighten. They
went down to the shore through the sodden woods.

Tringad came into the cove as he had promised, almost to the hour, and dropped two strong anchors. The activity along the wet shore did not escape him. All innocence, he asked what was the matter, and heard vehement replies. Their hospitality had been abused, Nemed's men said, their treasure stolen and their lady attacked. Although conscious, she lay ill, and might be days in mending. Tringad was fittingly appalled.

"I came here hoping for some trade, or at least a day's guesting," he said, after wishing that Vivha would recover swiftly, and her assailants be taken. "I suppose none of that can happen until you've settled this matter, now."

"You suppose aright," answered the warrior who had greeted him. "Maybe not even then. We're suspicious of strangers because of all this."

"Am I a stranger? Well, but I can't spare much time. A day or two at most, and since there's nothing here for me, I'd rather depart with the next tide." Tringad did not explain why. He had a reason if one should be demanded, but giving it unasked could make him seem too eager to convince.

"None is stopping you," the warrior said, "so long as your crew grows no larger before you leave. If any come to your ship trying to bribe you for an honest purpose like carrying them across the sea, give them to us. They might look like anybody, for there are masters of glamor among them. They number about five, though."

"Five?" Tringad shrugged. "Well, I've more men than that in my crew. They can't steal my ship, if they are desperate enough to try, and if I need help, no doubt you will give it."

"Help will be as close to you as the waves to your hull."

True to his promise, the man dispatched a boat with six warriors in it, to fasten their craft by lines to the ship's stern and watch Tringad closely. He welcomed them aboard. Talking genially, he offered them food and ale, awaiting his moment. If he knew Siala's children at all, it would come.

It did. One of the warriors looked over the stern and cried out in surprise. Their boat was drifting away. Since Tringad had seen them moor it to his ship with two ropes, he felt sure it was no accident, even though anything was possible when landsmen tied knots. He made a surreptitious gesture to his crew. Then he seized the nearest pair of warriors, cracked their heads together, and stepped aside while they fell. This brought him within reach of another, who had begun to draw his sword. Lowering his head, Tringad butted him hard in the midriff. He took two inadvertent steps backward. His spine met the stern railing. Tringad tipped him over by the ankles. The splash almost obliterated the grunts and blows being exchanged behind him. Tringad did not look around; he had confidence in his crew. He wanted to see what happened to the man he had tossed overboard. He couldn't be allowed to swim ashore, and Tringad already had an inkling that he wouldn't reach it.

Watching, he saw a powerful figure rise out of the water beside the man, seize him, and go under with him. Even while he recognized the naked form as human, Tringad's hair prickled with the dread of mermen which all mariners felt. Presently the dark head broke the surface again, its hair soaked sleekly down. On one huge bare shoulder lolled the head of an insensible man.

"The lord Oghmal?" Tringad asked softly.

"Yes, it's I. Fine it is to see you again, captain. How many friends did this one have?"

Tringad told him. "We've dealt with 'em all. Come aboard and see."

"Haul this one up first. I won't leave him to drown. And how *dealt with*? Are they alive or dead?"

"Knocked out with cudgels, sir."

Streaming water, the senseless warrior was dragged aboard, to complete the row of his dry companions. Their boat continued to drift. Oghmal loomed like a naked war-god over the captain, his brother's sword slung on his back. Two of the scars marring his white skin were fearful. Among them, the others wrote his history.

"You did well, Tringad," the champion said. "I'd thought I would have to climb aboard and begin the fighting. Your pardon for that."

"Given," Tringad said succinctly.

"And they are all alive. That's even better. There has been killing, and there's more to come, but these at least won't go to Anuven before their time. When can you depart?"

"With the next tide, lord. Now what of your kindred? Will you be taking that boat to fetch them?"

"No. They come now. Do you see?"

Tringad gazed through the rainy mist. For long moments he saw nothing. Then he beheld a half-submerged, sluggish shape in the bay, moving toward his ship as though drifting. Its jagged protuberances made him think of some deformed monster. It

proved to be a tangle of driftwood and kelp, lashed together by
Cena's party and propelled by their steadily kicking legs as they
clung to it. Nesting in the middle of it like an egg was the
cauldron of plenty.

In short order they, too, were aboard. Their prize, nondescript
in its wrapping of a plain cloak, did not look worth all the
striving. They stowed it among the cargo beneath the stern,
while their driftwood raft nudged the ship, lifted by the small
waves. Two of Tringad's sailors slipped into the water to break it
into its constituent bits again, while two others swam after the
boat Oghmal had turned loose as a distraction. There was still
some time to go before the tide ebbed, and Cena wished everything to look natural from the shore.

It was a long few hours for them all until they could go.

Too late, as Tringad put to sea, did the watchers ashore know
that something was far wrong. Too late did they launch their
boats and row after the seaworthy bark. The raiders were away,
and none of the prince's metal-hulled ships of sorcery remained
at home to pursue them. The entire fleet had gone to harry
Firbolgs on the waters of Sabra.

"We've done it!" Cena shouted. "Adored goddess! *We've
done it!*"

She threw her arms around Lygi, her brothers, and Alinet. In
sheer exuberance she linked arms with Carbri and danced, her
bare feet flashing over the deck. Alinet joined in with Lygi.
They celebrated their triumph in a glory that mounted and mounted.

The sailors cheered and beat time. The captives by the rail
watched in glum silence. Alone of the five raiders, Oghmal had
not moved. He watched his kindred revel, and smiled, but he
also looked southward from time to time, and an aura of dark,
compressed brooding emanated from him. Cena, breathing deeply,
noticed.

"Brother! Are you made of petrified wood? We have done it!
There will be no war! It's over, Oghmal, over!"

"Almost," the champion answered. His ice-grey gaze turned
southward again. "There is Tavasol to bring home, and then
there is Nemed. Remember how the Antlered Rhi demanded his
life from us? After that, it will be over—not before."

Chapter
Eleven

The vessel which entered Sabra in search of Nemed's fleet was no wide-beamed trader. Cena's own longship carried them now. Forty warriors drew on the slim oars, their war-gear close to hand, their persons groomed and resplendent in the manner of Danans going to fight. The Rhi and her brothers went clad as befitted their station, in bright embroidered linens, jewelled like the sky. They wore their own faces, to Oghmal's vast satisfaction.

"May I never sneak about behind a semblance of illusion again!" he declared. "Only the quest could have made me do it this time."

"You're too proud, brother." Carbri looked at his twin, dressed in crimson and white now, his hair confined by a plain leather band, a new sword at his side. "Didn't you enjoy fooling an enemy?"

"I'm pleased with it now that it's done. The people no longer face destruction, and that is like having a mountain off our backs. Maybe there was no other way to achieve it. But the hiding and feigning—no, I did not care for it, brother. I like this better."

"I too." Cena's eyes smoldered fire-blue. "I want to see Nemed's cheating face when I give him the news. I want him to see mine!"

Tringad snickered. He wanted to see that himself; it was one reason he had offered to come along as their pilot in the dangerous waters of Sabra. He might have remained in Tirtangir with his own ship and heard of the outcome secondhand, in perfect safety, but he wanted to witness it. A man abandoned safety each time he went to sea, anyhow.

Alinet had come for a like reason; to see the end, and to flaunt her glory before the man she had helped to hoodwink. She remembered the terrors of the White Land in acid-etched detail. Besides, her kindred might desperately need her when they encountered Nemed's fleet.

Nothing could have made Lygi remain behind. The matter of Nemed aside, and even loyalty to his lord, he had been Alinet's lover for those brief, splendid days in Tirtangir. She had told him honestly that when it was over she would return to her family's dun, yet her company was a delight, and he reckoned it fitting that they should finish this venture together. Nor would he wait at home for news of Tavasol's fate.

They came to the haven which Nemed must have attacked by now, if his avowed purpose of preventing the theft of any more holy stones was a serious one. From the Circles of Heaven, the Firbolgs dragged and sledded their heavy plunder to the sea. Then they loaded each stone on a platform supported across three of their dugout canoes, for the demanding eastward voyage. The task called for skilled workers and mariners in large numbers, besides concerted effort over years—but the Firbolgs had the numbers and the persistence. Like marauding black ants, Tringad thought sourly.

They rowed boldly into the haven, to find it deserted. The burnt remains of two canoes lay on the beach. Leading a scouting party up the Firbolgs' transport road, Lygi found a smashed sled and some broken harness-ropes for oxen, among signs that fighting had taken place there, days earlier.

"Where are the execrable Firbolgs, then?" wondered a companion of Lygi's who knew nothing about them. "They have had time to return and start work. Lazy, they must be, or afraid."

"We'd probably find them at the end of this road, taking apart the Circles of Heaven," Lygi guessed. "When they have sledded a few more stones down to the sea, the canoe-men will come to get them. And Nemed will be back to sink them as soon as they take to the water.''

Tringad enlightened him on that point, when he returned to the ship.

''It's none so simple, lad. You landsmen think it is. Oh, ships like the prince's—except that there aren't any ships like his, in our age, and won't be again—ships like his can destroy a set of dugouts burdened with stone, easy as a lynx can destroy a fat pheasant with its wings broken. But he has to find 'em first. Look yonder.''

Tringad allowed Lygi plenty of time to survey the shore they were passing. The thickly forested land—with its coves, islands, many anchorages, and tricky tides—offered all the chances one could wish for concealment or disaster.

''Nemed knows these waters, though,'' Lygi argued. ''Why, he was homeless for seven years, and lived off the sea, mainly here.''

''The Firbolgs know them even better. Besides, it's not as though they are everywhere, easy to be found. If they carry as many as a dozen stones in a summer, it's a mighty industrious summer, and there is a deal of coast to search. The only places Nemed can be truly sure of finding them are at the haven, where they begin, and at the eastern river-mouth, where they unload. Then the river boatmen take over, to carry the stones into the very heart of Alba, and the Firbolgs are always there in force to protect what they ha' taken. So never be amazed if we don't see them anywhere else. I'll be happy, so, if *I* can find *Nemed*. But five ships like his are something conspicuous.''

Yet even that guarded bit of optimism was not borne out for long days. Cena's longship nosed into many a creek-mouth, marsh, and bay, sought many a promising site for sea-ambushes, and moved ever deeper into the waters of Sabra. Once they had to fight off an attack by Firbolgs themselves. The tall Iberians in their leather boats fought grimly to take Cena's ship, but the Danans shook them off and rowed away, leaving the foe to paddle futilely in their wake. Normally, those who sought trouble with Cena found her willing to give it, but she had not come to battle Firbolgs. That was Nemed's business.

Aside from that skirmish, they found one other sign of Firbolgs. Tringad espied a carved wooden float riding the waves, anchored to the sea bottom by a long cord. The carving proved to be Iberian work. Clearly it was a marker for the men who carried the stones, signifying a safe place to ride out bad weather or contrary tides, and only a sharp-eyed man who knew the sea well could have spotted it without knowing in advance that it was there. Had Nemed passed that way, he too would have noticed it. Whether he cut the float free or left it would depend on how foresighted he was.

The Danans stopped on a densely wooded shore for a couple of days to hunt fresh food. Although they kept watch from the highest ground nearby, they saw no sign of the prince's ships. Cena began to fear he had already gone home. He would be having a furious quarrel with Vivha if he had.

"Maybe," Oghmal said, "though I judge him to be more persistent than that. Let's copy him and fare on. He may have gone all the way to the end of the Firbolgs' sea-route, if he found no prey elsewhere."

"We're getting deep into Sabra," Tringad warned. "Nay, we're almost at its end. Slight chances we'd have of leaving it ahead of those metal ships, supposing we met them now. And they are five to our one."

"That is why I am here," Alinet said. "Oghmal is right. Let's fare on."

"If it comes to a sea-fight, we will lose," Cena told them, "unless Nemed has divided his fleet, and he surely would not do that hereabouts. Captain?"

"He would not," Tringad agreed emphatically.

"Then we'll settle this with a single combat. The only question is which of us fights him, and I am the Rhi. Besides, I want him. You all know how I want him." Cena spoke the last words between her teeth.

"First we must find him." Oghmal looked searchingly into his sister's eyes. "Yet I have a claim, too. I am the champion, the tribe's hand against its enemies. It was I he shamed when he stole the cauldron from my side. You cannot want him more than I do. He must be mine."

Carbri hid a smile. He knew his brother. All that Oghmal said, he meant; yet there were other things he was not saying. One involved his conviction that Nemed would certainly kill Cena if she fought him. Although sly, his might as a warrior was unquestioned, and he would, after all, be a man against a woman. Skill, courage, and spirit being equal, Nemed's greater strength must prevail.

"No, brother. You do have a right, but mine is greater. He

disgraced me before the Freths, and all of us with me, so he must answer to me with weapons, and all of us with me." Her seriousness fell away then. "I saw the look that passed between you and Carbri! I'm your sister, but I am the Rhi! You cannot protect me."

"Do you think you can defeat him?"

"He's my better with weapons; I'm his better with magic. And there is always luck. It should be an equal fight."

"Cast me dice for him," Oghmal requested.

"No, brother, no! My mind's made up. Take my throne first, and then you may have Nemed. Besides, I promised the Antlered Rhi that I would send Nemed to him through the portals of death, and a vow is binding."

Oghmal knew when it was useless to persist. One other thing he knew. If Nemed did slay Cena, he'd have to deal with her brothers, and after them with her entire people. He'd done Tirtangir harm enough.

They reached the eastern end of Sabra, and the river-mouth through which the sacred bluestones were taken. Here they saw a Firbolg camp, uncouth in their sight, but vigorous and strong. The dark men turned out with bows strung at the sight of them, inviting them by gestures to come ashore and perish. Cena declined the invitation. Nemed was not there, nor did she see signs that he had paid a visit.

"I suppose we must turn west again," she said. "Can you think of any reason why he would cross to the southern shore, Tringad?"

"Oh, I can think of reasons, lady, any number, but not to convince me. The best chance of finding him lies along the Firbolg seaway."

"And Tavasol," Lygi reminded them all. "He will have questions to answer if he returns to the long valley."

"Tavasol isn't forgotten," Oghmal said. "When we find Nemed and challenge him, Tavasol will know what to do. He'll need but the chance."

They put about and returned as they had come. Some Firbolg craft pursued them for a while, the craggy-faced swart men hurling all their power into the strokes of their paddles. They failed to catch Cena's longship; paddles were no match for oars. They kept coming, nonetheless, until the Danans had passed from sight. The lookout at the masthead announced that they had finally turned back.

"No sign of metal ships?" Cena asked.

"None, lady."

She breathed a sigh. "Then, if there's none by tonight, I will take a dolphin's shape and seek them."

"Will that be so ill?" Carbri asked. "You say it as though it meant bathing in lead. You are able to work sorcery again."

"So I am, brother. Never fear, I would not do it if I thought the price too high. Why think you I brought my dolphin's skin, if not for this? Better it would have been to find Nemed by natural means, though. As I discover him, his wizards may discover me."

"You are worth all his wizards together," Carbri said, and played a dismissive few notes on his harp. "That isn't your fear. You have changed your shape many times lately, and now you wonder if you may become a dolphin for all of your life. Isn't that so, sister?"

"You know that it is. Why mention it? There is no choice, for if we are too tardy about finding him, the Antlered Rhi will claim his price from us. Rather would I be a dolphin, Carbri! They have a fine time of life."

"But the Antlered Rhi can ride on a track of moonlight across the sea. He'd still find you. Maybe you could change me instead of yourself. I'd seek Nemed until I found him."

"Not with a dolphin's mind. That takes a discipline which has to be practiced. Also, I doubt whether you have the strength of desire to track down our trickster prince that I have! This is my task, if it has to be done at all."

The day passed, and no glint of metal in sunlight was seen, nor any sail but their own. With the fall of night, Cena took the white dolphin's skin from her compartmented chest, set up her sorceress's wands and lay down between them, drawing the skin closely about her. It covered her legs, then her red-gold hair, and finally joined over her breasts. The sleek form struck the water. Its inpudent snout lifted towards the ship in farewell, and it vanished. Alinet looked after her cousin with a trace of envy.

"Would I could take different shapes," she said. "Yet I could search for Nemed's fleet, too, on the wing, and maybe find it before she does!"

"Maybe," Lygi said. "A second sun in the sky would be noticed, though, and if word has come to Nemed from his lady, he'd know what it signified. You did enough in his country for any mortal, Alinet—and you may still have to do more. Let the Rhi take her part. She may not have other chances for adventure.''

"This has been *my* first chance," Alinet said. "Seldom did I go beyond my family's dun before—not in human shape. I want to, Lygi, many times again. Will you ride there and visit me? My kindred will try to hold me there like a treasure, just as Vivha would have done. You may not have a kind reception.''

"Well, and that's fair warning. From them, or from you?''

"Guess. Do you think I'd receive you kindly, or not?" Alinet moved close enough to touch him with her shoulder and hip. "But don't mistake me. It's a friend I want to see come riding, not a man hungry with lust. Stay away, if that's all.''

"If I live, and you live, I will come," Lygi promised.

The longship remained where it was for three days. Its crew, particularly Carbri and Oghmal, grew more concerned with each sun that set without the white dolphin's reappearance. On the fourth morning, the white flukes and jaunty nose broke the surface. Cena frolicked about the ship, squealing. Even before she returned to human shape and uttered intelligible sounds, her brothers could tell she had discovered something of importance. When she shed the dolphin's skin and stood up in the water, a long-haired woman with flesh healthy as new cream, they knew by the brightness of her eyes what it was.

"I've found them," she said.

She clambered aboard, the heavy dolphin skin trailing from her hand, cast over her shoulder. She carried it without strain. Hanging it up like a cloak to drip its water, she turned to receive the garment Carbri gave her. She was older than the twins, their mother's first-born. She looked younger.

"They are not especially happy," Cena went on. "I heard them talking. Once they raided the haven, and ever since they have been seeking Firbolg mariners with bluestones, that they may punish them. They haven't found any. The Firbolgs have been too cunning. Now the prince intends to go where we went, to the main Firbolg camp at that eastern river-mouth, and destroy it. He isn't going to arrive, my kindred. He'll meet us first.''

"Indeed," Carbri said. His smile was wicked. "And if they reckon themselves jaded now, they have no idea how miserable they are going to be very soon.''

"The Firbolgs will owe us a debt before we're done." Tringad grinned.

He's coming, it throbbed in Cena. *Deceiver, betrayer, thief, my greatest shame since I lost the Battle of the Waste, he's coming within my reach. I can wipe the cunning laugh away from his face with a word—before I slay him!*

At her orders, they began to row. The nearer to their home they were when they met Nemed, the better. In the early afternoon they intercepted him, the steady beat of their oars taking them ever closer to the shining blue hulls which sliced through the sea like oiled knives. Cena touched the oaken rail of her own ship affectionately. If the Danans had forgotten some things, they had learned others.

The fleet's men recognized a Danan longship when they saw one. Here on Sabra, where the Firbolgs had overrun most of the desirable harbors and anchorages, such had become an uncommon sight. The prince knew more. He recognized Cena's longship at a glance, and came to the rail with his languid, agile gait. His armor, of the same ancient, nameless metal as his ships, glittered like a shirt of tiny mirrors. Across the narrowing gap of water, he greeted her sardonically.

"Welcome, Cena, Rhi of Tirtangir! How is it with you?"

"It's most excellent," she answered in a honed voice. "Better than ever I suspected it would be again, when a guest and comrade-in-arms stole from me what was not mine to give, and ran like the sneaking worm he has proved himself to hide in Alba which once had the good sense to exile him. Do you know why I have taken the trouble to find you? I'll tell you. To say this to your face before your men!

"You are a thief, Nemed; a thief, a liar, and a breaker of hospitality. Are you a coward as well? Will you fall upon me now, five ships to my one, or dare you give single combat for your offence? With me, Nemed. You needn't tremble in your pretty armor for fear that you will have to face my brother Oghmal! I am the one who calls you a cur without honor."

"Her brother Oghmal repeats it, though, Nemed," the champion said loudly. "Before all your men I repeat it, and pledge my own honor that it's true. You are Cena's meat; she has the first right to carve you. But if you'd rather fight me, if you have the manhood to insist upon it, I won't deny you. Indeed, I'd be grateful to you for as long as you live."

Cena kicked his ankle lightly. "Quiet, brother! Nemed is not the only cunning thief hereabouts, I see. But you may not steal him. Ah! Look at him squirm. See him hunt for a way out. Now come the counter-accusations, the insults in return. When he thinks he has confused the matter enough, he will order an attack. I know him now. Pity it is that I did not know him before."

Nemed opened his mouth, and the predicted flood came. "Do you say so, Rhi? You forget most conveniently who fought the Freths on your behalf. I did! I harried them from the sea while you lost your battles by land. I, Nemed, overthrew the Revolving Fortress for you when you could not. After you were conquered and I had returned to Alba, who came back again to help you rebel against your brute overlords? It's due to me that you won at last. You promised me any payment I desired"—a lie—"and when the time came, you refused. Therefore I took it. In return for your compliments to me, I can name you liar and oath-breaker, and I see now that you have a tongue of slander in your head besides. You are not worth troubling with. Move out of my sea-path and I will let you live. Otherwise—" Nemed shrugged. "Nothing but wreckage afloat will mark the place of your end."

"Fine, noisy words," Cena sneered. "None of them offer to defend your honor with bronze as I have done. But then you have none to defend, have you? As for slander, I do not lie or break my oaths. Your trick with the false Undry sent us to the White Land, *prince*. We came back. While there, we ate from that other cauldron, the one of pearl-rimmed silver which never cooks the food of cowards or perjurers. It cooked ours, and we fed there. I take the Anglered Rhi himself to witness, and his unnamed lady—and I repeat my challenge. Will you fight me? Or dare you not?"

A murmur of doubt went along the oar-thwarts in Nemed's own ship. None invoked lightly the powers Cena had named. Nemed heard the doubt, and pressed his lips together over the command he was about to give. His warriors might obey it, falling on the lone ship from Tirtangir and slaying all aboard her—but later they would remember. Their prince would have refused a challenge to defend his honor, while Cena of Tirtangir had come to face him boldly in a single ship which could not even outrun the slowest of his five. It was the sort of gesture that Danans loved. Supporters he badly needed would forsake him if he did not match it. He felt sure he could beat Cena, and might not even have to slay her; but then Oghmal and Carbri would both want to fight him.

Then Carbri went too far. As words were his craft, he had to have his share. Projecting the trained voice of a bard, with the greatest inflaming sting possible in its timbre, he declared:

"Yes, betrayer! Dare you not? And that isn't the half. The cauldron you stole is not in your manor any longer. We went there, we took it back as you took it from us, by trickery and stealth—and now it rests at Ridai for Sixarms to claim when he comes! Not that it matters to you! When you had the Undry, you still lost your battle. You are little use as a war-leader, that is now manifest. Forget your dream of sweeping the Firbolgs out of Alba; you cannot feed the hosts you would have to gather!"

A howl of pure fury rose from every ship in the fleet. Not a man there but remembered battles with the loathed, encroaching strangers, the hiss of their black arrows and the thud of their impact in flesh, the desecration of Alba's holy stone circles. Now it was as though these foreign Danans boasted of being Firbolgs' allies. His warriors' doubts of Nemed were consumed in sudden, overwhelming anger. The same passion flamed high in the prince as he listened and sickeningly believed. He forgot calculation, forgot consequences, forgot all but the desire to destroy the ones who had broken his greatest dream.

"They have sold us to the swart ones! Let none of them live!"

Cena wasted no time castigating her copper-haired brother. She cried, "Out of here, my companions! Straight through them! *Alinet!*"

The little Sunwitch transformed upon the word. Her clothes became a shining haze about her, and her second form flew up, its beating wings wider in span than the ship. Tringad gave sharp, precise orders which translated Cena's command into action. Oars dipped and bit.

A sandy-haired figure sprang to the rail of Nemed's ship and dove cleanly into the sea. Oghmal pointed to him and roared, "Take that one aboard unharmed!" Then he descended into the ship's waist to see that it was done, while the Tirtangir longship sped through the midst of Nemed's fleet, taking the swiftest way to freedom. Javelins thudded into her from all sides until she looked like a lean hedgehog.

Tavasol came aboard, dripping, through the hail of sharp-pointed bronze. He ducked for shelter, untouched. Oghmal and Lygi embraced him.

The wooden ship sped clear of the fleet, and gained some headway as the rowers continued to ply their oars for their lives. Behind them, Nemed's vessels got in each other's way as they turned about to pursue. That action cost the furious Albans time, yet they knew that once they were headed aright, they would overtake Cena's ship before dusk. She would find neither shelter nor allies along this coast.

A light breeze from the east began to stiffen. Nemed's captains blessed it and spread their sails, sure now that they would run down their quarry in a couple of hours. They reckoned without the Sunwitch.

Alinet swooped from the sky, her plumage incandescent, to brush her wings along the rearmost ship's bright sail. It began to burn, even as she wheeled to pass over the next and leave two sails hotly blazing. Her cry of triumph rang over the water, lifting above shouts of consternation and rage from the glittering hulls.

Rising again on flame-pinioned wings, she drew the power of her lord the sun into herself. From dazzling she became intolerably, blindingly brilliant. Men in the third and fourth vessels she torched had to shield their eyes and turn their heads away as they cast spears at her. None struck her, and she left both sails ablaze when she flew away.

Her radiance dimmed. She could not give off such intense refulgence for long. Regret touched her that she had not been able to burn the hulls and ribs, but that nigh-indestructible metal was beyond her power to affect. At least she had deprived them of their sails. Nemed's own ship remained.

"No, girl, no!" Cena wailed. Her knuckles whitened on the shaft of her spear. "It's enough, and more! No spells of protection are on you this day. Come back!"

Alinet couldn't hear. She dove like a burning arrow on the prince's ship. Very coolly, he took a barbed javelin in his hand, spoke an incantation over it which violated his mouth and twisted his throat, then looked at the fiery bird through narrowed eyes. As his sail began to hatch flames, he threw and hit.

Alinet tumbled seaward with a scream. Fire consumed the javelin as she fell. Its savage barbs melted within her flesh. Thrashing her wings frantically, she escaped plunging into the water, and flapped her way towards Cena's ship, crying forlornly. Her flight, which had been so gloriously sure, was now a labored thing. She veered; she dipped. Her tortured efforts to gain height failed.

The sunbird had almost reached Cena's prow when she slipped sidewise into the waves, her strength gone. The brine hissed and seethed about her. Cena struck the water almost as soon as Alinet, with Lygi a heartbeat behind. Tringad spilled wind from the wide sail and had the rowers stroke backward, ready to pick them up. Nemed's fleet was still trying frantically to douse or jettison its burning sails.

Lygi forged past Cena with smooth, violent strokes to reach the Sunwitch. She was human again, the golden child-woman as capable of stubborn unreason as sweetness, and she was sinking. Lygi turned on his back, passing an arm about her to support her while he swam with the other. His hand touched a wound in her side which horrified him.

Cena upheld her cousin on the other side, timing her strokes smoothly with Lygi's. The ship drew closer. Men lowered oars for them to grab; friendly hands hauled them aboard. Lygi lowered his love tenderly to the deck and looked at her side. The javelin's barbs had torn a great, deadly wound through her rib cage, and she had instinctively burned them out of her body as she fell. That had hastened the end. The effort of flying to the ship had been Alinet's last. Without moving or uttering a sound but one very faint sigh, she seemed to shrink and lose color. A shadow covered her face.

Lygi looked up from his knees at the chief bard of Tirtangir. Very softly, with the face of an enemy, he said: "This is your doing, you fool, you loud-mouthed, braying fool. Are you pleased with it? Lady, if you deal justice, it's him you will curse with the long tongue of a freak, and let him wag it all his days."

Then he choked, and his tears brimmed. Carbri whitened like the land under falling snow. He had satirized men for much less than that, and his satires had broken the morale of armies. He made not the least move to retaliate now.

He could not, because it was true.

Chapter
Twelve

"They are following," Tavasol said from the masthead in a tonelessly grim voice. "Nemed's ship has a sail and rigging again, but none of the others do. Maybe there was only the one spare set among them. They are keeping up well with the oars, though—thus far."

"They cannot row at that pace forever." It was Oghmal. "While the wind holds for us, Nemed can only catch us if he leaves his other ships behind. Then it will be a fight in equal strength, if he wants one."

"He does not," Lygi said savagely. "He's a coward. By the Mother, if he had only accepted your challenge, my Rhi—"

"Alinet would live." Cena avoided looking at the shrouded form near the stern. "Alas, that's something we cannot know, unless Vivha deigns to tell us. And few things are as useless as knowing what *would* have happened. Forget it, Lygi. Such is my command. And I do not think Nemed is a coward. He'll follow us alone if he must. He has a wrong to avenge now—or he believes he has."

"Let him believe what he likes, so long as it brings him within our reach. How I would like to strike at him myself!"

"You may have that chance. Remember, all of you—if it comes to a sea-fight, *Nemed must die*. It makes no difference who strikes him down."

Nods of understanding, murmurs of assent, acknowledged her charge.

The wind shifted, to blow from the northeast. Since they had almost cleared Sabra in any case, Tringad chose to run directly before it, and Cena acceded. If they slew Nemed and then were followed vengefully by his other ships, there were worse destinations than the Isle of Tin, which was where this wind would blow them.

"He's coming on," Oghmal said. "I see him myself now. He'll catch us soon."

"I hope he does," Lygi snarled.

"Tavasol, what of the others?"

"Barely in sight, lord, even for me, and they are beginning to falter."

"This is fine," the champion said, reaching for a tunic of hardened ox-leather. "We can take Nemed's ship and go home in that."

Carbri smiled bitterly. Strapping on a chest protector of enamelled bronze, he slung his loved harp on his back and stared with yearning at the oncoming longship. Truly, his careless mouth had precipitated this. But for him, Carbri, Nemed might have been shamed into single combat with Cena.

Yes, and he would probably have slain her. Carbri tested his sword's edge. Now it looked like a sea-fight on even terms, in which anything could happen. With Oghmal and Cena on his side, and some of Ridai's finest warriors, Carbri liked their chances. He took a sling and a pouch of lead ball missiles, and waited for the metal ship to come within range.

It had an unnatural look, he thought. Belike it was good that such things grew rarer, as they finally wore out or were destroyed, and none knew how to replace them. Danans were still the masters of all arts, crafts, and skills, as this ship beneath his feet showed. She was every bit as graceful and seaworthy as the sleek blue monster which hunted them down, able to sail as close to the wind, as nimble to turn, and if she happened to be less swift, why, she could be repaired at need. He, Carbri, given time, could sing a ship into existence without the need of mal-

lets, pegs, or other tools. Nemed's only advantage was that his
ships moved more swiftly.

Even that could work for his enemies.

Carbri whirled his sling, marking the figure in the famous blue
armor, now donning a matching helmet. The cruelly heavy lead
ball flew, to kill or main the man it struck, and as Carbri
released it the ship bucked. Nemed escaped; the ball flew over
his head. Then missiles rained from ship to ship as they approached each other, while Carbri waited behind his shield.

Men threw ropes with three-tined hooks on the end, binding
the ships together, dragging them close. They met with a grinding squeal, and Danan fought red-haired Danan on water infested
with an enemy who threatened them both.

This was real enough to Carbri, and he joined the heaving,
shoving mass at the rail, striving to batter a way through their
defence while Nemed's men struggled to smash theirs. Spearheads darted through gaps like snakes, sometimes biting. Carbri
chopped the head from one as it flashed past his eyes. He sent
his sword's point darting back in retribution, and felt it enter the
soft heaviness of flesh, sliding through until it met bone. Pulling
it back, he drove his shield forward with all the power of his
body, from braced feet to heaving shoulders. The line creaked.
Someone swept an axe down towards his unprotected head, and
Carbri instinctively tried to raise his shield, but it was caught in
the jam of overlapping targes massed along the rail. Carbri
thought his time had come. Then someone unseen behind him
covered his head with another shield, and the axe-head split it
across but wrought no other damage. Carbri, alive, drove his
sword's point into the throat of his attacker and again strained to
go forward. This time he discovered a weakness, the smallest
trace of yielding. With a great yell of *"Tir-tan-giiir!"* he flung
himself against it and suddenly broke it to a gap.

He promptly widened it. Slashing backhard, he cut through
the nape of a foe's neck and saw him begin to fall. A thrust in
the other direction met a leather war-shirt like Oghmal's and
failed to pierce it. That particular man vanished from sight as the
melee whirled Carbri onward, a half-dozen warriors with him.

Oghmal came next, at home amid the carnage, seeing in all
directions at once. He made killing seem so easy it was as
though his sword had knowledge and a will of its own, striking
just where a vital spot was unguarded for an instant, then flashing onward. For any man to delay him longer than moments was

rare. Nemed's warriors began hesitating to meet him. It did them
no good. Oghmal carried the fight to them, granting no mercy.
Meanwhile men of Nemed's had swarmed into Cena's ship and
gained some ground there. The battle remained anybody's, the
cries of "Nemed!" and "Cena!" resounding equally loud.

Cena found herself fighting beside Carbri, her red spear a
lightning-stroke. Suddenly a gray-haired warrior turned her point
aside with his shield. The spearhead skidded across the bullhide
covering. He rammed the shield's edge into her shoulder and
arm. Cena felt sudden weakness devour the strength of that limb,
and covered herself with her own shield as her weapon-arm sank
low. Carbri, howling their war-cry, met the man in her place and
fought him for long minutes. In the end, he killed his man.

Cena knelt on the timbers between two thwarts, her spear
broken. While Carbri guarded her, she discarded her shield, then
drew her sword awkwardly, with her left hand. Rising, she
advanced beside Carbri, who covered her undefended side. They
fought like that from then on.

One of those curious brief pauses, like calm moments in a
thunderstorm, had interrupted the fight. In the hiatus, Oghmal's
voice was heard, as it rang harshly from his mouth. He called
Nemed's name.

The prince answered. Mirror-blue mail splashed with red, the
helmet scratched though undented, he came through the pack of
suddenly quiet fighters to stand before Oghmal, and look at him
with utter hatred.

"So you took the Undry," he said, "or was that a lie?"

"It is no lie," Oghmal said. "We tricked your lady into
bringing it out, and then we took it. The Undry has been back in
Ridai these several days, as Cena said. Shall we fight?"

"I believe I was promised a fight with the Rhi," Nemed
reminded him, his face vicious. "You may wait your turn."

"That was my word," Cena answered, coming forward, "but
my sword-arm won't answer at present. You will have to be
satisfied with Oghmal, as he will be content with you."

"Well content," the champion affirmed.

"A lie," the prince said contemptuously. "I'd have thought
more of you had you refused in the beginning, Cena."

"It's no lie," one of Nemed's own warriors said. "She has
been fighting left-handed, without a shield, while her brother
wards her side. That is a long way to go for a lie."

"Thanks, weapon-man," Cena said, and looked carefully at

the speaker to be sure of knowing him again. "Are you satisfied, prince? Single combat? We to surrender if Oghmal loses, your men to surrender if you lose, and in either case, the prisoners to be honorably treated, then sent home? Who agrees?"

Nemed looked at the champion. There was nothing about Oghmal as an adversary that appealed to him. Yet his ox-leather tunic had been many times slashed and rent in the fighting. Nemed felt the reassuring weight of his own vastly superior armor, and the helmet which only he wore, every other man on both sides fighting bare-headed. With his skill and equipment, he was sure to prove victorious, even if Oghmal was somewhat the better man.

"I agree," he said. "Oghmal?"

"Yes."

The warriors on both sides looked at the harvest of their fighting so far, while their inflamed blood cooled. They were all Danans, quickly ablaze, quickly burnt out, with vivid, lively imaginations. In every hideous wound, every trampled corpse, they saw their own immediate future if the fighting went on, and in each moan of agony they heard their own voices. In ones and twos, they uttered their agreement.

"Then swear it," Oghmal said, "by the Gates to the White Land and your hopes of rebirth, never to return to the ridge of the earth if you forswear."

The oaths were taken, in sixty voices, and men drew apart, to watch in both united vessels, while steersmen and rowers cast lots for the duty of holding them steady in the sea. The combatants took new shields, long wicker ovals covered with hardened leather, and two javelins each. They also took wide-bladed stabbing spears and sheathed their swords, to finish the duel if they should be needed.

The prince stood his floor-planks like a seaman born, while Oghmal braced himself too hard. Swift as thought, he sent a javelin hurtling at Nemed's legs. The prince jumped high to avoid it, and Oghmal flung the second spear at his body, with all his strength behind it. The missile would have penetrated any other armor; thrown so powerfully, it would have penetrated a slab of oak. The force of it knocked Nemed flat. He lay croaking, feeling the impact in every particle of his torso, unsure at first whether he had been impaled or not. The leather and padding beneath his scale tunic had saved him from cracked ribs, though not from torment.

As he recovered the power to move, he saw Oghmal standing but a short distance from him, and remembered that he still had two javelins to cast. Cena's brother evidently meant to give him the chance. Nothing had prevented him from charging with his stabbing spear to pin Nemed's throat to the boards, as Nemed knew he would have done in Oghmal's place. Getting to his feet, the prince breathed for a while, testing his body for damage, then reached for his first throwing weapon.

He decided not to hurl them swiftly, as the champion had done. Twice he pretended he was about to throw. Oghmal neither jumped nor made careless movements. The third time, Nemed threw straight and hard for his enemy's stomach. Oghmal knocked the flying javelin aside with his stabbing spear. Nemed deliberately aimed for Oghmal's body again, shifted his aim to the throat, and then threw for the body after all. Oghmal barely moved his feet. Swaying his shoulders and torso aside, he deflected the javelin downward to stick trembling in the floor-timbers, a feat which drew interested comment from the watchers.

"It's a sure eye their champion has. It was well done, too, allowing the prince to use his javelins. Many wouldn't."

"Aye. Look now!"

Oghmal moved toward the prince. The stabbing spear had a short, tough shaft, with a carved grip and a long, broad head which could virtually shovel out a man's lungs if driven hard beneath his ribs. Very much a close-quarter weapon, even more than the sword, it passed the advantage clearly to Oghmal, with his height and vast strength, or it would have done but for the prince's armor. Nemed showed no dismay with his flickering, shifting glances, only appraisal. The big man's war-shirt had rents in it which might well admit a spearhead.

Nimble as a wolf, the prince crouched, shield held close to his body. Moving in short, curving steps which brushed the planking, he feinted and jabbed. Then, in an instant when the ship lurched a little, he thrust at Oghmal's side, in behind the champion's shield. Knowing it was too late to dodge, Oghmal extended his arm to the limit in a thrust at Nemed's brow, hoping to pierce his skull—or at least to rattle his brains and blind him with blood. Nemed lowered his head a little. The spear's point glanced shrieking from his helmet.

Oghmal's tunic held. From Nemed's quick stab he got nothing worse than bruised ribs. He decided to take the prince's shield away. He already had as much protection as any man needed.

"Your oxhide is more trusty than I thought," Nemed gibed. "I'll seek entry through one of the tears. Among so many, there's room to pick and choose."

He did just that, darting and jabbing at the weak places, which made Oghmal sure he had something else in mind. Crowding the prince closely, he stabbed for his face and throat, always thwarted by the shield Nemed carried high. It covered him from jaw to knees. Oghmal had used his own for nothing but defence so far—but a shield also made a potent weapon of attack:

He thrust again, not at Nemed's face this time, but at the shield itself. Such was the power of his blow that the point went through spell-toughened bullhide, the wicker frame, and emerged on the other side with a hand-span of broad blade following. In the next instant, Oghmal slammed the prince mightily on Nemed's weapon-side, and slid his foot forward so that Nemed tripped over it as he staggered. He fell, not headlong but to one knee, banging that knee badly, although he never noticed. He was occupied with driving his spear up between Oghmal's thighs.

The watchers sucked air through their teeth.

Oghmal bent one leg and straightened the other, moving to the left. The spear'e edge cut a groove across the outside of his thigh. He battered Nemed further with his shield's surface and edge, never letting him rise, while his other hand twisted the stabbing spear. Most of the watchers thought these were attempts to free it from Nemed's shield. His kindred saw that he was really bending the spearhead so that it should not pull loose. Cena leaned forward, aching to shout encouragement but knowing better.

Oghmal's attack had partly dazed the prince. Stabbing at his adversary's belly, he lurched upright. Oghmal slanted his shield between them, then drove it forcibly at Nemed's weapon-side, at the same time kicking his feet from under him. Nemed fell with a crash. The champion gave a great heave on his trapped spear, and tore Nemed's shield wholly from his arm. Oghmal moved backward, in possession of both shield and spear, while Nemed rose to his feet, enraged. Oghmal placed a foot on the long spearhead to straighten it, and pulled it out of the shield, which he kicked away behind him. Now Nemed's only protection was his tunic and helmet.

Straightening the latter, which had come askew in the fall, Nemed carried the attack to Oghmal. There was nothing of the bantering fox about him now. He sought implacably to kill, with no surface mockery to lacquer the intention. Tossing his spear to his left hand, he drew his sword with the right and fought with both weapons.

"Spawn of a raddled cow!" he taunted. "You cannot kill me! My armor is all the protection I want. What would you like? The sword or the spear? You may have your choice of ways to die!"

He sent the wide-bladed spear leaping at Oghmal's side. The champion turned it, then parried a cut from Nemed's sword, using his spear. Metal clashed; the bullhide shield boomed like a drum.

Now Oghmal attacked. All that he owed Nemed went into his blows as he struck for the face and throat. The prince dodged, almost dancing, his two weapons constantly awhirl as he sought to disable his foe. Oghmal sought single-mindedly to kill. He stabbed at the small, difficult targets of face and throat as though under a spell. Carbri watched in growing concern. He could understand why his twin wasted no effort on Nemed's armored body, but he might at least vary his attacks and try to surprise the prince.

Oghmal saw a chance. Ramming his spear upward at a narrow angle, he sought to drive its point under Nemed's chin. The prince ducked his head forward, turning to the side a little, so that Oghmal's point would pass over his shoulder. Oghmal instantly halted the stroke and reversed his hand, so that his point was aimed downward, between their bodies, at the same narrow angle. He punched it ferociously into Nemed's thigh. In the same instant, Nemed's sword bit his side through the slashed leather shirt.

The spear-point entered just below Nemed's metal tunic. Angling down through the thigh's muscles, it entered the knee-joint with barely diminished force, to pierce cartilage and crack bone. Behind it, the wide blade gouged a great triangular wedge out of the muscle. The spearhead broke. Part of it remained lodged in Nemed's leg, with blood spouting around it. Oghmal moved swiftly back, throwing the rest of the spear away. Redness began to seep from his side.

Drawing his sword, he returned to the attack. Nemed was somehow still standing, ashen but defiant. Oghmal circled him, forcing him to turn upon his ruined leg. It gave way beneath him. As he sank to the floor-timbers, he slashed at Oghmal with an agonized cry of *"Alba!"*

His blade hacked into the rim of Oghmal's shield. Then the

champion's own sword, like a flash of summer lightning, found its mark at last in Nemed's throat, and all words ended there.

Time to triumph or crow there was none. Oghmal turned to the warriors who had witnessed the fight. Through the swelling groan of the Albans, and the cheer of his own countrymen, he cried to the former to throw down their weapons, if they wished to see their homes again. He trod close to their leader now that Nemed was dead, the warrior Brasc.

"What do you say?" he asked. "Will you take your life from me?"

"From such a man as you, Oghmal," Brasc said, "I will take it."

He allowed Oghmal to remove his weapons.

"You will have these back from me personally, and your freedom with them," the champion promised, while blood from his wound ran down his leg. Nemed's remaining men surrendered their weapons to the jubilant Danans as Carbri came to his brother's side. Cena had taken charge of the yielding Albans now.

"Let be, brother," Carbri said. "You have done your part, Maker of stars, but you did it mightily! Now let me see to that wound."

He cut the thongs of Oghmal's battle-tunic and pulled the hacked, sweaty, bloody object off. The gash in Oghmal's side bled faster. Although skin and muscle had been slashed, the cut had reached no organs; it needed only cleaning, stitching closed, and bandaging. Carbri sighed with relief.

"It looks as though you will live to see Tirtangir again."

Oghmal nodded. "Aye, Tirtangir. It didn't feel mortal, brother. I knew Nemed had failed his last try when I could keep moving and finish him. We're free now of the Antlered Rhi's threat. But there are two who won't go home."

"Neither will we," Tringad grunted, "if we waste time getting these ships under way! For the other four ships of Nemed's fleet have given us no oaths, and there they come."

The mirror-bright hulls of Nemed's unsailed ships flashed in the sun. Cena's mariners worked like men with their lives at stake, which they were, and the bright sails filled again. Timber ship and metal one fled side by side, half of the defeated warriors in each, guarded by armed men of Tirtangir. Looking back, they saw the oarbeat increase and the pursuit begin to gain.

Their lead had been slender to begin; if the rowers lessened it much more, or the wind failed, they would be overtaken.

"They surely cannot maintain that pace long," Cena said.

They maintained it until she thought she would have to eat her words, and maybe the edge of a weapon with them. Then the oar-rhythm faltered and the pursuit fell back at last, though not in despair. The quartet of ships hung on Cena's sea-trail all the way to Tirtangir, straining to catch her each time the wind weakened or shifted, keeping a steady pace behind when it favored her. Four times it seemed that their grim patience would be rewarded; four times fortune and Tringad's seamanship deprived them of their prize. The men from Tirtangir ran by night and day, sleeping by turns, rowing or sailing as seemed best, and still the Alban ships stayed with them.

They reached their own shores at last. Racing north with the Albans behind them, they rounded the haunted point where many ships had come to grief, and watched for the rest of Nemed's fleet to appear.

They did, in time. All four had survived, though at a cost, it seemed. They stayed close together and their speed was less. The seas had battered them.

"If they have the hardihood to land in Tirtangir, they could carry out a raid to remember," Cena said, staring aft. "They are persistent, that I'll grant them."

"Too much so. Sister, can you become an eagle one last time?"

"I think I must. I've been trying to avoid it, but now we are harried so—yes, Carbri, I can."

The commander of the Alban ships saw a great she-eagle rise from the deck of the vessel he hunted. Knowing what that meant, he inveighed burningly against Cena for a long time, and called upon the powers of earth, sea, and sky to forsake her.

"She will rouse her men at Ridai, and have them meet the ships at a place arranged," he snarled. "So would I do in her shoes. We must run them down quickly or lose them."

"The men cannot row harder, Muilrin. They can barely maintain this pace. We won't catch them now until they land."

"And when they do," Muildrn said, as though swallowing something bitter, "they will still have hostages to bargain with. Maybe the prince, if he's still alive. Their Rhi has escaped us. We're on their coasts, and could be trapped here." He drew his sword and drove it deep into the mast. "Still, I'm not for turning back. We may have a chance to make worm's meat of them yet. A bare chance.''

He clung to that hope until he saw the bay where his quarry had landed. Beyond the beach lay rocky heights where a handful of men could stand off a thousand, and a wind blowing out of the east sent strong waves rolling in to the shore. It would be easy to enter that bay, far less easy to come out again, and a force from Ridai could be expected at any hour.

"We have lost," he said bitterly. "All we can do now is bargain, peacefully and humbly, for their hostages and Nemed—or his body.''

He was allowed to depart with that, and with the captives Cena had taken. She did not even impose a vow of peace upon him, and she kept the metal ship she had conquered.

"It's my rightful prize,'' she said. "Considering all that your prince did to us, it is the least he owes me—his life aside, which did not profit me. If ever your lady, Vivha, wants to know the full truth of the matter, she is welcome to come to Ridai and ask. Without weapons.''

"Rhi of Tirtangir, I know her. If she comes it will be with point and edge.''

"That will be her disaster,'' Cena answered, "and yours, if you are with her. The best thing she can do now is look to her land and her people, as I shall look to mine. Let her protect it with her own craft and powers, rather than counting on sunbirds or magic cauldrons.''

She watched Muilrin depart to his ships. Then she rode home to Ridai, through the living greenery of late summer, past fields of maturing grain. The Earth-Mother promised a rich harvest this year.

Sixarms waited at Ridai, gross, ugly Sixarms, who was also the wisest and most patient ruler Cena knew. The Undry was his again. Gravely, he saluted her. That he had set her no easy task he had always known. Now that it was achieved, he felt as glad as she.

"Midsummer has passed,'' he said bluntly. "The months I allowed you have lapsed and more, Cena. It's almost harvest time.''

"Yes.'' Cena's heart hammered with dread, even as she met Sixarms's gaze levelly, wondering if it was to be renewed war after all. "We failed to get back the Undry within your appointed time, that's true. Yet we did regain it. We fought battles

against Danans and Firbolgs, we were cast living into the White
Land of Death and came back, and before our task was finished
two of us were slain. Nothing made of flesh and bone could have
striven harder than we did, Sixarms.''

"That I know." The deep voice which always seemed to echo
from caverns deep in the earth was quiet and serious. "You had
a mighty task, nearly impossible, but I tell you, mine was no
less, to hold the Freth tribes back from outright war when
Midsummer came and went with no sign of the cauldron. Every
voice of man and woman was against me.''

"Did you succeed?"

Cena couldn't wait for the answer to be offered in Sixarms's
own time. She had to ask. Tensely, she scanned the weathered,
bearded visage before her, trying to read whatever feelings might
be inscribed in the lines of that ridged forehead, the sagacious
eyes, the heavy, impassive mouth. It baffled her, as Sixarm's
expressions always had, until he smiled.

"There will be no more fighting," he rumbled, from far down
in his churnlike chest. "No fighting at all. No curses upon your
herds and crops from our old women. I'll carry the Undry from
tribe to tribe and prove that the Danan Rhi keeps her word at
whatever cost. My folk will retell the story for as long as this
island stands above the sea.''

"Thank the Mother," Cena whispered. "Thank you,
Sixarms . . . and yet . . . you can do another thing before
all of that.''

Sixarms waited.

"Two of us died. And others, in the sea-fight. I want you to
come to their feast and honor them.''

"With a true will," Sixarms said.

There was an empty table at that feast, with empty places set,
and supplied with anything living folk might require, in case the
slain should come in from the night and dine with their kindred.
Those places would be set for them each Winter Eve, and at the
dark of every moon. Their comrades would think of them, then
and at many other times, knowing that they ate from that other
cauldron in the land of Anuven whose contents were only for the
brave. One day they would be reborn, changed irrevocably, as
all were changed by living and dying, so that they and their
fellows of the quest for Undry would not know each other again.

What they had done would have its fruit in the world, though.
Cena looked at their empty seats and silently promised them not

to waste what they had bought for all the Tirtangir Danans. Time. Time for the crops and children to grow. Time for the bitterness bred by the late war to ease, for its festering poison to pass. There was a hundred years' work in that for herself and Sixarms, while the wounded earth renewed its forests. It would still be unfinished when they had to leave it to others.

Heavy thoughts, Cena mused, lifting herself out of them. She had done what she must. Their debts to Sixarms and Nemed were paid; that sufficed. Sixarms was her guest tonight, not quite as he had been in former times, but still her guest, and that sufficed, too.

She met his deep-set eyes over the rim of her cup, held them, and drank.

FANTASY FROM ACE--FANCIFUL AND FANTASTIC!